On The Line

Sonja Myburgh

On The Line

Published by Sonja Myburgh at Createspace.

Copyright 2012 Sonja Myburgh

All rights reserved. No part of this publication may be reproduced, stored in a retrieval system, or transmitted, in any form or by any means without the prior written permission of the author.
References that are made to well-known brands and places are done without the consent of the specific company or place, and is not in any way endorsed by them for advertising purposes.

This publication contains references of real people and actual events, but is still a work of fiction and should not be considered or used in any way, except for entertainment purposes. All characters in this publication are fictitious, except the aforementioned, and any resemblance to real persons, living or dead, is purely coincidental.

Thank you for respecting the author and the work that has been put into this publication.

Acknowledgments

To Heather, my proofreader and editor, for all the advice and suggestions, and for believing in me. I appreciate it more than you will ever know.

To my husband Mark, my tennis encyclopedia, for your patience, love and neverending support! You are one in six billion!

On The Line

Sonja Myburgh

Prologue

The sun peeked over the horizon, setting the sky alight with a mixture of red and orange swirls, just as Nathan started his early morning run. Washington, just before the sunrise, was Nathan's favourite place in the whole U.S. All exaggerations aside, it really was. He had lived in Washington his whole life, but as most of his family was scattered all over the U.S, he had been from San Francisco, to Miami, to Boston, and everywhere in between. Nothing beats Washington, though. The historical sights, the lush green grass, the great people, and his absolute favourite place, the Lincoln Memorial Reflecting Pool. That's where he went to think, to get away from the drama that consumed his family home on a daily basis. No matter how hard he tried to keep his mind clear, it always seemed like an impossible task. His sister was giving him endless grief about yet another season of tennis, even though he had agreed that this year's tournament in Las Vegas, was the last one. His father wanted him to finish his degree in architecture, but according to Nathan, he was way too young to retire. He was only twenty-three, how on Earth could they expect him to retire? Sure, he had been playing since he was seven, turned pro when he was only sixteen years old, won numerous tournaments and was rated number two in the U.S. last year. His father thought that Nathan was wasting his life and that he needed to grow up. His mother on the other hand, was very supportive of his decisions, as she had been his whole life. Nathan was so used to his father frowning upon the choices that he made, never agreeing with anything he does, that his father's comments didn't matter anymore. They rarely spoke, and when they did, their neighbours usually ended up calling the police to break up the fight.

    Nathan shrugged and quickened his pace, and attempted for the second time to clear his head. He focused on his breathing, with every stride, pushing himself harder and faster, until he reached the reflecting pool. He wiped his face and ran his fingers through his brown windblown hair, breathing shallowly. "Not as fit as you would like to be, hey Nathan? How do you expect to get anywhere if you can't even run a twenty mile without breaking a sweat? Those guys are going to eat you for breakfast!" His sister's comments whirled through his mind. He shook his head angrily and drove the voices away. "No! Stay with it,

Nathan, focus! You are better than them! All of them!" He wiped his face again and stared at the water in the pool. He stared at his reflection for a second and then grinned. "Right, let's do this!" He started running again back home, even though he was reluctant to do so, knowing what was waiting for him when he got there.

"I can't believe this!" Emilie ran her hands angrily through her blonde hair and bent down to pick up her racquet. She shook her head as she felt the grip press against her palm. Her morning practice was not going as she had hoped it would. Her right knee was aching profusely and she could hear by the tone of Spencer's voice, he wasn't impressed either. "What the hell was I thinking? I can't do it like he did..." She could feel the agitation build up inside her and she growled to herself.

"You almost had it." She heard Spencer say.

"Yeah right." She muttered to herself and shook her head. She twirled her racquet a couple of times and looked up at him, standing on the opposite baseline, his eyebrows pushed together.

"Try it again. Make sure that your feet aren't too far apart, and get your centre balanced before you swing." Spencer tugged at his cap and he walked over to the ball launcher behind him.

"Right." Emilie nodded at him and gripped her racquet tightly. "Centre, balanced, got it."

She had to do better, there was no other alternative. In two months she needed to be on top form for the American Open in New York City. She had to be ready. After her knee injury nine months ago, she had struggled to make a come back, but this was her time to shine! Nothing could stop her! She bent her knees and felt the pain in her knee increase and she felt her shoulders slump. She thought of her brother, Jeremy, and felt a shiver run up her spine. His smiling face reminded her why she had not quit, but she can't seem to get her volley right. He was the one that taught her how to hit the perfect volley, quick and powerful. She thought back to the night of the accident and her heart ached. She remembered the look on Jeremy and Spencer's faces and could still feel the cool metal of the keys against her palm. A mixture of rusted metal and gasoline filled her nostrils and she heaved.

"Emilie." She heard Spencer's voice and looked up, driving a bad memory away. He had a worried look on his face and walked towards her. "Are you okay?"

"I'm fine." She nodded.

"Should I call Shannon...." Spencer asked.

"Spence, it's okay. It's just an ache." She smiled weakly and tugged at her racquet's strings. She would rather have a physical ache than an emotional ache. The former eventually heals, but the latter doesn't. Ever. She sighed miserably and her heart yearned for her brother, his teasing laugh, the way she always felt safe with him, invincible. The only thing that could stop her from being invincible, wasn't a busted knee, it was a busted heart. She bent her knee a few times and smiled sadly as she felt the pain subside. "Right. Let's do this." She nodded, tightly gripping the handle of her racquet, waiting for the next tennis ball to launch towards her. She would be ready to play, but she knew in her heart that she would not be ready for the questions. Not at this rate. The funeral was hard enough, and the only question she was asked was 'How are you doing?'. Her answer was always the same. "I'm fine." She wasn't in denial, some days were easier than others, but those days didn't happen very often. Somehow she hoped that her answer would make the questions stop, but they never did.

CHAPTER 1

Emilie rested her head against the headrest of her seat and looked out of the small window. The sky was a bright blue and the city of Washington DC was growing smaller and smaller by the second, as the airplane ascended higher into the air. She took a deep breath and closed her eyes for a brief moment. There was a long, deep beeping sound and a voice sounded over the intercom that the captain has turned off the seatbelt sign. Emilie opened her eyes and undid her seatbelt, bending over to reach for the bag on the open seat next to her. Just as she took her phone out of her bag, someone walked passed her seat, and she felt a hand brush against her head. She felt a jolt of electricity, static probably, and felt her phone slip out of her hand, and onto the carpet of the plane.

"Excuse me." A deep sultry voice said and he reached for her phone on the floor.

"That's alright. Don't worry about it." She shook her head lightly and looked up.

The stranger met her eyes and she stared at him for a brief moment. She could feel her heartrate accellerate and her palms dampen. Strange, that was how she felt minutes before a game. "No distractions, Emilie Hayes! No distractions!" She said to herself.

"I believe this is yours." The hottie grinned and held out her phone to her.

"Yes, it is. Thank you." She blinked and smiled shyly, taking her phone from him.

He smiled at her, hesitating for a moment too long, and walked briskly down the aisle to the front of the plane. Emilie exhaled and ran her hands through her hair. She flipped open her phone and looked at a text Shannon sent her.

> Emmy, flight's been delayed, sandstorms, got sand EVERYWHERE! literally....so won't be there for your arrival, or your first press. sorry Em! will make it up to you, promise! will come straight after I check in. 1417 as always? see u soon! much love, shan xx

Emilie chuckled at the text, just imagining Shannon at Austin Airport, holding on to her stetson, in a sandstorm. Shannon Moore, her best friend for the last fourteen years, was quite a character. Originally from Austin, Shannon had a proper Texan accent, but it completely disappeared when she was plastered. She never went anywhere without her cowboy boots, and had a pair for every occasion. She was the only person that could wear cowboy boots any time, anywhere and still look good. With her dark auburn hair and her striking green eyes, she was one of the prettiest Texans Emilie had ever seen and she was smart as hell. Most people Shannon met couldn't believe that she was a qualified physiotherapist. They always assumed she owned a ranch with horses or some lame stereotype associated with Texans. The only horse Shannon owned was a red 1969 Ford Mustang called Sting and had a bulldog called Socrates. She was an outspoken girl, always the life of the party, up for any kind of fun and the greatest friend Emilie could have ever asked for. Emilie smiled and wished Shannon was here with her. Usually they travelled together, but Shannon had to make sure that Socrates would be well looked after before she left. Emilie rested her head against the headrest and smiled. She turned her head and saw the hottie walking towards her. She almost laughed at her own stupidity as she realised he wasn't walking towards her, he was going back to his seat. Their eyes met and she tilted her head slightly to the side and smiled. The guy winked at her and walked passed her. She looked down at her phone and typed a text to Shannon, with a smile.

Everywhere? that sucks. don't worry, I'm a big girl, besides I got in-flight entertainment! wish you were here, he's hot! Spence will pick me up at NYA. will see you soon! 1417 as always! love you, Em.

Emilie grinned to herself and put her phone back in her bag. Slowly she looked over her shoulder, trying to find the hottie, trying to be as inconspicuous as she possibly could. She spotted him four rows from the back, on the opposite side of the aisle, looking straight at her, giving her a crooked smile. "Oh crap." Emilie quickly turned around and shifted uncomfortably in her seat. She covered her face with her hands, and felt the heat rise to her face. How embarrassing! She looked out the window and shook her head in disapproval.

"Excuse me?" She heard his voice beside her.

She looked over her shoulder and into the green eyes of the hottie. He was resting his elbows on the headrest of the seat next to her, grinning.

"You're busted, pretty girl." He gave her a crooked smile.

"Pardon me?" Emilie frowned.

"You are busted." He repeated.

"I don't know what you mean." She blushed.

"Don't feel bad, I couldn't take my eyes off of you either." He winked, leaning forward.

"Wow, you are about as subtle as a handgrenade." Emilie frowned.

"Speak for yourself." He chuckled.

"Sorry. I didn't.." Emilie looked him in the eyes.

A voice over the intercom sounded, the captain has turned on the seatbelt sign.

"Looks like I gotto go." He gave a sad smile, with a hint of disappointment.

"Pity." Emilie nodded. "But I am sure we will run into each other again."

"I hope so." He grinned, clearly impressed by her answer.

A stewardess walked over to the hottie. "Please, sir, the captain requested all passengers back to their seats please. We are currently experiencing some turbulence."

"Yes, ma'am." He saluted, smiled at the stewardess, and turned around.   He held out his hand to Emilie and smiled. "I'm Nate, by the way."

Emilie took his hand and grinned at him. "Emilie."

"See you around then, pretty girl Emilie."

Nathan nodded, still holding on to her hand.

"You too." Emilie nodded casually and looked at Nathan's hand over hers.

Nathan paused another moment and let go of her hand, walking back to his seat. Emilie sat back in her seat and looked out the window again, her hand still hot from Nate's touch.

Nathan spotted the pretty blonde, Emilie, standing by the conveyer, waiting for her luggage. She looked a slight bit agitated, fiddling with the handle of her luggage cart. She looked at the conveyer, tapping her fingers impatiently on the handle. Her long, blonde hair was pulled to the side and a few loose strands hung in her face. He grinned and walked over to her.

"We meet again, pretty girl." Nathan smiled at her.

She shifted her gaze from the conveyer to him and smiled shyly. "That's logical, as we shared the same plane."

"I suppose so." Nathan chuckled and looked at her.

Emilie looked over at the conveyer and spotted her bags. "Oh, there's mine."

"All of them?" Nathan looked shocked.

Emilie grabbed hold of her three large white

and light blue bags and pulled them off the conveyer. "Yes." She looked at him with a frown and nodded, looking puzzled.

"Let me help." Nathan smiled at her.

"Sure, if you don't mind." Emilie blushed slightly.

"Not at all." He shook his head and helped Emilie put all her bags onto the cart.

"Thank you." Emilie grinned at him and chuckled. "Normally I don't travel this light."

Nathan raised his eyebrows and laughed light-heartedly. "This is light?"

"Yes." Emilie laughed as well and looked at him.

"You're not from around here, are you?" Nathan asked.

"Is it that obvious?" Emilie smiled.

"Just a little. Ordinarily, people don't usually travel with three bags and hand-luggage." Nathan grinned. "But that's okay, because you are definitely far from ordinary."

"Thank you." Emilie tilted her head and grinned.

"You're welcome." Nathan smiled.

Emilie studied his expression for a few moments and raised her eyebrows.

"So where are you staying?" He asked, suddenly, stunned by his frankness.

"Why?" Emilie eyed him suspiciously.

"Well, I just thought you'd like to share a cab, with me." Nathan grinned. "But considering all your luggage we might need an eighteen wheeler."

"Alright, you made your point." She laughed and looked at Nate. "Actually, my driver is picking me up outside. He should be here already."

"Your driver? Is that what you call your boyfriend?" Nathan frowned, intrigued by this girl.

"No, it's not my boyfriend." Emilie shook her head.

"Do you have a boyfriend?" Nathan pressed.

"No, I don't have a boyfriend." Emilie grinned.

"You don't? Well that's good news for me then." Nathan smiled at her, digging his hands into his pockets.

"You reckon?" She lifted her brows at him.

"We should go have some coffee, to celebrate." Nathan smiled at her.

"I'd like to, but I can't, my driver is probably outside already. Sorry." She looked down at her watch and looked at him. "Some other time?"

"Right." Nathan sighed, his voice laced with disappointment. "So you're sure you don't have a boyfriend?"

"Yes, I'm sure." Emilie giggled and looked at him.

Nathan held his hand against his heart and smiled. "You just made my day."

"Well, I'm glad." Emilie smiled and pushed her cart passed Nathan.

"You know what would make my day even better?" Nathan turned around and touched her arm.

Emilie looked over her shoulder. "What?"

"If you gave me your number." He grinned at her and she hesitated for a second. "I'm not a psycho, I promise."

"Only psychos say things like that." Emilie laughed.

"Please." Nathan flashed her a sexy smile and she sighed.

"Do you have a pen?" Emilie asked.

"Here, it's easier." Nathan handed her his phone.

Emilie smiled at him and took the phone from him. She typed her number in and stored it. She gave the phone back to him and he smiled.

"So when can I call you?" Nathan asked and Emilie looked at him. "You didn't give me a bogus number did you?"

"No, I didn't, but I'm only in town for three

weeks." Emilie said.

"So am I." Nathan frowned. "You're from Washington, right?"

"Yes, Weaver Terrace." Emilie nodded.

"Chancery Court." Nathan smiled.

"Really? Oh my god!" Emilie shook her head in disbelief. "That's so cool."

"I agree." Nathan nodded.

Emilie looked at her watch and frowned. "Listen, I have to go. I'm really sorry."

"That's alright, so do I actually. I'll speak to you soon, then." Nathan said.

"Yeah." She smiled over her shoulder and walked to the exit.

Nathan gave a slight nod and grinned at Emilie, walking away from him. He noticed two lonely bags on the conveyer and ran over to them, with a laugh. He grabbed his phone from his pocket, flipped it open and dialed a number. "Hey, I've just arrived. Give me a call when you get this."

"You're very quiet, Em." Spencer looked at her as they walked down the corridor to her room.

"I'm just tired, I guess, and I miss Shannon." Emilie sighed.

"Apparently the sandstorms are quite bad down there." Spencer nodded. "Let's hope all her boots blow away."

Emilie looked at Spencer and slapped his arm. "Don't be mean, that's my best friend you're talking about."

"You know I'm kidding." Spencer laughed. 'So why always 1417, Em?"

Emilie gave a soft sigh and Spencer knew it had something to do with Jeremy.

"I read somewhere that if you are on the fourteenth floor, no-one can see you from the ground." Emilie said.

"Really?" Spencer frowned.

"Apparently." Emilie nodded.

"And the seventeen?" Spencer asked, but he already knew the answer.

"Jer's birthday." Emilie and Spencer said at the same time.

Emilie nodded and smiled at Spencer. "He would have been thirty-one next month."

"Are we that old already?" Spencer frowned.

"You are, I'm not." Emilie shook her head.

"Don't be a wise-ass, Em." Spencer chuckled and stopped in front of 1417. "Here we are, Em."

Emilie looked over her shoulder at Spencer and her father, walking behind her as she opened the doors of the hotel conference suite of the New York Four Seasons. Her father, Tom Hayes, seemed very uncomfortable, but Spencer smiled encouragingly and nodded at her. The doors swung open and hundreds of journalists and camera crews turned towards them. Cameras flashed and Emilie blinked a couple of times, making her way to the front of the room as fast as she possibly could. How she wished Jeremy was here with her. Tom and Spencer stood by the doors and smiled at Emilie as she walked to the front of the room. Emilie walked up the two stairs and sat down on one of the five chairs. Next to her, on her left, there was Kelly Shaw, a pretty brown-haired girl and, on her right, there was Brandon Campbell, a dark-haired guy with a pensive expression on his face. She smiled at Kelly and looked at the chaos in front of her. Each journalist was yelling their own question, creating a rumbling of noise, which pierced through Emilie's skull. She closed her eyes for a second and rubbed at her temples. The noise quieted down and she looked at Brandon. He met her gaze and the corners of his mouth curled up, his chocolate eyes twinkling. She felt herself blush and she quickly looked away. She could hear a soft laugh coming from him and she grinned to herself. The CEO of the International Tennis

Board, Jack Huxley stood up from the other end of the table and cleared his throat. Suddenly, the doors burst open and two guys stood in the doorway. Emilie looked up from the table and glared at the two cocky guys. The one with the dark hair she had never seen before, but the other guy she had. She frowned as she recognised him from the plane, and the airport yesterday morning. It was Nate.

"Nice of you to join us, Nathan, Zac." Jack frowned at the two guys.

"The pleasure is all mine, Jack." Nathan grinned at Jack and looked over at Emilie. His face lit up when he saw her and gave her a friendly nod, while walking over to the front of the room, followed by his friend. They took their seats next to Brandon, and the press conference started. Emilie sighed helplessly, like she needed any more distractions!

"Next question." Jack pointed to a blonde journalist.

"Nathan, are you feeling more confident, knowing that your biggest rival is out of the American Open this year?" The blonde journalist lifted her microphone and looked at Nathan.

"If he was my biggest rival, he would have

been here, wouldn't he?" Nathan grinned, cockily.

Emilie frowned heavily and parted her lips, shocked. Such a cocky idiot! What an unbelievable answer! She looked over at him and shook her head a little. He was breathtakingly gorgeous, but just as cocky, and arrogant! She couldn't believe she actually dreamt about this guy last night. She preferred the Nate in her dream, he was gorgeous and humble. This Nathan was cocky and arrogant! All that he is, is a distraction. She took a deep breath and wiped her face.

"He is here, Nathan, he is just not playing this year." The journalist said.

"He probably did not feel like losing this year, again." Nathan gave a soft laugh and he looked over at Emilie from the other side of the table. She stared at him for a second, confused, trying to figure out who they were talking about. He flashed her a sexy smile and she turned her face away. Distraction! she yelled at herself. But he is so hot! No Em, stop it! She looked over at the journalists and the flashing cameras and sighed. She rested her elbows on the table and rested her chin on her palms.

"Emilie, how is your recovery going after your accident? And has it discouraged you, having such a long recovery time?" Another journalist asked.

Emilie sat back in her chair and smiled. "It did not discourage me at all. Sure, it was an extremely long recovery time, but it has helped me recover fully. You don't realise what you had before it is taken away, and I never gave up, it has made me work even harder to achieve the results I wanted." She said confidently.

"Has the death of your brother had any impact on your recovery?" Another journalist asked.

Emilie shifted her gaze to the journalist and opened her mouth to answer, but no words came out. She felt her heart beat in her throat and swallowed loudly. She shifted uncomfortably in her chair and felt all their eyes on her. Right, there it is, Emilie, the first of many questions to come. "I...uhm, I don't discuss my personal life, at all."

A moment of silence washed over the room, and Nathan looked at Zac. "Impressive."

Zac nodded and the rumbling of voices rose again.

"Brandon, the rumors going around that you are newly single, is there any truth to that?" A female journalist asked.

"Why, are you interested?" Brandon

answered with a cocky smile.

Laughter echoed off the walls of the conference centre and Emilie shook her head.

"The rumors are quite true." Brandon said simply.

"Kelly, you were last years winner, do you feel threatened now that there is a new girl on the block?" A male journalist asked her.

"Of course not. I've been the womens champ for three years in a row, I don't feel threatened at all." Kelly smiled.

"Care to comment on that, Emilie?" The journalist said.

"Well, Kelly better not count her chickens before they've hatched, that's all I will say." Emilie answered as diplomatic as she could.

"At least I have two good knees." Kelly muttered.

Emilie looked at her and raised her eyebrows.

"I could have two unjured knees, and I would still beat your ass." Emilie commented with a scowl. "So watch what you say, befcre you embarrass youself."

The rumbling of voices grew louder in the conference room and Jack Huxley stood up and raised his arms in the air. "Quiet, please."

"She's so feisty." Zac grinned at Nathan and Nathan nodded with a laugh.

"But Kelly is a bitch." Nathan nodded. "We all know that."

The noise calmed down and Jack frowned at the table of players. "Such a lively bunch." He muttered. "No more questions." He motioned to the security guards to take all the journalists out of the room and the room started to clear. Emilie shook her head and stood up from her chair.

"You like embarrassing people?" Kelly sneered, grabbing her arm.

"Let go of me. You embarrassed yourself." Emilie snapped and pulled her arm away. What the hell was this girl's problem? She felt her blood boil, but took a deep breath and calmed herself. She was walking towards the doors when she heard a voice behind her.

"Hey you."

She turned around and looked at Nathan and his friend standing there. "Are you following me?"

"You should be so lucky." Nathan laughed and shook his head.

"You didn't tell me you were in the tournament." Emilie crossed her arms, narrowing her eyes at him.

"Neither did you." Nathan put his hand on his hip.

Emilie was at a loss for words and just

shook her head lightly. She extended her arm and smiled at the other guy. "Emilie Hayes."

"Zac Gilmore." Zac shook her hand. "This is Nathan Connor."

"Nathan, huh?" Emilie looked at Nathan.

"My friends call me Nate." Nathan said nonchalantly. Emilie nodded, not amused, but smiled anyway.

"Wait, Hayes, as in Jeremy Hayes?" Zac asked.

"Yeah, he was my brother." She nodded grimly, looking at Zac and then at Nathan.

"I'm so sorry. He was a great player, and a really nice guy." Zac said apologetically.

"You knew him?" Emilie asked, not really surprised. Everyone knew Jeremy.

"Yeah, I had the privilege of playing him a couple of times." Zac nodded.

Emilie tried to smile, but failed miserably. She avoided Zac's eyes and looked at Nathan. He met her gaze and stared into her blue-grey eyes, seeing a deep sadness at the mention of her brother. She blinked and smiled sadly when he folded his arms and lifted an eyebrow at her.

"Emilie." A voice behind her said.

She looked over her shoulder and saw her father and Spencer standing behind her.

"Ready to go?" Tom asked.

"Sure. Dad, Spencer, this is Nathan and Zac." She introduced them.

"Good to meet you, boys." Tom nodded.

"Same here, sir. Nice to see you, Spencer." Nathan grinned at Spencer, remembering their match last year, in Los Angeles.

"Connor." Spencer frowned at Nathan.

"Wait, you two know each other?" Emilie frowned.

"You could say that." Nathan grinned at Emilie and dug his hands into his pockets.

"Something like that." Spencer studied him for a brief second and looked at Emilie. "Em, we have to get going." Spencer lightly touched Emilie's shoulder and grinned at Nathan.

"Okay." Emilie nodded at Spencer. "You go on ahead, I'll be right out."

Spencer frowned, but nodded and turned away, walking back to Tom.

"I though you said you don't have a boyfriend." Nathan lifted his brows.

"I don't, he's my coach." Emilie shook her head and put her hands in her jean pockets.

"Spencer Byrne is your coach?" Nathan grinned and cleared his throat.

"Yeah." She frowned. "Something wrong with that?"

"Not at all." Nathan shook his head. "Listen, if you're not too busy getting coached, there's an opening party tonight, for everyone, on the top floor, if you want to come." Nathan looked at Emilie and dug his hands into his jacket pockets. "No coaches allowed."

"Noted." She laughed with a nod. "Can I bring a friend?"

"Is your friend a she?" Zac asked over Nathan's shoulder.

Emilie laughed out loud and nodded. "Shannon is very much a she."

"Of course, the more the merrier!" Zac grinned.

"We'll definitely be there!" Emilie tilted her head and looked at Nathan with a smile.

"Great! See you then." Nathan gave a satisfied smile.

Emilie gave him a small smile and turned to the double doors behind her, leaving the conference room.

"Where'd you meet her, Nate? She's hot." Zac elbowed Nathan in the ribs. Nathan pretended to wince and Zac laughed.

"On the plane. I told you to fly with me, but no!" Nathan smiled, looking at the way her hips swayed in her tight jeans.

"Let's hope Shannon is as hot as Emilie." Zac grinned.

"Highly doubtful." Nathan murmured and looked at Zac with a grin. "Come on, let's go check in."

"I can't believe her!" Jennifer exclaimed and stood up from the sofa in her hotel room.

"Who?" Kelly looked up from her magazine and at her best friend. Jennifer's dark eyes flashed and she paced the room.

"Emilie fucking Hayes. I can't believe she has the nerve to embarrass you in front of everyone in the conference room!" Jennifer sighed and waved her hands dramatically in the air. "It's totally unacceptable!"

"Jen, it was nothing." Kelly shrugged and looked at her magazine again.

"Kelly Shaw!" Jennifer grabbed the magazine from her and threw it on the floor.

Kelly looked at her with an exasperated look on her face. "I was reading that!"

"You can read it later." Jennifer crossed her arms. "Are you seriously not pissed off about what she did?"

"No." Kelly frowned, leaning forward to pick up her magazine on the floor.

"Not even a little bit?" Jennifer pouted.

"No, Jen, I told you. It's fine." Kelly rolled her eyes. "Why do you always insist on getting even with everyone?"

"Because that is what I do, my dear friend." Jennifer smirked. "I just need to figure out how...."

"Forget it, Jen!" Kelly crossed her arms.

"Oh come on!" Jennifer exclaimed.

"Like I told you, it's no big deal. She obviously felt threatened enough, so just leave the poor girl alone. She's been through enough." Kelly sighed.

"I can't believe that you are actually going to allow her to get away with this!" Jennifer exclaimed.

"Jen, just let it go!" Kelly shrugged.

Jennifer looked at her friend and shook her head Jennifer, pouting slightly.

"Please, don't give me that look." Kelly glared at Jennifer.

"What look?" Jennifer lifted her eyebrows.

"You know exactly, Jen." Kelly shook her head.

"You are so lame." Jennifer muttered. "What are we doing tonight then?"

"Well, there's a party tonight on the top floor." Kelly said and looked at Jennifer.

"Players only?" Jennifer smiled.

"No, for everyone actually." Kelly said.

"Perfect." Jennifer smirked, rubbing her hands together.

Kelly looked at Jennifer and pointed at her. "I am only going to take you with, if you promise to behave."

"Don't I always?" Jennifer smiled.

Kelly lifted her eyebrows suspiciously at Jennifer and stood up from the couch.

CHAPTER 2

Emilie eyed herself in the bathroom mirror and picked up her lipstick. She was wearing a pair of cream shorts, a white vest, a short grey jacket and a pair of grey high heels. Her blonde hair was loose, hanging down her shoulders. There was a loud knock on Emilie's door that made her jump and drop her lipstick in the basin.

"Shit..." She mumbled, and fished the lipstick out of the basin, putting it down on the counter. She wiped her hands with an anti-bacterial wipe and threw it in the bin. Another loud knock came from the door.

"Coming!" She yelled and walked briskly to the door. The moment she saw her best friend, and physiotherapist, Shannon, she hugged her tight.

"Whoa, did you miss me or something?" Shannon laughed, pulling free from Emilie's grip.

"Just a little. The press conference was a nightmare. I almost cried when they started asking about Jer, and I snapped at Kelly Shaw in front of everyone!" Emilie confessed to Shannon.

Shannon raised her eyebrows and shook

her head. "Looks like I got here just in time, then!"

Emily laughed at her friend and looked at her. Her straight dark brown hair just touched her shoulders and her cheeks were flushed. She wore a pair of denim shorts, a tight black top with an AC¥DC logo on it and a pair of dark brown cowboy boots.

"How come you get such a cool room?" Shannon walked passed her and raised her eyebrows, looking around the hotel suite.

"Maybe because I am a player and you're just a physio." Emilie grinned light-heartedly.

"Just a physio, huh?" Shannon frowned dramatically.

"I don't make the rules, Shannon Moore." Emilie shrugged.

"I guess, but when you are famous one day, please ask for adjoining suites." Shannon looked at the room in awe.

"I will remember that." Emily nodded.

Shannon looked her over and frowned. "Why are you all dressed up, Em?"

"You feel like going to a party?" Emilie asked.

"Sure, sounds like fun." Shannon grinned. "Player invitation?"

"Yes." Emilie grinned.

"Do I know him?" Shannon narrowed her

eyes.

"Actually, it turns out that he was my on-flight entertainment." Emilie grinned.

"Interesting, and he did not know who you were?" Shannon asked, intrigued.

"Nope. Apparently he knows Spencer." Emilie said flatly.

"How?" Shannon frowned.

"Rivals probably. You should have seen the way they glared at each other this morning." Emilie giggled. "It was quite entertaining, I must say."

"Like a couple of vikings." Shannon rolled her eyes. "Men."

Emilie laughed and looking at her wristwatch. "Shoot, we've got to go."

Shannon nodded and followed Emilie out of the room.

"So how's the knee?" Shannon asked when they stood in the corridor, waiting for the elevator.

"It's fine." Emilie said flatly and avoided eye contact with Shannon.

"Are you sure?" Shannon narrowed her eyes at her friend.

"It's not my knee that's hurting." Emilie sighed.

"Aaah, Em." Shannon put her arms around Emilie and hugged her tight.

"The press was horrible, Shan. I completely froze." Emilie rested her head on Shannon's shoulder.

"You didn't have a downpour did you?" Shannon asked.

Emilie shook her head and looked at Shannon. "Nope, I just said I don't discuss my personal life." Emilie shook her head.

"Good girl." Shannon smiled and watched the elevator doors open. They stepped into the elevator and the doors closed. Emilie pressed the button marked 25 and it lit up. The doors closed and Shannon looked at Emilie.

"Doctor Gilbert called me as I was getting off the plane." Shannon grinned and Emilie looked at her. "He is in Rome with Doctor Gerrard, working on that new corticosteroid injection...."

"Shan, don't." Emilie groaned agitatedly and glared at Shannon.

"This could really help you." Shannon frowned sympathetically. "Don't you dream of having full function of your knee again? To be able to move like you want? To be able to walk without a limp?"

"I'm sorry that my limp bothers you so much." Emilie glared at Shannon and crossed her arms.

"That's not what I meant, Em. I just...." Shannon sighed.

"You just what?" Emilie asked.

"Nothing." Shannon shook her head as the elevator doors opened. "Why are you being so negative?"

"I'm not being negative, okay." Emilie frowned and walked out of the elevator.

"Then what is it, Em?" Shannon asked, following Emilie.

Emilie stopped in the middle of the corridor and crossed her arms, looking at Shannon.

"You know you can tell me anything." Shannon sighed.

Emilie glared at her and felt tears stinging her eyes.

"Em..." Shannon turned to her.

Emilie stared at Shannon but did not say a word. She blinked back her tears and shook her head. "It's nothing. I'm fine."

Shannon raised an eyebrow and looked at Emilie. "Maybe you should..."

"Shannon, just let it go. I told you I'm fine!" Emilie snapped.

"Fine then." Shannon raised her eyebrows.

"I'm sorry, Shan. I didn't mean to snap at you. I've just had enough drama to last me a lifetime, you know." Emilie said apologetically.

"That's okay." Shannon smiled.

"Can we just have some fun?" Emilie shook her head. "Even if it is just for tonight."

"Maybe not just tonight. Maybe your in-flight entertainment becomes mandatory entertainment." Shannon winked at her and Emilie laughed.

"The door isn't going anywhere, man." Zac called to Nathan with a laugh.

"I know." Nathan looked at his friend.

"You should know women by now, Nate. They are never on time." Zac rolled his eyes.

"I suppose." Nathan frowned and walked over to the bar.

"Have a shot, man." Zac grinned and Nathan raised an eyebrow at him. "One shot, Nate."

"Zac, we both know it never ends up being just one shot." Nathan shook his head and took a shot glass full of a bright green liquid from Zac.

"Very true, my friend, but the night is still young." Zac nodded.

"What is this?" Nathan frowned, holding the glass up into the light.

"This, my dear Nate, is the drink of the tennis gods! It will give you incredible strength and supernatural endurance that mortals only dream about!" Zac announced triumphantly.

Nathan gave a crooked smile, suspiciously eyeing the ominous green liquid.

"Don't tell me you never had absinthe before?" Zac looked horrified.

"I can't recall that I have, man. Doesn't that stuff make you hallucinate?" Nathan looked at his friend.

"An old wives' tale, man." Zac said nonchalantly. "Drink up."

Nathan still eyed the shot glass and shook his head. This was going to be one interesting night, by the looks of things. Nathan brought the glass up to his mouth and swallowed the green liquid. Nathan felt a fire ignite in his throat, going all the way down to his stomach. He pulled a disgusted face, but Zac did not take any notice of him. Zac nudged him in the ribs with his elbow and pointed to the door.

"Look who just walked in." Zac grinned.

Nathan looked at the door and saw Emilie, looking gorgeous in a pair of cream colored shorts, and a pretty brunette with cowboy boots. "I'll be right back." Nathan smiled.

"Bring them over for a drink, I'll pour." Zac lifted his hand in the air and Nathan high-fived him.

Nathan walked towards the two girls and wondered who Emilie's friend was. She was pretty, sure, but she looked too high-maintenance for his liking. He strolled over to them, the horrible after-taste in his mouth from the absinthe still burning his throat. Hopefully, Emilie won't be as repulsed by the smell, and taste, as he was. He chuckled to himself and took a deep breath.

"Oh dear god! Look at all this talent!" Shannon exlaimed as they entered the top floor suite.
Emilie laughed at her friend's frankness and looked around the room.
"Looking for someone in particular?" Shannon wiggled her eyebrows up and down.
"Just seeing if I recognize anyone." Emilie shook her head.
"Spencer would know everyone." Shannon looked around. "Why isn't he here?"
"He wasn't invited." Emilie mumbled.
"Em, you don't need an invitation to come to an open party." Shannon frowned and looked at Emilie. Emilie smiled and Shannon grinned. "Right, I see."
Emilie nodded and tugged at her jacket. In the far corner of the room, she spotted Kelly and an unknown girl with dark red hair, chatting. She shrugged and looked at Shannon, literally salivating over all the hot guys in the room. She chuckled and tucked a strand of

blonde hair behind her ear. Emilie looked over her shoulder and spotted Nathan, looking absolutely gorgeous in a dark grey shirt and dark jeans, walking over to them. She could feel her knees go a little weak and her heartrate increase. She looked over at Shannon and leaned closer to her.

"There he is." Emilie whispered.

"Good work." Shannon nodded with approval and Emilie giggled.

"Glad you could make it." Nathan walked up to the two girls and smiled.

"Hey! You too." Emilie nodded with a smile. "Nathan, this is Shannon, Shannon, this is Nathan."

"Pleasure to meet you!" Shannon smiled.

"Likewise." Nathan nodded. "Are you also competing?"

"Oh god no, tennis is such a barbaric sport. I'm Emilie's physio." Shannon frowned.

"Barbaric?" Nathan grinned.

"Yes, absolutely. Em is the only reason that I am here." Shannon said, but her attention was elsewhere.

"And the parties." Emilie smiled at Shannon.

"Yes, and the parties." Shannon nodded, looking at Nathan.

Emilie and Nathan laughed and looked at Shannon. There was a loud, piercing whistle coming from the other side of the room and they looked over at the bar. Zac waved his arms in the air and motioned them to come over.

"Oh great, there's a bar!" Shannon grinned and was the first to walk towards him.

Nathan looked at Emilie and held his arm in the direction of the bar. "After you."

Emilie tilted her head and smiled sweetly. "Thank you."

"Welcome, welcome! I'm Zac. You must be the lovely Shannon." Zac held his hand out to Shannon.

"That's me." She shook his hand. "Are you the barman?"

"Tonight, I will be whatever you want me to be." Zac winked at her, slurring a slight bit.

"Please excuse him, he's been drinking the drink of the tennis gods." Nathan smiled apologetically at Emilie and Shannon.

"You have absinthe?" Shannon leaned against the bar and her eyes twinkled with mischief. "That's fantastic news!"

"I like you already!" Zac applauded.

Shannon laughed and stepped onto the barstool. She sat down on the bar counter, crossed her legs and smiled at Zac. He placed four shot glasses on the counter and poured the bright green liquid into each of the four glasses. Emilie hesitated when the others took a glass.

"Scared?" Nathan raised his eyebrows at Emilie.

"Not really." Emilie looked at Nathan and he studied her face for a second.

"Are you sure?" Nathan's green eyes twinkled.

"Em is completely fearless." Shannon smirked.

"Is that so?" Nathan grinned.

"Absolutely." Emilie grinned, and drank her shot, without wincing or pulling a face. She put her shot glass down on the counter and looked at him. Emilie could feel the burn in her throat, but fought against it, just to prove a point.

"That's impressive." Nathan smirked, trying not to pull a face. He watched her put the shot back on the counter and tilted her head at Zac.

"What else have you got back there?" Emilie asked Zac.

"Vodka, bourbon, champagne and tequila." Zac answered with a smile.

"Tequila sounds good." Emilie and Shannon agreed.

"Tequila for the girls, coming up." Zac nodded, spun the bottle on his hand and the girls clapped.

Nathan grinned at Emilie, and Shannon, cheering at Zac's party-trick. He leaned against the bar and watched as Emilie and Shannon raised the shots in the air and yelling 'Ole!', before drinking their shots. Emilie wiped the corner of her mouth and placed the glass back on the counter. She turned to him and leaned against the bar. Nathan studied her expression for a moment and grinned to himself.

Emilie's eyes met his and she smiled at him. "What?"

"Nothing. You just took me completely by surprize." Nathan smiled.

"And why is that?" Emilie asked.

"You don't look like the type of girl that can drink down a shot of absinthe, followed by a shot of tequila, without showing any sign of distaste." Nathan said.

"You make it sound like a bad thing." Emilie smiled.

"Not at all." Nathan smiled at her and she felt her heart pounding in her chest.

"Right, enough with the chit-chat! I think it's time for another round!" Zac exclaimed and Emilie and Shannon laughed.

"Oh, my, god!" Jennifer nudged Kelly from across the room.

"What?" Kelly choked on her drink.

"It's her!" Jennifer pointed cross the room.

Kelly looked over at Emilie and Nathan, chatting and laughing, and wiped her mouth. "Looks like they are having a good time. Good for him." Kelly muttered.

"Why is he talking to her anyway?" Jennifer exclaimed.

"Maybe he likes her." Kelly shook her head.

"Ugh." Jennifer mumbled. "She's got some nerve showing up here..."

"Jen, just let it go." Kelly frowned.

Jennifer looked at Kelly in disbelief and shook her head.

"Just enjoy the party. Brandon is here somewhere, why don't you go find him?" Kelly sighed.

"No need, he's over there with Eileen, Samantha and Maria. They're are like a bunch of flies around a big pile of....." Jennifer shrugged.

"Jen!" Kelly shook her head.

After a moment of silence, Jennifer's eyes widened. "Oh my god! I got it!" Jennifer exclaimed.

"What?" Kelly frowned and looked at Jennifer.

"Oh, this is going to be fantastic!" Jennifer rubbed her palms together.

"What are you talking about?" Kelly frowned.

"I know how we are going to make her pay for embarrassing you!" Jennifer rolled her eyes. "Please keep up, Kel!"

"Jen, no. I told you, leave it alone!" Kelly sighed.

"Kelly, you're my friend. Nobody embarrasses my friend and gets away with it." Jennifer said.

"I appreciate the gesture, but don't." Kelly said. "Please Jen."

"But..." Jennifer frowned.

"Promise me, you'll leave it alone." Kelly looked at Jennifer.

"I promise to leave it alone." Jennifer rolled her eyes.

"Thank you." Kelly nodded and turned around.

"Where are you going?" Jennifer asked.

"To the bar. My drink is empty." Kelly said.

"But she's there..." Jennifer crossed her arms and looked at her in disbelief.

"It doesn't matter, Jen." Kelly shook her head and walked to the bar.

"It matters to me." Jennifer grimaced and glared over at Nathan and Emilie.

"That was the best party I've been to in a

long time!" Shannon slurred as she, Emilie, Nathan and Zac stepped in to the elevator. Emilie reached over to the button marked 14, but Nathan beat her to it.

"That's my floor too!" Emilie giggled and looked at him, leaning against the wall of the elevator, looking at her with a casual smile.

Zac pressed the button marked 16 and Shannon giggled.

"What? Is that your floor?" Zac exclaimed and Shannon nodded.

"Such coincidences." Emilie leaned against the wall next to Nathan and looked at him. He looked at her and smiled with a nod.

The elevator came to a stop and the doors opened. Zac high-fived Nathan and Emilie hugged Shannon.

"See you tomorrow, superstar!" Shannon called out to Emilie.

"Bright and early on the court, Shan!" Emilie laughed.

"I'll need a wake-up call." Shannon mumbled.

"I can give you a wake-up call, if you like." Zac put his arm around Shannon's shoulder and she giggled.

"I'd like that!" Shannon laughed.

"Oh dear." Emilie laughed as they watched the elevator doors close in front of them.

"She seems like a handful." Nathan grinned. "Poor Zac."

"Hey, that's my friend you are talking about!" Emilie playfully smacked him on the arm, and she looked at him.

He was leaning against the wall again, holding on to the horizontal bar, looking at Emilie. She gave him a soft smile. "Are you really on floor fourteen?" She asked.

Nathan narrowed his eyes at Emilie and grinned. "What do you think?"

Emilie stared at him for a few seconds, trying to read his expression.

"I think you should walk me to my door." She grinned when the doors opened.

"Of course." Nathan grinned, dug his hands into his pockets and followed Emilie down the corridor. He walked beside her and occasionally looked at her. She caught him looking at her and smiled at him.

"This is me." She pointed to the door marked 14-17.

"Impossible, this is my room." Nathan smirked.

"Nice try, Nathan." Emilie crossed her arms and smiled at him.

"Please, call me Nate." He grinned at her.

"Okay, Nate. Thanks for a fun night." Emilie looked up at him.

"We should do this again sometime. Just without all the people and the absinthe." Nathan nodded.

"I totally agree." Emilie smiled shyly.

"How about tomorrow night?" Nathan looked at her, searching.

She smiled at him. "We need to focus on our games."

"I am focused." He was looking straight at her, not blinking or looking away.

Emilie could feel her heart rate increase rapidly and tried to keep her breathing under control. Nathan took a step towards her and took her hand. He pulled her towards him and she held her breath. He brought her hand up to his face and kissed the top of her hand softly.

"Do you need a wake-up call too?" He murmured.

Emilie, still holding her breath, just stared at him. She saw him raise his eyebrows and she exhaled. "I'm good." She whispered, breathlessly.

"Unless you want to come to my room and keep me company." His voice was like velvet.

"Nate...." She whispered. "I can't."

"Well, I'm in fourteen twenty-three, if you change your mind." He smiled at her, unaffected by her response.

Let's hope I come to my senses." Emilie frowned.

Nathan laughed softly and kissed her hand again. "Good night Emilie."

Good night Nate." She smiled at him and watched him walk away. He looked over his shoulder at her and she smiled at him. She opened her door and went inside. She locked the door behind her and leaned against the wall. She took a deep breath and laughed at herself. Focus, Emilie, focus!

Nathan took off his shirt and threw in on the floor. He undid his jeans and took them off, leaving them on the floor. He sat down on his bed and looked at the telephone on the bedside table next to him. He smiled, picked up the receiver and dialled 1-4-1-7. It rang a few times and Emilie picked up.

"Hello?" She sounded confused.

"Any chance of you changing your mind yet?" He smiled, leaning back and resting his head on the pillow.

"I'm not that easily persuaded." Emilie smiled.

"Looks like I've got my work cut out for me." Nathan chuckled.

"You sure do." Emilie laughed.

There was a brief silence on the line, but

Nathan could still hear Emilie's shallow breathing on the line.

"Well, good night then." Emilie said finally.

"Good night." Nathan smiled and heard the call disconnect. He put the receiver back in its place and stared at the ceiling, grinning. This girl had taken him completely by surprize. He closed his eyes and pictured her in front of him, those tight shorts that she wore tonight, her perfect legs, the way her hips move when she walked, the way she laughed, her gorgeous blue-grey eyes, her small pouty mouth. He felt a warm feeling wash over him, opened his eyes and sighed.

"This is gonna be a long night." He stood up and walked to the bathroom.

CHAPTER 3

"So?" Emilie asked.

"What?" Shannon asked.

"You and Zac? Last night?" Emilie picked up her spoon and scratched around in her bowl.

"A lady doesn't kiss and tell." Shannon grinned, shoving a spoonful of muesli into her mouth.

Emilie tilted her head to the side and glared at Shannon. "Since when?"

"Since now." Shannon grinned and chewed on her muesli.

"Spill it, Shan." Emilie shook her head as she watched her friend grab a napkin and wiped her mouth.

"Well, let's just say, DC Zac can show those Texas cowboys a thing or two!" Shannon whispered with a giggle. "So, what about you, superstar? How was your in-flight entertainment?"

"Well, if you want to know what happened, nothing happened." Emilie said.

"I'm am so disappointed in you." Shannon looked at her with a straight face.

"That's your type of thing, not mine, Shan. Besides, we sort of have a date tonight." Emilie looked up from her breakfast at Shannon.

"Sort of have a date?" Shannon frowned. "What does that even mean?"

"I told him to come over to my room tonight at six." Emilie put down her spoon on the table and crossed her arms.

"You're in one of the greatest city in the world and you invited him to your room?" Shannon exclaimed.

"Well, it is a pretty great room." Emilie shrugged.

"Don't rub it it now!" Shannon pointed her spoon in the air. "I guess it is more private..."

"I didn't know what to say. I called him up this morning..." Emilie said.

"Wait, you called him?" Shannon frowned.

"Yeah, last night he walked me to my room and he said if I wanted to keep him company he is in fourteen twenty-three." Emilie frowned.

"He gave you his room number?" Shannon exclaimed. "Just like that?"

"Yes." Emilie narrowed her eyes at Shannon, who looked completely stunned. "So I asked him to have breakfast with me this morning, but it turns out that he and Zac are going to go practice their serves this morning...." Emilie said.

"Yes, Zac mentioned that in the shower this morning." Shannon nodded, deep in thought.

Emilie raised her eyebrows, looked at her friend with wide eyes and shook her head. "Well, atleast now I know he didn't just brush me off."

"Yip." Shannon nodded, still chewing on her muesli.

"So, anyway, then he asked if we could so something this afternoon, but I told him that Spencer wants me to do laps in the pool, so he asked if I was going to be in a bikini, and I said maybe. Then he wanted to know if Spencer was going to be there, and he sounded relieved when I said no." Emilie said, with a small smile.

"Jealousy is a good sign." Shannon mumbled.

"There seems to be a vibe between him and Spencer." Emilie frowned.

"Of course there is, Em. Don't you watch the news?" Shannon asked in disbelief.

"What do you mean?" Emilie asked intrigued.

"Last year, Nathan beat Spencer's ass in the open final." Shannon whispered. "Spencer hates him."

"Hate is a pretty strong word, don't you think?" Emilie frowned.

"Em, Nate likes you, that's pretty obvious. Spencer, being your coach and all, gets to spend a lot of time with you, plus he gets to see you in a bikini." Shannon looked at her.

"But it's Spence." Emilie shrugged.

"Sure, but Nathan is obviously jealous. If you were in his shoes, wouldn't you be jealous?" Shannon pointed her spoon at Emilie.

No, of course not." Emilie looked at her unfinished breakfast in front of her.

"Em." Shannon raised her eyebrows and glared at her.

"Okay, maybe a little. But that doesn't mean anything." Emilie narrowed her eyes at Shannon and Shannon rolled her eyes.

"You like him, admit it." Shannon eyed her and Emilie glared at Shannon, narrowing her eyes.

"I don't blame you, he's quite a catch, I hear his family is loaded." Shannon smiled.

"Just because he's rich, does not mean he's a catch, Shannon. You know things like that don't matter to me." Emilie rolled her eyes.

"Well, besides that, he's charming, a complete gentleman and those arms!" Shannon purred.

Emilie rested her chin on her palms and sighed, dreamily. "Yeah. He has the most gorgeous green eyes, and his smile, and the way his hair falls when..." She stopped when she heard Shannon chuckle and glared at her.

"Busted." Shannon sang and took a sip of her water.

Emilie scowled at her and crossed her arms.

Shannon smiled and thought for a little while. "What time do you finish with your laps?"

"At about quarter to five." Emilie frowned. "Why?"

"Right, leave everything to me. Just make sure you are at your room at five sharp." Shannon took out her phone.

"What are you going to do?" Emilie frowned.

"There are a lot of people in this city that owe me." Shannon winked at Emilie.

Nathan grabbed a ball from the grass and walked to the baseline. He bounced the ball twice, shifted his weight and threw the ball in the air. As soon as the ball descended to Earth, Nathan raised his racquet and hit the ball with massive force, towards Zac. Zac ducked out of the way and the ball hit the back net.

"Are you trying to kill me?" Zac looked at Nathan.

"Sorry." Nathan smiled and lifted his white sunglasses from his eyes.

"Looks like you had a good night last night."

Zac laughed and picked up the ball and hit it back to Nathan. "You have been cheery all morning."

"You could say that." Nathan smiled and effortlessly hit the ball back to Zac. "I'm seeing her again tonight. In her room."

"So little Miss Fearless put out? Do tell, Nate." Zac hit the ball back at him.

"There's nothing to tell, Zac." Nathan ran towards the net and hit a powerful volley shot that passed by Zac's shoulder. Zac stopped in his tracks as the ball flew passed him. Nathan raised his hands and frowned.

"What do you mean? Nothing happened?" Zac was shocked and looked at him.

"Nope." Nathan pulled at the strings of his racquet and pulled his face at Zac.

"I'm disappointed. It's not like you." Zac shook his head and looked at him.

"Zac, come on man." Nathan shook his head.

"Girls can not resist your Connor charm, which is completely unfair, by the way." Zac said. "She turned you down, didn't she?"

"Nope." Nathan shook his head.

"What's wrong with you, man?" Zac frowned.

"I don't know, Zac. It's just, I'm tired of meaningless flings that don't mean anything."

Nathan shook his head.

"This girl is changing you already." Zac frowned.

"Maybe it's not the girl, maybe I want to change. It just feels different this time. She's different." Nathan looked at his friend.

"No man. Girls are all the same." Zac shook his head.

"I disagree, there's something about her." Nathan looked at Zac with a smile.

"Dude, what about Spencer? He's not going to give in that easily, you know that." Zac raised his eyebrows and picked up the ball behind him.

"Spencer is the least of my worries, Zac." Nathan grinned at him. "I know how to handle him. I always have."

"Just don't lose your focus, dude." Zac shook his head.

"Funny, that's exactly what she said." Nathan laughed.

Emilie sat on the grass, shaking her head at herself. Her mind was definitely not on her game, she was as distracted as hell. Nathan Connor seemed to occupy her mind ever since she woke up this morning. She looked at the light silver criss-cross scar on her knee and traced it with her finger.

"Emilie!" Spencer ran over to her. "Are you okay?"

Emilie looked up at him and she lifted her arms up. Spencer pulled her up from the ground and looked at her.

"It's not my knee, Spencer, it's my head." She laughed.

"Well get your head straight, Em. Tomorrow is your first round." Spencer growled at her. "The last thing you need now is to be distracted."

"Yes, I know." Emilie pouted, tilted her head and looked at Spencer.

His dark hair, electric blue eyes and tanned skin made him quite popular with the girls he coached, but he has only ever had one love. And that was tennis. He and Jeremy were best friends and they trained together ever since she could remember. Jeremy and Spencer were in the finals of the Grand Slam last year, but Jeremy beat him by two sets. Spencer had been more excited when Jeremy won the championship point than everyone else, Jeremy included.

She looked at him standing beside the net and he turned to look at her. Just looking at Spencer made her heart ache for her brother. She felt her heart cramp up in her chest, she threw her racquet down on the ground and marched over to him. He saw her approach him and frowned at her. She grabbed hold of him and put her arms around his waist. He put his arms around her shoulders and hugged her tight. After a few moments, Emilie pulled herself free and walked back to the baseline, picking up her purple racquet.

"What was that for?" Spencer frowned.

"You are the only thing that I have left of him, Spence." Emilie shrugged, adjusting her visor, then hitting her palm against the strings of her racquet.

Spencer smiled sadly and cleared his throat. "Right, keep going with your volleys."

"Sure." Emilie nodded and smiled at Spencer.

Tom Hayes sat in the hotel's restaurant, reading the Telegraph's front page. He opened the newspaper and his eyes widened. The was a picture of Emilie and Kelly glaring at each other in yesterday's press conference, with a headline that read 'Ready to Rumble?'. Tom sighed and read how Kelly and Emilie verbally attacked each other. He shook his head and adjusted his glasses. Right, Tom, this is the first headline. At least Emilie was not caught on camera with a guy or doing something irresponsible, like drinking or doing drugs. He thought back to the night of his son's death, when he got a call from Spencer to say that they have been in an accident. Three minutes later, Jeremy died. Tom arrived at the scene ten minutes later, and Emilie was still holding her brother's hand. Emilie was bleeding profusely from her right knee, but she did not care, she just held onto her brother and sobbed. There were pools of their blood all over the scene and Jeremy's silver Escalade was on it's roof, completely wrecked. Spencer tried to get Emilie away from Jeremy and into the ambulance, but she refused. She stayed with her brother until the coroner officially declared him dead. Emilie and Spencer had to be rushed to hospital for emergency surgery, and Tom waited alone in the waiting room for nine hours. The emotions hit him hard, and he was reminded of his wife, Paige, who had died fourteen years ago, in a similiar accident. He felt tears stinging his eyes and quickly wiped them away.

    Nathan put his racquet in his bag and zipped it shut when Jennifer walked up to him on the court.
    "Hey little brother!" She smiled.
    "Jennifer." He eyed his sister standing in front of him. He stood up from the bench and

swung his bag over his shoulder. "I haven't got time to talk."

"Not even for your favorite sister?" Jennifer crossed her arms and pouted.

Nathan stopped in his tracks and looked at her, unimpressed.

"I saw you at the party with that blonde girl last night." Jennifer grinned, blocking his way.

"Yeah, and since when is my social life any of your concern?" Nathan sneered.

"I'm just concerned that your head's not going to be in the game tomorrow." Jennifer tucked a strand of dark red hair behind her ear.

"I'm focused." Nathan looked at her, angrily. "Now get out of my way, Jen."

"You don't look focused to me, little brother." Jennifer lifted an eyebrow at him.

"Whatever, Jen!" He pushed her out of his way and marched angrily out of the tennis arena.

He looked at his watch, it was 14:00. Emilie should be alone at the pool already, he smiled. He walked briskly across the road and through the doors of the indoor swimming center. He looked through the glass window of the door and recognised Emilie's light blue and white bag on the bench and looked at the pool. He saw a blonde girl doing laps in the pool and knew it was her. He pushed the door open and walked into the arena. He put his bag down on the wooden bench and walked closer to the pool. He reached the railing of the ladder and leaned against it. Emilie surfaced and wiped her face. She looked at Nathan with a smile and swam to the side. Nathan knelt by the edge and smiled down at her.

"Glad you could make it." She grinned.

"At least you have another sport to fall back on in case tennis does not work out." He looked at the pool.

"I highly doubt that." She shook her head. "This is just to .."

"To relax your knee, I get it." He nodded. "Is it okay? Your knee?"

Emilie nodded, a small smile forming. "It's fine. I got through a whole practice today without having to stop for a rest."

"Wow. How about that?" He laughed, impressed by her endurance and looked around the arena. "So are you alone?"

"Yes. Do you want to join me?" She smiled slyly.

Nathan laughed and looked at her. "I'm not much of a swimmer."

"Neither am I." Emilie raised her shoulders. "It's nice after a session on the court. Cools you down."

Nathan stepped out of his slops and sat down on the tiles, his feet in the water. He looked at her and gave her a cocky smile.

Emilie swam over to the ladder and climbed out of the pool. Nathan looked at her, in a white and pink bikini and raised his eyebrows. She was hot! He could feel his pulse quickening and he looked around the arena.

"He's not here, he's with my dad." She grabbed her towel and dried herself. "They're having a late lunch at the Waldorf, or something. apparently they have the best lunch in the area."

"Huh." Nathan looked at her and grinned. "I should remember that, for future use."

"You want to take me for lunch?" Emilie smiled at him.

"Maybe." Nathan looked at her and he could see her cheeks flush slightly. "So, you're sure that Spencer is only your coach?" Nathan tilted his head at her.

"Spencer is just my coach, Nate." Emilie narrowed her eyes at him. "What is with you two anyway?"

"Some people lose gracefully, and some don't." Nathan said, looking at the water.

"And I'm guessing that Spencer didn't." Emilie frowned.

"You guessed correctly." Nathan dropped

his hands onto his lap.

"He always taught me to be a graceful loser, because from every defeat you learn more than from a win." Emilie sat down next to Nathan, her feet also in the water.

"Sounds like something a loser would say." Nathan laughed.

"It happens to be true." Emilie narrowed her eyes at him.

"I wouldn't know." Nathan said.

"What? You've never lost?" Emilie raised her eyebrows.

"Nope." Nathan said.

"Are you serious?" Emilie asked, slightly shocked.

When Nathan nodded with a grin, her jaw dropped. "No way."

"Does that surprise you?" Nathan looked at her.

"I guess not." Emilie pulled a face. "Did you ever play my brother?"

"Unfortunately not." Nathan shook his head.

"That's why you never lost." Emilie grinned and Nathan chuckled.

"I would have loved to have played him, though. I watched him at last year's Slam and I was really impressed. He had the most incredible footwork. The crowd absolutely oved him." Nathan nodded and looked at her.

"Jer could work a crowd without even realizing it. People couldn't get enough of him." She laughed sadly. "I couldn't get enough of him."

"I'm sorry about what happened." Nathan softly touched her arm.

"Thanks. Jer would have liked you." She smiled and their eyes locked. She stared into his green eyes and felt her head spin.

"Can I ask you something?" Nathan asked, after a brief pause.

"Sure." She nodded, looking away.

"Isn't it painful to be around Spencer, seeing as he and Jeremy were so close?" Nathan leaned forward and rested his hands on his knees.

Emilie turned to face him and smiled sadly. "Sometimes it feels like a dream, like at any moment he is going to come walking out onto the court and start yelling at me for getting my serves wrong. It is painful, I admit. If Spencer was not around so much, I would feel completely lost. It's like Spencer is the only thing I have left of Jer, you know."

"That's not true. You still have your tennis." Nathan touched her damp hair and she nodded. "And your dad."

Emilie raised her eyebrows and shrugged.

"That's not entirely true."

"Why do you say that?" Nathan frowned.

"My dad hates me, and I know that he doesn't want me to play tennis. He's never been to one of my games, ever." Emilie said.

"Never?" Nathan frowned.

"Never." Emilie nodded. "Ever since my mom died, he was never really....available, if you know what I mean."

"So why does he come along, if he does not come to watch?" Nathan asked.

"To check up on me? To ease his conscience? I honestly don't know." Emilie raised her shoulders and sighed.

"Don't let him put you off, Emilie. Just do what you love, the rest doesn't matter." Nathan smiled.

"Good-looking and profound. Who knew?" Emilie smiled at him. "Is it a Connor family trait?"

"Nope, I'm one of a kind." Nathan gave her a crooked smile.

"You aren't full of yourself at all." Emilie laughed and looked at him.

"Well, only sometimes." Nathan smiled.

"Yeah, especially when there are cameras around." Emilie nodded. "Then you're too cocky for your own good!"

"That was only to impress you." Nathan

laughed.

"Oh really?" Emilie playfully shoved Nathan.

"Yes. Really." Nathan laughed.

"You didn't need to." Emilie looked at the water.

"And why is that?" He looked at her.

"I don't impress that easily." Emilie giggled.

Nathan laughed and just stared at her. She looked at him and he saw a smile formed on her lips. Nathan had to fight every urge inside him, not to kiss her.

"You know what?" Nathan grinned.

"What?" Emilie tilted her head.

"I think I will join you after all." He stood up, took off his sunglasses, put them on the bench behind them and took off his shirt. "Finally." Emilie laughed, and looked at him over her shoulder. The sight of him took her breath away and stood up slowly, suddenly feeling a little light-headed. He walked to her, bare chested and she took a deep breath. He was perfect, completely perfect. His skin was damp from his practice on the court and his stomach, chest and arm muscles made her feel weak in the knees. She blinked and looked away, feeling an overwhelming rush of blood flowing to her face.

"See, now you're not the only one walking around half-naked." Nathan grinned, his green eyes twinkling with mischief.

Emilie nodded and looked at the water. "You wanna race?"

"Races are for swimmers." He grabbed hold of her and jumped into the water.

Emilie felt his strong arms around her waist and she let out a scream just before they hit the water. The cold pool water washed over her, but could still feel the heat of his arms around her, almost burning her skin. Emilie and Nathan surfaced at the same time and she laughed, wiping her face.

"Told you I wasn't a swimmer." He ran his hands through his hair and looked at her.

"It's all about tactics, huh?" She grinned and looked at him. His brown hair was dishevelled and wet, standing in all directions, not a look that she ever imagined on him, but he looked good. Correction, he looked fantastic! His green eyes were sparkling and the corners of his mouth curled up in a crooked smile. Nathan swam a bit closer to her, and their faces were only inches apart. Emilie could feel his breath on her face and felt her heart beat in her throat. Nathan tilted his chin up and Emilie could feel his lips brushing against hers. She could also hear Spencer's voice in the distance and the center's double doors slammed open. Emilie and Nathan looked up at the doors and at Spencer, shocked and embarrassed.

"What the..." Spencer exclaimed.

Nathan looked at Emilie, swimming to the opposite end of the pool, then looked at Spencer. "Spencer, good to see you!"

"What are you doing here, Connor?" Spencer tugged at his cap.

"Swimming." Nathan smiled.

Emilie closed her eyes and shook her head.

"I can see that, but there are seven other pools. Couldn't you have picked a different one?" Spencer snapped and Emilie glared at him.

"This one seems to be my favorite, actually." Nathan looked at Emilie and she smiled at him.

"Is that right?" Spencer crossed his arms.

"Actually, Emilie told me how swimming was good for relaxing tight muscles." Nathan grinned and swam for the ladder. He climbed to the top of the ladder and walked towards his bag.

"Well according to my knowledge, Emilie has a healed knee injury. What injury do you have, Connor?" Spencer crossed his arms and glared at him.

"My disfunctional brain, mainly. But I don't think that will ever heal." Nathan looked over at Emilie and winked at her. She suppressed a giggle by covering her mouth with both her hands.

"Neither do I." Spencer scowled.

"Ooh, aren't we in a bad mood today. Was the salad at the Waldorf not as good as you'd hoped?" Nathan grinned at him, pulling his shirt over his head and slipped his slops on.

"Just leave, Connor." Spencer still glared at him.

"Okay, okay, I'm going." He put his sunglasses on his head, picked up his bag and slung it over his shoulder. "Thank you for the swim, princess. We should definitely do it again." He smiled at Emilie, and she gave him a small wave. "Take it easy, Spencer." He walked briskly passed Spencer, giving him a cocky nod and pushed open the doors.

Emilie raised her hand out of the water, grabbed hold of the edge of the pool and lifted herself onto the tiles. She grabbed her towel and wiped her face. She looked over at Spencer, now glaring at her.

"What, Spencer?" She frowned.

"Him?" Spencer exclaimed.

"What about him?" Emilie snapped at him, wringing her hair.

"I don't want you near that guy." Spencer shook his head.

"Spence, it was just a swim, and you didn't have to be so rude to him " Emilie rolled her eyes and dried her arms.

"That was still being nice." Spencer muttered and shook his head.

"Just relax, Spence, you're far too uptight." Emilie put her hands on her hips and stared at him.

He glared at her and shook his head. "How do you suppose you are going to stay focused with a guy like that distracting you?"

"He's not a distraction." Emilie dried off her legs and her stomach.

"Of course he is, Em. Don't be stupid." Spencer shook his head.

"It's not about being stupid, Spencer...." Emilie ran her hand through her damp hair.

"Anything regarding him is, Em. He's a cocky kid that thinks the sun shines out of his ass and he can get any girl. Do you want to be just another notch on his bedpost, Em?" Spencer crossed his arms. "Because that is all that you will be to him! I know him, Emilie! That's what he does!"

"That is not true, Spence! He's not like that!" Emilie frowned and crossed her arms.

"Oh and you know him like I do?" Spencer looked at her, eagerly awaiting an answer. Emilie looked at him, hesitantly and Spencer shook his head. "You don't know anything about this guy, Em!"

"Just because you hate him, does not mean that I have to as well!" She walked passed him and threw the wet towel at him.

"Em, don't be like that.." Spencer tugged at his cap.

"Screw you!" She marched to her bag, pulled a pair of shorts on, threw her bag over her shoulder and walked to the double doors.

"Em, don't leave...." Spencer turned around and she could hear his voice was filled with regret.

Emilie looked over her shoulder at him and shook her head. "I'm done for the day, Spence."

Emilie felt her blood boil as she crossed the road and pushed through the glass doors of The Four Seasons. She avoided everyone's eyes and headed straight to the elevator. She pressed 14 and watched as the doors started to close. An arm reached into the elevator and the door opened again. It was the girl she saw with Kelly last night at the top floor party. The girl looked at the already lit 14 and stood beside Emilie with a grin.

"Your floor too?" She smiled, amused for some reason.

Emilie glanced over at her and nodded. "Yes.

Unfortunately." She mumbled, more to herself.

"Do you play?" She asked, gently tugging at Emilie's bag.

"Yes." Emilie nodded. "You?"

"Nope, I write."

"You're a journalist." Emilie said simply.

"You say that like it's a bad thing." The girl laughed. Something was familiar about her laugh, she just couldn't place it.

"Journalists aren't exactly my favorite people in the world." Emilie admitted.

"I'm Jennifer Grayson, I'm with the Telegraph." The girl held out her hand to Emilie with a smile.

Emilie took her hand and gave her a friendly smile. "Emilie Hayes."

"It's a pleasure to finally meet you!" Jennifer exclaimed. "I was a big fan your brother. I'm so sorry to hear what happened."

"Thanks." Emilie frowned.

"Look, I don't want to push my luck here, but you wouldn't happen to be interested in doing an interview, would you?" Jennifer asked.

"No." Emilie said simply, looking at Jennifer.

Jennifer opened her mouth to say something else, luckily the elevator doors opened and Emilie rushed out.

"Just one interview...." Jennifer gently grabbed her hand, but Emilie glared at her dissaprovingly.

"Look, Miss Grayson, what part of no don't you understand?" Emilie scowled.

"I was just..." Jennifer tried again.

"Making a nuisance of yourself, I agree. I would appreciate it if you wouldn't ask me again. Ever." Emilie snapped at her and whirled around, heading down the corridor to her room.

"Alright then." Jennifer's smile faded and she crossed her arms as she watched Emilie walk away.

Emilie stopped in front of her door and took her keycard out of her side pocket. She looked over her shoulder at Jennifer, confidently walking further up the corridor, like nothing had happened. Emilie frowned at herself, shook her head and opened her door. She felt her bag slide from her shoulder when she looked at the chaos going on inside her room.

Nathan was stretched out on his couch, his hands under his head, staring at the television. There was a soft knock on his door and he jumped up from the couch. Expecting it to be Emilie, he ran to the door and opened it with a smile.

"Glad to see me?" Jennifer smirked and leaned her head against the frame.

His face dropped and he let out an irritated groan.

"Or maybe expecting someone else?" Jennifer laughed and pushed passed her brother.

"What do you want?" Nathan closed the door behind him.

Jennifer sat down on the couch and crossed her legs. "I met Emilie in the elevator a few minutes ago."

Nathan walked over to her and opened his mouth to say something.

"I was perfectly civil, don't stress, little brother." Jennifer lifted her hand up in the air. "She's...uhm, really nice."

"Jen, you..."

"Relax, little brother." Jennifer rolled her eyes. "Why are you so uptight?"

"I know you by now, sis." Nathan scowled.

"I think you two would make a really adorable couple." Jennifer said, looking at Nathan.

Nathan looked at her and frowned. "What are you up to?"

"Nothing, I swear. Kelly is the one that wants her out, not me." Jennifer said.

"Kelly? Why?" Nathan sat on the couch

opposite Jennifer.

"Who knows, she's such a deceptive vengeful bitch." Jennifer sighed.

"Speak for yourself." Nathan lifted an eyebrow.

"Hey!" Jennifer raised a finger in the air. "Be nice."

Nathan rolled his eyes at her and stood up from the couch.

"I can tell you one thing, little brother." Jennifer lifted an eyebrow at him, grinning wickedly.

"And what is that?" Nathan crossed his arms.

"She's got such an amazing coach." Jennifer stood up and grinned.

"Jen, don't start." Nathan growled.

"Temper, temper." Jennifer pouted. "So defensive already, and you haven't even slept with her yet. Could it be that my brother is falling for her?"

"You're crossing a line, Jen." Nathan crossed his arms again.

"Don't worry, Nate, I won't tell." She put her finger against her mouth and pouted. "Actually, I am rather happy for you."

"Why?" Nathan frowned at his pestering sister.

"She's blond and pretty, not like that other

one..." Jennifer looked at him. "What was her name again?"

"Jen!" Nathan growled again.

"And she's very feisty. She turned me down for an interview, and before I could even ask her to reconsider, she dismissed me, completely. She's got guts! Any girl willing to do that, with complete grace I might add, is worthy to date my precious little brother!" Jennifer winked at him and walked to the door.

"Why are you being so nice?" Nathan was shocked.

"Who knows? I guess I am turning over a new leaf. Or something like that." Jennifer grinned and opened the door. "Toodles, little brother!"

Nathan stood there, in his room, staring at the door, in disbelief. Since when has his sister believed in turning over a new leaf? He didn't trust this at all. He was going to have to tell Emilie about Jennifer. Maybe Jen was right, he thought to himself, maybe he is falling for her. That's impossible though, he was not the type of guy to fall for a girl he barely knows, so quickly. In most situations, it was just to impress girls with the things that he did, but with Emilie he felt different, like he did not need to try so hard to make her smile. He looked at his watch and sighed. It was 15:15, two hours and forty-five minutes to go. He honestly did not know how he was going to make time fly, just so he could see her again. He frowned to himself and shook his head.

CHAPTER 4

Shannon stopped in her tracks when she saw Emilie standing in the doorway, looking at her in disbelief. Everywhere Emilie looked there was food and candles and clothes and flowers. Emilie put her bag down on the floor and walked slowly towards Shannon.

"Shan?" She almost whispered. "What's going on in here?"

"Preparations, what else, honey?" Shannon looked at her for a second, brought her hand up to her chin and nodded. "Good thing you finished early. You're a mess!"

"Shan!" Emilie sighed.

"Come, sit!" Shannon ordered and Emilie sat down on the sofa. "Desiree, Francine, she's over here." She called out.

Two young women came running to Emilie and smiled at her. The one, Desiree, with platinum blond cropped hair started combing out her hair and the other one, Francine, with bright red curly hair, was wiping Emilie's face with a damp cotton wool pad.

"Shannon Moore!" Emilie exclaimed and everyone froze, the room suddenly silent. "Get your butt over here!"

Francine and Desiree looked at her with

wide eyes and then exchanged looks. Shannon walked towards her and sat in front of her on the opposite sofa, gently resting her hands on Emilie's knees.

"Okay, my friends, here's the deal. You sit and let these two fabulous women make you even more beautiful than you already are, they'll do your hair, your make-up, get you dressed, while Louise and I take care of the food and the setting. Then, when all goes according to plan, you and your in-flight entertainment will have a magical night beyond your wildest expectations!" Shannon grinned.

"Do I have a choice?" Emilie frowned at Shannon.

"Hey, you were the tart that invited him to your room in the first place. Just deal with it." Shannon put her hands on her hips and Emilie nodded. Shannon clapped her hands excitedly and smiled. "Ah, I wish Socrates was here to see this."

Nathan paced around his room, wearing a black shirt and dark jeans. His hair was standing in all directions as he frequently ran his hands through his hair. He kept looking at his watch, but time seemed to stand still. He glanced over to his laptop in the far corner of his living room and walked to the desk. He sat down, powered up his laptop and checked his emails. There was one of his mother, saying how she misses him and how she knows he will do well. He opened another email, from the International Tennis Board and he scrolled through all the names of the players. Right at the bottom was a paragraph on Jeremy Hayes. "Emilie's performance will be dedicated to her late brother, and tennis great, Jeremy Hayes. He will remain in the hearts of everyone that knew him, and even those who did not." Nathan read out loud. He frowned and closed his emails. He opened Google.com and typed 'Jeremy Hayes death' and clicked on 'search'. He opened the first headline and scrolled down to read the articles. He frowned as he read how Jeremy, Spencer and Emilie were driving from an undisclosed location to the New York Hilton, when Jeremy lost control of the car and it flipped over and skid onto the opposite side of the road hitting a solid concrete wall. Emilie and Spencer were lucky enough to make it out of the car alive, but Jeremy died on the scene from extreme hemorrhaging on the brain, before the emergency vehicles could get to the scene, in his sister's arms. Spencer had a broken right leg and dislocated his left shoulder, whereas

Emilie tore every ligament in her right knee and shattered her kneecap, along with other multiple scratches and bruises. It said that Emilie refused treatment and stayed with her brother until the coroner officially declared him dead. Emilie and Spencer were rushed to the Manhattan Hospital, were they had to have emergency surgery. The doctors initial progonis concerning Emilie's knee was not good, and her surgeon, Doctor Aiden Gilbert was convinced that she would never walk normally, let alone play tennis, ever again. Nathan frowned as he touched his right knee and pictured the scene in his head. If the car flipped over onto the other side of the road, Emilie's left knee would have gotten hurt, not her right. Right? But then again, if the car flipped over, it would be the other side, wouldn't it? Maybe he could ask her about it. Later. He scratched his head and scrolled down to look at the crash photographs. He winced as he saw the crumpled up silver Escalade, flipped over on its roof. He heard some commotion in the corridor, but took no notice of it. He rested his elbows on the desk and sighed at the thought of   Emilie going through all that. Even though she had lost her brother and that she was told that she could never play tennis again, that through all that pain and heartache, she had picked herself up and here she was, competing for the title of the US open. Damm, he admired her perseverance! She never quit, she deserved to be here more than anyone. He kept thinking about her right knee and frowned again. He shook his head free of all the questions and the doubt and closed his laptop. The last thing that she needed was to be cross examined.

    He glanced at his watch and grinned. It was 17:57. He jumped up from the chair, leaving his wallet, and also his room-key that he had completely forgotten about at the time, on the table. He bolted for the door and closed it behind him. He walked down the corridor and stopped a few feet from Emilie's door. 14-17. He took a deep breath and looked at his watch. 18:00. Right on time. As usual. He smiled at himself, and firmly knocked on the door. He waited for a few seconds and knocked again. The door opened and the sight of her took his breath away. She was wearing a short white halterneck dress and black peeptoe high heeled shoes. Her hair hung down her shoulders and there was a small flower pinned on the right side of her head, keeping her hair out of her face. She tucked a strand of hair behind her ear and he noticed that her lips were a glossy, kissable pink. Her eyes were smouldering and a hint of glitter made her skin glow. She smiled when she saw him in his black shirt and dark jeans, and she opened the door for him.

"Hey there." She smiled at him.

"You look gorgeous." He tilted his head and looked at her again, entranced.

"Thank you, you too." She nodded slightly. "Come on in."

He nodded with a smile and walked into her room. More like a penthouse! The room was twice, no three times, the size of his room, with a massive living area, which now, had been converted into a dining area. The couches were moved out of the way, there was a fluffy blanket on the floor, with a picnic basket and candles all around. The shades were opened all the way and the New York skyline made for a spectacular view. There was soft, slow music playing in the background and the lights were low. He glanced over at her and raised an eyebrow. "I'm so impressed." He smiled at her.

"I'm glad to hear that." She picked up two glasses of champagne and handed him one.

"Wow, here's to you." He grinned at her. "For surprizing the hell out of me."

"And here's to you." She laughed. "For looking really good and for showing up."

"Like I would dare to stand you up." Nathan laughed with her and stared at her again. Their two glasses made a clinking noise as the glasses connected with each other and they took a sip of champagne.

"Isn't this beautiful?" She smiled as they walked over to the window. "Even the moon favoured us tonight."

"I've never seen anything like it." Nathan looked out the window at the moon. "It seems that I like your room better."

Emilie put her glass down on the table, looked over at him and narrowed her eyes. "And why is that?"

Nathan looked at her intensely and grinned. "Well, the logical answers would be, the size of the room, the view, or even the fabulous band gracing us with their vocals tonight, but to me, none of those answers comes to mind, at all."

"Not even a little bit?" Emilie turned to face him and stared into his green eyes.

"Nope. Not even a little bit." He smiled at her, and put down his glass of champagne.

"Then tell me, Nathan Connor, why do you seem to like my room better than your own?" Emilie looked at him.

Nathan lifted his hand to her face and brushed her cheek. "Because you are in this room." Nathan's hand cupped her face and stared at her for a second, then shifted closer to her. He stared into her pale-blue eyes and brushed a strand of hair out of her face. Emilie held her breath and she closed her eyes as Nathan's head leaned in closer to hers, his lips pressing gently, yet urgent, against hers. She felt his mouth move and she parted her lips. His tongue, still tasting of champagne and toothpaste, gently moved against hers and she moaned indulgently. His hands gripped her waist and she held on to his arms, as if they were the only things holding her down, incase she might just float away. The kiss simmered down and Nathan was the first to pull away. Emilie opened her eyes and Nathan was captivated from the start.

"That was a really good answer." She breathed, with a smile. She pulled him against her and she could feel his body tense up, in a good way.

"You think anybody can see us from up here?" Nathan broke the silence.

Emilie looked over her shoulder, out the window. "That's the beauty of the fourteenth floor. We're invisible to the naked eye." She raised an eyebrow and grinned at him.

"So, even if we continued kissing in front of the window the whole night, nobody would know?" Nathan's voice had that velvety tone again.

"Not unless we told someone." Emilie looked out the window again.

He grinned. "Not that I would, of course."

Emilie's eyebrows shot up and she put her hand on her hip. "No?"

"Of course not, I'm not that kind of guy." He grinned.

Emilie took a large gulp of champagne and smiled at him. "So, what kind of guy are you?"

"Let me show you." He smiled at her and took her hand. He twirled her around and pulled her close to him, slowly dancing to the sound of Parachute playing in the background.

Jennifer knocked on a door marked 15-18 and Kelly opened her door a few moments later.

"I have some news!" Jennifer beamed.

"Somebody better be dead." Kelly rolled her eyes.

"You look tired, Kel." Jennifer looked at her.

"I was just on my way to bed, Jen. I have a game on tomorrow, in case you have forgotten." Kelly motioned to herself, already in her pajamas.

"Oh, this will only take a second, I promise!" Jennifer pushed the door open and walked into Kelly's room.

"When has it ever taken a second?" Kelly sighed and closed her door.

"This very moment, as we speak, Nate is in her room....." Jennifer exclaimed.

"Jen, I don't care if he is in Huxley's room giving him head, I want to sleep." Kelly interrupted with a frown and rubbed her eyes.

Jennifer looked at her friend and scowled. She opened her mouth to say something, but Kelly pointed a finger at her.

"Not a word." Kelly shook her head. "Get!" She motioned to the door, irately.

"But...." Jennifer tried.

"Out Jen!" Kelly pointed to the door, her eyes closed.

Jennifer's shoulders slumped and she walked to the door, pausing and looking over her shoulder.

"I said out!" Kelly's voice echoed off the walls and Jennifer stared at her.

"Night Kel." Jennifer said before exiting the room.

Kelly sighed and walked back to her bedroom. She fell into bed and looked at the clock next to her. 20:55. She pulled a face and rolled over onto her back. Gone were the days when she could stay up until the sun rose, partying the whole night long. Now she had to be in bed by eight thirty, or she would be totally ruined the next morning. She couldn't believe Jennifer was acting so stupid about this whole Emilie Hayes story. Frankly, Kelly did not care if Emilie embarrassed her or not, she would prove her wrong on court, not with some stupid, pathetic attempt to ruin the poor girl off the court. That was not fair! Tomorrow morning she would tell Jennifer to grow up and get a life, not that Jennifer would be too happy about that, but Kelly did not care. All she wanted to do now, was focus on her games, the rest was just unneccesary bullshit. She closed her eyes and drifted off to sleep.

"So you're confident you're going to win this year?" Emilie grinned, took a bite of cucumber and rested her head against Nathan's shoulder as they sat on the blanket, their backs leaning against the sofa.

"You sound like my sister." He frowned, putting his arm around her shoulder.

"You have a sister?" Emilie looked at him.

"Yeah. I think you met her already. Jennifer Grayson." He nodded.

"That's your sister?" Emilie exclaimed, feeding him the rest of the cucumber.

"Unfortunately yes." Nathan nodded again and chewed loudly. "She's the evil twin."

"You're twins?" Emilie exclaimed.

"Yes. Thankfully we don't look alike." Nathan nodded.

"Is she married?" Emilie asked.

"Nope, she just changed her last name when she moved here. Apparently it sounds more professional." Nathan sighed.

"She looks nice enough." Emilie grinned.

"Looks can be deceiving." Nathan sighed.

"So have you got any other twins in your family?" Emilie asked.

"My cousins in Malibu, and my aunt and uncle in Chicago." Nathan said.

"Wow, the Connors are all over the place." Emilie giggled and rested her hand on his chest.

"No, they're from my Mother's side of the family. My cousins, Scott and Jason, are the greatest. One Spring break they tried to teach me how to surf, but that was a complete disaster! Scott told me to rather stick with tennis." Nathan laughed.

"So is it just you and your sister?" Emilie asked.

"Yes." Nathan took her hand and sat up a bit. "Apparently we were more than enough for my parents to handle."

"Are both your parents still alive?" Emilie asked, studying his face.

"Yes, and no." Nathan looked at the giant question mark on Emilie's face and he smiled sadly. "They're both still alive. My dad was, still is never at home, so even though he was there, he wasn't really there at all. He's an architect and he wanted me to join the Connor family business. I did it for two years, but it was not what I wanted to do. My dad could not understand this and eventually just gave up on me. My mom was the one that supported me, no matter what I did. She never had a problem with me giving up my studies, as long as I was happy. I still call her every other day, just to check on her. Ever since I started travelling so much, she is all alone in the house."

"She sounds sweet!" Emilie smiled.

"She is. She's one of the best people I have ever known." Nathan nodded. "Unlike my father."

"Is he really that bad?" Emilie rested her head on his shoulder.

"You have no idea. Everything that my mom is, he is the total opposite. He's so detached from our family, he does not care about anyone but himself." Nathan shrugged.

"Another thing we have in common." Emilie nodded and looked at him.

A long silence filled the room and Emilie

shifted uncomfortably. Nathan studied her expression and smiled at her. "So, correct me if I'm wrong, but this is your first US open, because I would definitely have remembered you from last year." He grinned at her and squeezed her arm.

She looked at him and the corners of her mouth curled up slightly. "Yes, this is my first. Believe it or not, but eighteen months ago, I was still sporting amateur colors, but I turned pro about thirteen months ago."

"Is that so? No wonder Shannon calls you Superstar." Nathan laughed, clearly impressed. "So why the US open then?"

"Well, I entered last year's qualifiers with...with Jeremy and Spencer, and the three of us made it through all the elimination rounds. Then after the accident and my...my brother's death, I swore I would never play tennis again. Ever. My recovery went excrutiatingly slow, and I wanted to quit, many times. But Spencer, he was the one that told me to keep fighting. You know, Doctor Gilbert thought I would never be able to walk normally again, let alone play tennis." She said sadly.

"But here you are, a little superstar." He grinned at her. He tilted her chin upwards with his hand and kissed her lips tenderly.

Emilie pulled away and looked at him. Nathan glanced at his watch and felt his body jolt up. It was 22:35. "Shit, is that the time?" He sat upright and looked bewildered at Emilie.

"You want to go?" Emilie smiled sadly.

Nathan looked at her and cupped her face with his hands. "No, I don't, but I should." He shook his head lightly and kissed her softly on the lips. Nathan stood up from the floor and pulled Emilie onto her feet. They crossed the room and Nathan shoved his hands into his pockets, frowning.

"Something wrong?" Emilie looked at him, puzzledly.

"I can't seem to find my key." Nathan went through his pockets again. "Looks like I'm going to have to sleep here tonight."

"You planned this, didn't you?" Emilie crossed her arms, with a slight grin on her face.

"I can understand how you would say that, but actually no. I really did misplace my key." Nathan shook his head.

Emilie burst out laughing and Nathan joined her. Their laughter subsided and they stared at each other again.

"Come on, let's go get you one from the front desk." Emilie reached for the door.

Nathan grabbed hold of her hand and shook his head. "Do you really think that is such a good idea? Aren't you afraid someone might see us, together? This time of the night. Asking for a room key?"

Nathan could see Emilie thought about it for a second and saw the sense fill her head again. "You're right. Way too obvious." She nodded. "Not that I care what people think..." She added.

"Same here, but don't you think we better not do this, uhm, publicly?" Nathan kissed her on her lips and looked at her.

"I suppose." She sighed dreamily. "But how am I going to be able to keep my distance from you?"

"It's going to be difficult." He smiled.

"But worth it?" Emilie looked up at him.

"Absolutely." He nodded. "Plus your dad and Spencer might flip."

Emilie narrowed her eyes at him, but he returned with a sexy smile, which melted away her annoyance at the way he said Spencer's name, and she smiled dreamily.

"So, I guess this is good night then." Nathan nodded and kissed the top of Emilie's hand.

"You don't have to go yet." She tilted her head to the side and sighed.

"I tell you what, tomorrow night we can

rendezvous in my room." Nathan smiled crookedly.

"Promise?" Emilie smiled.

"Yes, and then after we win the US open, I'll take you for lunch at the Waldorf, and for martini's at the Hilton!" He grinned at her.

"That sounds nice." She smiled and he frowned. "More than nice, fantastic."

"Better." He laughed and kissed her tenderly on the lips and opened the door. "Good night superstar." He smiled at her and walked out into the corridor.

"Night." She smiled shyly and leaned against the door frame. She watched him walk down the corridor, towards the elevator, when he paused and looked over his shoulder at her. He smiled at her and gave her a nod. She gave him a small wave and closed the door with a giggle.

Nathan walked out of the elevator on the ground floor and headed in the direction of the front desk. He whistled under his breath as he walked up to the counter and smiled to himself.

"Good evening Mister Connor." The woman behind the desk smiled at him.

"Good evening. I seem to have misplaced my room key." Nathan grinned at the woman's name tag on her chest. "Marilyn, would you kindly arrange a replacement for me. Fourteen twenty-three." He leaned over the desk, towards Marilyn, flashing her a smile.

"Certainly Mister Connor." Her face flushed and she typed frantically on her keyboard. She took a card out of the drawer and swiped it through a machine. She typed again on her keyboard and handed the card to Nathan.

"I will be forever in your debt, Marilyn. I thank you. Have a pleasant night." He smiled at her, taking the card from her and spun around.

"Lost your key?"

Nathan looked up and into the dark, cocky brown eyes of Brandon. "Not that it is any of your business, but yes." He smirked. "I'm surprised to see you are still awake at this hour."

"Good boys don't go to bed early." Brandon grinned at him.

"So why exactly are you still up?" Nathan frowned and crossed his arms.

"None of your business, Connor." Brandon sneered and walked to the elevator.

Nathan shook his head and followed Brandon to the elevator. Nathan watched the doors closing in front of them and he fiddled with his key.

"Rumor has it you and Hayes were quite cosy up in fourteen eighteen tonight." Brandon said, staring into space.

"Rumor has it?" Nathan narrowed his eyes at Brandon.

"Things don't stay a secret very long in this place. Everyone talks to everyone." Brandon gave Nathan a crooked smile. "Plus, the staff seem to be easily persuaded, if you know what I mean." Brandon smirked.

"I can't imagine that Jack will be too happy with the idea that you screw the staff, just to get your daily dose of inside info on who's screwing who." Nathan shook his head, disapprovingly.

"I just can't imagine how Emilie's father would react if he knew that you are screwing his daughter right under his nose..." Brandon sneered. "And Spencer would be furious, to say the very least. But then again, you always did manage to piss Spencer off when it comes to women..."

Nathan grabbed Brandon by the collar and pushed him against the elevator wall, with a growl.

"Easy, easy, I won't tell." Brandon laughed.

"Just for your information, I am not screwing her!" Nathan loosened his grip and pushed Brandon back against the wall.

"Sure, dude, whatever." Brandon shook his head. "But if you won't, I will."

Nathan felt himself lose control and punched Brandon in the face. Brandon fell to the floor of the elevator and Nathan stared down at him. "Don't you ever talk about her like that again! Do you understand me?"

Brandon gave him a weak salute and grinned. "Sure thing, Connor."

Nathan took a deep breath and stormed out of the elevator when the doors opened. He marched past Emilie's room and paused briefly in front of her door, raised his hand to knock, but he brought his hand up to his face instead. He rubbed his eyes and shook his head, and walked to his room, furious with Brandon, Spencer and himself.

CHAPTER 5

Emilie felt her heart beat in her throat as she stepped out into the sunlight, on court four. There weren't many spectators around, but seeing as this is only the first stages of the tournament, she didn't expect a full house. She looked over at her first opponent, a petite asian girl, Amirah Yanamoto, with large, dirt colored bulging eyes and an unstylishly tight pair of red shorts. To Emilie it seemed as if this girl either has no sense of style, or she is trying too hard. How she could play in shorts that tight? Apparently she was the only one that needed blood supply to her legs. She looked down at her own outfit, a pair of white skorts, a light blue vest and her trusty purple tennis racquet. She put her bag down on the chair next to the umpire's high chair and took a few deep breaths. She smoothed her hair out of her face and adjusted her white visor. She could feel Spencer's eyes on her and she glanced at him, over her shoulder. She felt a feeling of disappointment wash over her and sighed. If only her father could have been here. Even though she felt abandoned and upset by her father's absence, she gave Spencer a subtle nod and Spencer gave her a not so subtle thumbs-up. Emilie shifted her gaze, and searched the crowd for Shannon. Shannon was sitting with the on-site doctor in their own booth closer to the court. Shannon waved at her excitedly, and cheered. Emilie chuckled as she watched the doctor sitting next to Shannon frown heavily. She shook her head and raised her racquet at Shannon, before turning around and walking to the baseline. A short boy, aged eleven Emilie would guess, threw two balls at her, and she thanked him with a smile. The one ball she tucked under the elastic of her skort and the other one she held in her left hand. She subtlely scanned the crowd, for the slight chance that Nathan was there, but he wasn't. He had his own games to focus on. That was exactly what she needed to do now, to focus on her games. Starting with this one!

"Hayes to serve." The umpire said over the speaker.

She took another deep breath and looked at her opponent, waiting on the other side of the net. She bounced the ball once, twice, three times, tossed it up in the air and swung her racquet in a strong, swift motion, feeling the shock in her wrist as the racquet hit the ball. The ball flew over the net, bounced off the cement, and somehow deviated straight into Yanamoto's face.

"Love, forty. Match point." The umpire's voice sounded through the speakers.

Nathan grinned to himself, looking over at his exhausted opponent. He adjusted his black cap and bent his knees, waiting for the serve. His opponent, Timothy Gerrard, was sweating profusely and Nathan chuckled to himself. Already on his third game for the day, he was on a roll, winning with straight sets every single time. He thought, for a brief second, of Emilie and wondered how she was doing. If she was also doing as well as he was. He also hoped that her knee was not giving her any problems, and that she would hopefully get to see him play a game. He frowned as he realised how badly he wanted to see her play. He cleared his head and took a deep breath, trying not to think about Emilie. Nathan shifted his weight and watched as Timothy served, if you can even call it that. The ball flew towards Nathan and he did not even strain to reach it. He hit a powerful groundstroke that sent the ball flying towards Timothy. Timothy ran forward, towards the net and sent it flying high in the air. Nathan ran to the net, and raised his racquet, tilting it slightly to the left and smashed the ball towards the open court. Timothy, still close to the net, watched as the ball flew passed him and he threw his racquet onto the blue cement.

"Game, set, match, Connor." The umpire's monotonous voice sounded.

The small crowd of spectators cheered and clapped and Nathan lifted up his racquet up at them, giving them a cocky smile.

Nathan lowered his racquet and walked towards the net, where a clearly exhausted Timothy, picked up his racquet and walked towards him. Nathan shook Timothy's hand and gave him a quick nod."Good game, man."

"Whatever, dude." Timothy grimaced and reached for his towel.

Nathan grinned and heard cheers behind him. He looked over his shoulder at his 'fan club' and chuckled. A group of five girls were cheering at him and going crazy. He took a few steps towards them, took his cap off his head and threw it at them. The girls shrieked and all five of them tried to grab the flying cap. Nathan laughed at these silly girls, but secretly hoped that Emilie was there to see him win. The girls were still fighting over the cap, when Nathan turned around and walked back to his bag. He slid his sunglasses over his eyes and swung his bag over his shoulder. He left the court and pushed open the doors of the locker room.

"Well done, little brother." Jennifer was leaning against his locker, holding a microphone.

"Thanks." He said simply, sat down on the bench, looking for a towel and glanced at his watch.

"Her last game finished about ten minutes ago." Jennifer crossed her arms, smiling. "I just thought you'd like to know."

Nathan jerked his head up and stared at her.

"I am also glad to report that she won all her games and she advanced to next weeks' quarter-finals." Jennifer reported. "She's not half bad, actually. Her volleys are amazing, for a little girl like her, she has quite an arm!"

Nathan sat up and glared at her. "What's the deal with you, Jen?"

"What do you mean?" Jennifer asked with a frown.

Nathan put his bag down on the bench and eyed her suspiciously. "You know what I mean, Jen."

"Look, Nate, this may come as a surprize, especially to you, but I really am glad for you." Jennifer smiled.

"That's a first." He shook his head disapprovingly.

"All I'm saying is, keep your focus, Nate." Jennifer looked at him.

She turned around and walked out the doors. Nathan ran his hands through his hair and frowned at himself. His sister was acting weird, nice, but for her that was weird. Maybe she was coming down with some untreatable disease. Wishful thinking Nate, he thought out loud and shook his head.

Shannon walked into the lobby and spotted Emilie and Spencer. She grinned and ran to Emilie.

"Oh my god! I am so proud of you!" Shannon put her arm around Emilie's shoulder and squeezed it.

Emilie smiled at her. "It was all Spencer. If he was not so persistant, I wouldn't even have made it through the first round."

"Rubbish, that was all you out there!" Shannon frowned. "We have to go celebrate tonight!" She exclaimed excitedly.

"Shan, no, I'm tired." Emilie rolled her eyes and rested her head on Shannon's shoulder. "Rather tomorrow night, please?"

"Even superstars get tired, Shannon." Spencer said behind them.

Emilie and Shannon turned around and Emilie smiled at Spencer. "You were great,

Em." Spencer hugged her and her face flushed a little.

"I was just telling Emilie, that we should go celebrate tonight. A well deserved party!" Shannon looked at Spencer and tilted her head. "What do you say, Spence, you want to come?"

"Shannon, Emilie's had a rough day." Spencer shook his head.

"Party-pooper." Shannon crossed her arms.

"Yeah, Shan, I'm tired!" Emilie exclaimed.

"Yeah, I would be too." Shannon winked at her.

"And why is that?" Spencer frowned.

Emilie and Shannon exchanged panicked looks and stared blankly at Spencer. "Well, uhm, you just said so yourself. She, uhm, played THREE games today, and uhm, she did not sleep very well late, I mean last night." Shannon stuttered. "Right, Em?"

"Yeah, I was worried my knee was going to give me trouble today, it kept me awake a bit last night. But I'm okay." Emilie nodded.

Spencer narrowed his eyes, eyeing them suspiciously.

"So, is it okay if I take her out tomorrow night then, Coach?" Shannon smiled at Spencer.

Spencer looked at Emilie, wiping her face

with a towel, hiding her face, and then at Shannon, chewing nonchalantly on a piece of gum. "Sure, but no driving."

"Spence, this is New York City, nobody drives anywhere anymore, that's what taxi's are there for!" Shannon grinned and lightly patted her hand against his arm. "Don't worry, Spence, I promise to take good care of her."

"Do you really think that is such a good idea?" Tom shoved his hands into his pants pockets.

"Yes, I do, so does Shan, and so does Spencer." She sighed and looked at her father. "I need a day off, I really need this, Daddy."

"Just you and Shannon?" He eyed her suspiciously.

"Yes, Daddy."

"Is that safe?" Her father crossed his arms. "Maybe Spencer..."

"That's okay, really. We'll be extra safe, as we always are." Emilie pleaded.

"No boys?" Tom raised his eyebrows. "I don't want you galavanting with strange men."

"No boys, Daddy." Emilie shook her head. "I promise."

"Alright then. Be careful. Don't make me read about you in the paper. Again." Tom frowned.

"I was emotional, and she provoked me." Emilie defended. "It won't happen again, I promise."

Tom crossed her arms and looked at Emilie. "You're as fiery as your mother was."

"So you say, but she was French." Emilie looked at him and sighed. "No headlines, I promise."

"You and Shannon have fun." Tom nodded at her.

"We will. Thanks Dad." Emilie smiled and walked back to Shannon and Spencer.

"And?" Shannon lifted her eyebrows.

Emilie nodded with a wide grin and gave Shannon a thumbs-up.

"Fantastic!" Shannon shrieked and put her arms around Emilie's shoulders.

"And that's my cue to leave." Spencer rolled his eyes at the two overly-excited girls and walked to the front desk.

"What did you tell him?" Shannon shrieked.

"The truth. That we are going swimming now, and then have a sleepover in my room, and then we're going sight-seeing the whole day tomorrow." Emilie grinned.

"Genius! Absolute genius!" Shannon nodded. "But let's tweak the details a bit. Let's go swimming, as planned, do a co-ed sleep-over with Zac and Nathan, and go sight-seeing and clubbing with them tomorrow night." Shannon wiggled her eyebrows at Emilie.

"It's too public, Shan. I don't want any reporters following my every move. Besides, my dad would kill me! I promised him, no headlines, and no boys." She looked at Shannon with a pout.

Shannon tapped Emilie on the shoulder, pointing to the rotating glass doors of the hotel and grinning. "Honey, you don't have to worry about that. Because those, are not boys."

Emilie looked over at the doors and saw Nathan and Zac making their way towards them. Nathan looked completely irresistible in his baggy black Nike shorts and a white Nike vest, his hair slightly damp and standing in all directions, just the way she liked it.

"I see what you mean." Emilie exhaled and felt a wave of emotion crash over her as he looked at her and smiled. Her chin dropped slightly and she took a deep breath.

"Hey, Shannon!" Zac smiled at Shannon.

"Zac." Shannon nodded.

"Hey, you." Nathan stopped in front of Emilie and smiled, that oh-so-sexy smile of his.

"Hey!" She took a step towards him to take

his hand, but paused and cringed. "Sorry."

"Not as easy as you thought?" Nathan tilted his head at her.

"You have no idea." She tugged at her visor.

He smiled at her, and she felt her heart skip a beat. "I heard you are through to the quarters." Nathan shoved his hands into his pockets. "Congratulations."

"Yeah. I mean thank you, it feels good, I'm quite relieved actually." She nodded with a giggle. "I'm so sorry, I didn't even ask how you did? How did you do?"

"That's okay, it's a lot to take in. I think I did good, I'm through to the quarters." Nathan grinned at her, clearly amused. "And so is Zac."

"Wow, congratulations!" Shannon exclaimed and touched Zac's arm.

"That's fantastic! We should celebrate." Emilie smiled and gave him a small applause. He nodded with a smile and stared at her again.

"Good idea, Em!" Shannon blinked. "We should have a celebration in your awesome room tonight!" Shannon turned to Zac with a grin. "Do you and Nathan want to join us?"

"Sure, if we're allowed." Nathan grinned at Shannon.

"Of course you are allowed, silly." Shannon

put her hand on her hip. "And then we want to go sight-seeing tomorrow, see some of New York, while we are here."

"Lunch at the Waldorf, martini's at the Hilton?" Nathan grinned at Emilie and she smiled.

"That sounds perfect!" Shannon grinned, but Emilie elbowed her in the ribs. "Ow!"

"I'm in. Obviously." Nathan grinned and Emilie bit her lip.

"So, eight o clock tonight, her room." Shannon grinned. "We'll take care of dinner."

"Can't wait!" Nathan grinned and slid his sunglasses over his eyes. "See you girls later."

"Bye Zac." Shannon said, with a smile.

"See you later Shannon." Zac grinned and winked at Shannon.

"We'll rendezvous some other time." Nathan whispered to Emilie and she smiled. He winked at her, as she watched him turn around and leave the way that they came.

"Dinner at the Waldorf? Martini's at the Hilton? You hit the jackpot with that guy." Shannon whispered to Emilie.

"It's too public, Shan." Emilie sighed. "I promised my dad no headlines."

"There is nothing wrong with a bunch of people going to have lunch and martini's in a public place, Emilie." Shannon put her hand on her hip and smiled at her. "Besides, he seems to have his urge to kiss you under control..."

"I wish I could say the same." Emilie smiled dreamily and Shannon looked at her.

"Don't look now, but we're in trouble." Shannon elbowed Emilie and motioned to her right.

Emilie turned her head slowly and looked over her shoulder. Spencer was looking straight at her, his arms crossed, shaking his head slightly, in disapproval. Emilie grinned and looked at Shannon. "It's your fault."

"Oh, yeah, sure, blame the physio." Shannon laughed.

Kelly walked into the hotel lobby and saw Shannon and Emilie chatting and laughing. Kelly took a deep breath and walked towards them. After a few steps, she stopped abruptly and frowned. What was she going to say to them? Jennifer would have a fit if she was here, but Kelly did not really care what Jennifer thought of Emilie. Jennifer was pulling this whole thing out of proportion and she had to stop. Emilie seemed like a nice enough girl, even though she snapped at her at the press conference. Kelly never held a grudge, unlike Jennifer. Kelly sighed and decided to just walk passed the two girls, still laughing.

"How were your games, Honey?" Zoe asked.

"They were good, my footwork has definitely improved." Nathan grinned, taking a sip of coffee.

"That's good to hear. And how is your temper?" Zoe asked.

"My temper is fine, Mom." Nathan rolled his eyes and sighed. "Unless Jen is around, then I have to beat up someone."

"Nathan Connor..." Zoe exclaimed.

"Relax, I was joking." Nathan laughed. "You know I don't fight, Mom."

"You better not. Even though I know how you feel about your sister, it does not mean you can just hand out punches whenever you want. Don't make me come down there and show you some tough love." Zoe said.

"Actually, I would like that. If you were here." Nathan said.

"You know I want to be there..."

"So if you want to be here, just come. Screw what he says. He's not at home anyway." Nathan said.

"It's not that simple, Honey. You know that." Zoe said.

"Whatever you say, Mom." Nathan shook his head and rubbed his eyes. "I need to tell you something."

"What is it?" Zoe asked.

"It's kind of important." Nathan sighed.

"It sounds serious. Is everything okay?"

"Well, I kind of met someone." Nathan said.

"Nathan, please don't get mixed up in another...." Zoe sighed.

"No, wait. She's not like that. She's funny and beautiful and smart and she can probably kick my ass on the court any day." Nathan rolled his eyes again.

"Do you like her?"

"Yes, I do, and I have a feeling that she likes me too." Nathan blushed slightly.

"Well, that's a good thing. What is her name?"

"Her name is Emilie, and she's also from DC." Nathan smiled, still tasting her lips.

"Right. Local girls are always better." Zoe said.

"I totally agree." Nathan laughed.

"I'm happy for you, Honey, just be careful." Zoe said.

"I will, thanks Mom." Nathan nodded. "I'll speak to you soon."

"Have a great night. I love you Baby." Zoe said.

"Love you too, Mom." Nathan nodded and closed his phone, dropping it on the bed.

He stood up, taking a deep breath and walked to his closet. He grinned as he opened his closet and stared at his clothes. "Right, let's do this."

"So what are we wearing tonight?" Emilie sat on the floor, in the living room, staring at the mountain of clothes on the floor.

"Does it matter? It's a slumber party." Shannon opened a bottle of champagne.

"I am not wearing my pajamas, Shan." Emilie shook her head.

"Yeah, I know, mine's also too sheer." Shannon said flatly.

Emilie frowned and twisted her body around to look at the clock on the wall. It was twenty minutes to eight and the place was a mess! "Shannon, I need your help!" She called frantically and heard Shannon put down the champagne on the countertop.

"Let's see. Wear this." Shannon dug her way through the mountain and threw a pair of cropped jeans at Emilie. "And this." She pulled a pink top from the pile and also threw it at her.

Emilie caught them and put them on the couch. "So what about the rest of your stuff?" She looked at the clothes on the floor.

"For a little girl, you sure can make a mess."

Shannon put her hands on her hips. "Throw them in the hamper, it can go with housekeeping tomorrow morning."

Emilie nodded and picked up the pile of clothes, and shoving them into the hamper in the linen cupboard. She closed the doors and laughed at herself.

"Please do share." Shannon looked at Emilie and took a sip from the bottle.

"I feel like we are doing something illegal." Emilie looked at Shannon.

"Drinking from the bottle might be a bit unladylike, but definitely not illegal!" Shannon rolled her eyes.

"That's not what I mean, Shan." Emilie walked over to the kitchen counter and leaned her elbows on the cool marble. "Having them here, having them sleep over, going sight-seeing with them, without anybody knowing about it. It's exciting."

"Well, we're in the greatest city in the world, what did you expect?" Shannon handed her the bottle and Emilie took a big sip.

"To New York." Emilie pulled her face from the taste of the champagne.

"To the City that never sleeps!" Shannon grinned. "Now get dressed, our guests will arrive shortly."

Emilie laughed at Shannon's mister

Belvedere impression, grabbed the clothes from the couch and ran to the bedroom.

CHAPTER 6

"They're here." Emilie whispered to Shannon, standing in the kitchen.

"I know." Shannon whispered back to Emilie, an amused expression on her face.

Emilie stood up and followed Shannon to the door. Shannon looked at Emilie, winked with a smile and opened the door. Emilie could feel her heart bursting out of her chest when her eyes met Nathan's. He had a grey shirt on, with those famous dark jeans of his.

"Hey." Emilie and Shannon said breathlessly.

"Hey." The two guys grinned. They walked into the room and Shannon quickly closed the door.

"Shannon." Zac grinned and kissed Shannon on the cheek.

Emilie and Nathan looked at Shannon and Zac and Shannon laughed. "Oh don't mind us, just kiss her." Shannon looked at Nathan and winked. Shannon wrapped her arms around Zac's shoulders and she whispered something to him.

"Finally." Nathan sighed relieved and wrapped his arms around Emilie's waist, gently pulling her close to him.

She sighed, happy to be in his arms again,

and put her arms around his broad shoulders. She could feel his breath on her face and she lifted her chin, kissing him. She felt his lips part and she tasted the hint of toothpaste on his tongue. She ran her fingers through his hair and felt his grip tighten around her waist. He pulled back, breathless, and grinned at her.

"I have missed you." She breathed.

"You have no idea how good that felt." Nathan grinned at her.

"Better than beating Luke Taylor?" He heard Zac ask behind him.

He looked over his shoulder, still holding Emilie. "That doesn't even come close to this."

Emilie felt her falling head over heels for this charming, sweet, gorgeous man. Normally she wouldn't fall this easily, always being weary and careful. She had only been in love once before, but that ended so badly that she promised herself never ever again. Her guard was always up when it came to guys, but with Nathan everything seemed so easy, so natural. She looked at him smiling at Zac, and when he looked back at her, with a look in his eyes that she recognised, because that was how she also looked at him, she knew that he felt the same. She heard Shannon clear her throat, felt Nathan's arms let go of her waist and they looked over at Shannon. "You guys hungry?"

Emilie and Nathan looked at each other again and chuckled.

"I meant for food, you animals." Shannon rolled her eyes.

Nathan and Emilie laughed, Nathan put his arm around Emilie's shoulder and they walked to the kitchen counter. "Sure, what's on the menu?"

Emilie glanced over at Nathan, as the four of them sat on the floor in front of the plasma television, watching a slasher movie. Nathan grinned, still staring at the screen. "What?" He whispered.

"Nothing, I'm just happy that you're here." She smiled.

Nathan looked at her and brought his hand up to her face, brushing her cheek. "So am I."

"We all are! Now shut up, because somebody's going to get killed any second." Shannon threw a handful of popcorn at them.

Emilie and Nathan chuckled and Emilie rested her head on Nathan's shoulder. "Sorry Shan." She whispered.

"Won't happen again." Nathan also whispered.

Emilie turned her head towards Nathan's face and she grinned at him. He smiled at her and kissed her tenderly.

Suddenly, the girl in the movie let out a bloodcurdling scream and Shannon shrieked, sending the whole bucket of popcorn flying into the air, and landed all over the room. Nathan, Emilie and Zac jumped and looked at Shannon. Shannon scrambled for the remote control and she switched off the television. "I told you guys I don't like scary movies. Tell them, Em."

"Oh come on, Shannon." Emilie laughed at her friend, grabbed a handfull of popcorn that was on the floor in front of her and tossed it towards her. The popcorn, however, ended up in Zac's face and he tossed the remainder of the popcorn from the bucket, in Nathan and Emilie's direction, with a playful growl.

"Hey!" Emilie shrieked.

Zac and Shannon laughed and Emilie shook her head with a slight giggle. She looked at Nathan and he was also laughing. He reached out and gently removed a popcorn kernel from her hair and threw it on the floor.

Tom Hayes was very tempted to go down to his daughter's room and check on their girls night in, but he knew that Emilie would be furious with him if he did. He paced around the room and looked at the clock on the opposite wall. It was 21:46. Knowing Emilie and Shannon, they would probably be eating strawberries on the floor and talking about the outfits of the other female players, as they normally did when Shannon came over to their house for a sleep-over. He knew that he was overreacting completely by wanting to check on her. She had always been the responsible one, the one that never broke curfew, never skipped school, never got bad grades. She never lied to him and he completely trusted her. It was Shannon that made him doubt his daughter. Sure, Shannon had been Emilie's best friend since she was seven, when she and Jeremy lost their mom, when Tom lost his wife. It was Shannon that got Emilie to talk again, after not saying a word for two years. It was Shannon that attended every one of Jeremy and Emilie's tennis games, to support her friend and to check out her brother. It had been no secret that Shannon had the hots for Jeremy, but Jeremy only seemed to be interested in two things. Tennis and blondes. And Shannon was neither. After Jeremy's death, Shannon was really supportive of Emilie and she made it her life's mission to make sure that Emilie would be able to walk, and play tennis again. Even better than she had before. Tom was extremely grateful towards Shannon and he scolded himself for not trusting her! Shannon had the remarkable ability to bring out the best in Emilie, and her game, even though Jeremy was not there anymore. Tom stopped pacing and smiled to himself. His daughter was safe with Shannon, he should never had doubted her. She was Emilie's guardian angel. He nodded, satisfied that his internal struggle was resolved, for now, and he walked to the kitchen.

"Don't be a wimp, Em." Shannon tilted her head and looked at Emilie, rubbing her temples.

"I don't particularly like that stuff." Emilie pointed to the bottle of absinthe on the table and pulled a face. "If it were tequila I would not be complaining."

"Come on, stop being such a girl." Zac frowned at her.

"I thought you said she was fearless." Nathan winked at Shannon.

"Oh, I'm fearless, on the court." Emilie said, still looking at the bottle.

"But off the court she's a real wimp." Shannon shrugged.

"Isn't it on the court that matters?" Emilie pulled a face at Shannon.

"Come on, princess fearless." Nathan asked,

the velvet returning to his voice, and a twinkling in his green eyes.

Shannon, Zac and Nathan looked at her and she sighed. "Fine." She reached over to the table and took a shot. She could feel the bitter taste burn her throat and she grimaced. "That's disgusting."

"Was that so hard?" Shannon grinned.

Emilie looked at Shannon and coughed.

"Okay, Nathan you're up." Zac grinned.

Nathan picked up the top card from the pile and flipped it over. "The dare card." Nathan smiled and looked at Emilie.

"So who's the unlucky victim?" Zac smiled.

"Right, I dare Emilie, to go down to the front desk, ask for a key to my room and come back here, with the key, of course." Nathan grinned at her.

"Okay." Emilie said simply and Nathan raised his eyebrows.

"You're not going to protest?" Zac asked.

"No." Emilie frowned. "But I'm going to need some courage." She grabbed the bottle and took a deep breath. She unscrewed the cap and took a big sip.

Brandon was sitting in the hotel's bar, when he saw Emilie stepping out of the elevator, wearing a tight pair of cropped jeans and an incredibly clingy pink top, accentuating just in the right places. She looked a slight bit disorientated, but maybe she was tired. He looked at his watch and he understood why. It was 23:17. What the hell was Emilie still doing up, and what was she doing in the front lobby at this hour? He looked through the window and see her stepping up to the front desk.

"What are you still doing up, man?" He heard a voice behind him. He turned and saw Spencer, looking troubled.

"Just having a nightcap." Brandon lifted his glass in the air.

"Two more, please." Spencer said to the barman and the barman nodded.

"So why the troubled expression?" Brandon looked at him.

"Oh nothing." Spencer shrugged, watching as the barman put two tumblers of whiskey and ice in front of him and Brandon. He placed a bill on the counter and nodded at the barman. "Thanks man, keep the change."

"What gives man? You look seriously troubled." Brandon frowned.

"I get frustrated when things don't go my way, you know." Spencer looked at Brandon and spotted the blue-purple bruise just below his eye. "Geez, what happened to you?"

"Connor." Brandon stared at his drink.

"What did you do?" Spencer sighed.

"Nothing, I swear." Brandon frowned and Spencer scowled.

"I don't believe that. Connor is an asshole, sure, but he won't just give you a black eye for doing nothing." Spencer took a sip of his drink.

"I got under his skin a bit, that's all." Brandon grinned.

"Clearly a mistake." Spencer laughed.

"It felt good though." Brandon confessed. "Seeing him so pissed off. A bit of justice, you know."

"What did you say to him, anyway?" Spencer asked.

Brandon hesitated and looked at Spencer. Spencer frowned and turned to Brandon. "What?"

"I'd rather not say." Brandon finished his drink and stood up. "Thanks for the drink, man."

Spencer watched as Brandon left the bar and he frowned when he saw Emilie at the front desk.

Emilie stopped at the front desk and looked at the woman, Marilyn, behind the desk.

"Excuse me." She whispered, leaning closer to Marilyn. Oh my god! What the hell was she going to say to this woman? The truth is always a good idea, but it was too crazy to be taken seriously. Plus, she did not wat to make a schene. Her dad would kill her!

"Is there a problem, miss Hayes?" Marilyn frowned.

"Yes, but just a tiny problem. You see, I left my bag with a friend, and I remembered that there is something that I need in my bag. Urgently. Could you maybe get me a key for the room? Please." Emilie felt her heart beating in her ears.

Marilyn frowned and picked up the phone."What is the room number? Maybe I can phone him."

"There's no one there, I just checked." Emilie said quickly. "Please?"

"What room?" Marilyn looked at her.

Emilie sighed and stared at the counter. "Fourteen twenty-three."

"Mister Connor's room." She looked up at Emilie.

"Yes." Emilie nodded and bit her lip.

"Miss Hayes, Hotel policy clearly states..." Marilyn started, but Emilie leaned over the counter.

"Look, Marilyn, I know what you must be thinking, and I know that this looks really bad, but I really need to get into that room. The outfit that I had on today has to be rinsed out tonight, otherwise I am going to lose my quarter final match. You don't want that to happen, do you?" Emilie explained. It was a fake explanation, but nobody needed to know that!

"Lucky for you, I'm also a very superstitious person, so I understand." She swiped a card through the machine and typed on her keyboard. She took the card from the machine and handed it to Emilie.

"Oh my god, thank you! Thank you so much! You are the best!" Emilie exclaimed and took the card.

"Have a good night, miss Hayes." Marilyn grinned.

"You too!" Emilie nodded at her and walked briskly to the elevator.

"Em, wait!" She heard behind her as she entered the elevator. Her heart started pounding in her chest, as she realized it was Spencer.

"Shit." She mumbled and repeatedly pressed the button. Just as Spencer's face came into view the doors closed and Emilie breathed a sigh of relief.

"You think she did it?" Zac asked.
"I don't know." Shannon frowned.
"I just hope she didn't run into anyone." Nathan looked worried.

"Why does it matter?" Shannon looked at him.

"Nate is enjoying the secrecy thing." Zac grinned.

"It's not like that, Zac." Nathan shook his head.

"So what is it like, then Nate?" Shannon crossed her arms.

"Look, as I told Zac, if this gets out that we are...."

"Dating?" Shannon asked. "You are technically dating, aren't you?"

"Just so that nobody will notice." Zac said.

"Look, under any other circumstances I would tattoo her name on my face, but for now it needs to stay between us." Nathan looked at Shannon and Zac.

"Tattoo her name on your face? Are you serious, man?" Zac exclaimed.

"So I take it you are serious about her, right?" Shannon smiled.

"Yes, I am. I'm crazy about her." Nathan admitted and looked at the floor.

"Aah, that's so sweet!" Shannon sighed, with a smile.

Suddenly, the door burst open and the three of them looked at Emilie, standing by the door, smiling smugly. She held up the key card and waved it around. "Look what I got!"

"Seriously?" Shannon exclaimed.

Emilie shut the door, threw the card at Nathan and walked to them. "Of course!"

"How did you do it?" Nathan caught the card and smiled at her.

"Easy, I just used my powers of persuasion." Emilie sat down next to Nathan and batted her eyelashes.

"You are quite good at it." Nathan smiled suggestively at her.

"Wait a minute!" Shannon exclaimed. "How do we know it opens Nate's room?"

"Where's the trust?" Emilie looked at Shannon with a shocked expression.

"Not going to work this time, Hayes!" Shannon grinned.

Emily glared at Shannon and stood up. She grabbed the card on Nathan's lap, her own keycard on the counter, walked to the door and opened it. "Come on then." She watched as Shannon stood up hesitantly, but the guys did not move. "All of you." Emilie looked at them and they stood up quickly.

"Em, you don't have to do this." Nathan said as he, Shannon and Zac followed her out of the room and down the corridor.

"Yes, she does!" Shannon exclaimed.

Emilie turned to Shannon and pulled a face. "Seeing as my best friend thinks I am a liar."

"I just want proof." Shannon shrugged.

Nathan smiled and Emilie turned around again. The four of them continued down the corridor and they came to a stop in front of fourteen twenty-three. Emily took the card from her pocket and pushed it into the slot in the door. A green light came on and she opened the door.

"I told you!" Emilie sighed and looked at Shannon, shocked and impressed at the same time.

"Impressive." Shannon nodded and looked at the door.

Emilie held out the card to Nathan, but he shook his head.

"Keep it, pretty girl." He grinned at her.

"Are you sure?" She frowned.

"Of course, it's well deserved." He nodded. "Besides, I can't think of anything better than getting a surprize visit from the prettiest girl in DC."

"That's not a half bad idea, I might just do that." She grinned and put the card in her pocket. "And thank you."

"Come on guys, let's get back to the room." Shannon looked around her and took Zac's hand.

Nathan nodded and looked at Emilie. Emilie took his hand and he frowned. "What if someone sees us?"

"Well, I don't see anyone." She smiled and Nathan laughed.

The four of them, Shannon and Zac, hand-in-hand and Nathan and Emilie, hand-in-hand, walked back to fourteen seventeen.

"Think again, Emilie." Jennifer emerged from around the corner and she watched as they closed the room door behind them. She pressed 'stop' on her handheld voice recorder and smiled wickedly.

Nathan opened his eyes the next morning and stared at the ceiling for a second, realizing where he was. He turned his head to his right and smiled when he saw Emilie lying next to him. She was on her side, facing him, still asleep, her hands by her face. Next to Emilie, was Shannon and Zac, with their backs to each other. He rolled over onto his right side and gently touched Emilie's cheek. She stirred slightly, but did not wake up. He traced her lips with his finger and kissed her softly on the lips. She slowly opened those beautiful pale-blue eyes of hers and smiled sleepily.

"Good morning pretty girl." He whispered.

"Good morning." She smiled and ran her fingers through his brown hair. He softly brushed his lips against hers and she sighed happily. "Why can't I wake up like that every morning?"

"We could always arrange that." He smiled at her and wiped strands of blonde hair off her face.

She sighed happily and rolled onto her back. She looked in Shannon's direction and giggled. "Did they have a fight or something?"

"You mean you don't remember?" Nathan frowned.

"Come on, I wasn't that drunk." Emilie frowned. "Was I?"

"If you have to ask, then there are problems!" Nathan laughed heartily and Emilie grinned.

"Thin ice, Connor." Emile grinned.

"Not at all." He smiled.

"Would you like some coffee?" Emilie sat up, throwing the comforter off her.

Nathan nodded and stood up with Emilie. "I'll help."

They walked to the kitchen and Nathan took out four cups from the cupboard. "Those two are defintely also going to need some."

Emilie laughed and nodded, filling the coffee machine with enough coffee for Zac and Shannon as well.

"I want to ask you something." Nathan said

to her, placing his hands on the counter in front of him.

"Sure." She closed the lid of the coffee machine and switched it on. Emilie looked at him and frowned. "Everything okay?" She crossed her arms.

"I just want to know if you are okay with the idea of keeping us a secret for now?" Nathan looked at her.

"It's not ideal, but yes." She tilted her head at him.

"Are you sure?" Nathan frowned.

"Yes, I'm sure, Nate." She dropped her arms and put her hands on her hips. "Why?"

"I don't want you to think that I don't care about you, or that I don't want to tell anyone about us, because I do. The press would have an absolute field day and we will be in every front page in the world." He explained. "Not that I would mind, but I don't want your life to be disrupted. You don't need such disruptions and complications in your life, and neither do I."

"Nate..." Emilie shook her head.

"No, wait, Em." Nathan looked at her, taking her hands. "I'm crazy about you and I want to tell everyone, but I can't. At least not yet. As soon as this tournament is over...."

"It's okay. I understand, Nate." Emilie

smiled at him.

"You do?" Nathan frowned.

"Yes." She said simply.

Relief washed over Nathan and he nodded at her. "I am glad to hear that you understand." He smiled.

"Oh, and by the way, I'm crazy about you too." She smiled at him.

Nathan felt his heartbeat started to race and he pulled Emilie close to him. He tilted her chin up with his hand and kissed her.

"Ugh, get a room." They heard Shannon croak behind them.

Emilie giggled and turned to her friend. "Good morning Sunshine."

"Good morning you two." Nathan laughed, studying the expressions on Shannon and Zac's faces.

"Yeah, yeah, where's the coffee?" Shannon groaned.

Emilie pointed over her shoulder to the coffee machine and grinned.

"Please tell me I am not the only one that's hungover this morning?" Shannon pulled a face and took a sip of coffee.

"I don't get hungover." Zac frowned.

"Nope." Nathan grinned and put his arm around Emilie's shoulder.

"What about you, Em?" Shannon sighed.

"I feel good." Emilie looked at Shannon. Nathan kissed her forehead and she smiled at him. "Really good."

CHAPTER 7

Emilie and Shannon stepped out of the front rotating glass doors of The Four Seasons Hotel and stepped out into the sunlight. It was a beautiful sunny summers day, not a cloud in the sky. Shannon flicked her hair out her face and grinned to herself. Emilie put her purple sunglasses on and looked over at the taxi in front of them. She looked back at the doors and felt Shannon pull her towards the taxi.

"I don't think that this is such a good idea Shan." Emilie said somberly and looked at Shannon.

"You have to go there sometime, Em. And today is a good a day as any. So get in." Shannon grinned and opened the taxi door.

"I don't feel like crying or being upset today, Shan." Emilie glared at Shannon.

Shannon touched her arm and glared at her. "You won't, you're strong." Shannon gave her a serious look.

"Only on the court." Emilie sighed.

"That's bullshit and you know it." Shannon rolled her eyes.

"It's true, though." Emilie mumbled as they got into the taxi. Emilie closed the door and opened the window. She spotted Spencer coming out of the hotel and she froze. He obviously spotted her and Shannon in the lobby as they were leaving. He ran over to the taxi and smiled.

"Hey, where have you been?" He asked.

"Are we going, or what?" The cabdriver asked, irritatedly.

"Turn on the meter, dude." Shannon rolled her eyes.

"We've been in my room all morning." Emilie frowned. Technically...

Spencer frowned at her. "I just wanted to ask if we're okay."

"Of course. Why?" Emilie adjusted her sunglasses.

"I thought you were avoiding me on purpose." Spencer shrugged.

"Ding ding ding!" Shannon mumbled next to her.

Emilie rubbed her chin and shook her head. "No, we're okay."

"That's good to hear. So, where are you two headed?"

"Sight-seeing." Shannon snapped.

"Anywhere in particular?" Spencer asked.

"We're going to go ride the subway." Shannon tilted her head, sarcastically and started closing the window.

"Please excuse her." Emilie said

apologetically.

"It's okay, I have to get going anyway. See you Em." He waved at her.

Emilie looked at him through the glass and turned to Shannon.

"Twin Towers memorial sight, please." Shannon said to the cabdriver.

"Was that necessary?" Emilie glared at Emilie.

"Yes, he's annoying!" Shannon sat back in her seat.

"You're horrible, Shannon." Emilie shook her head, sat back and rested her head on the headrest.

Nathan looked up and saw a taxi stop next to the sidewalk.

"Hey Zac. They're here." He called to Zac. Zac turned skipped up the steps and walked to him. Emilie and Shannon got out of the cab and Nathan felt his heart set alight. Emilie, with her sunglasses pulled over her eyes, her blonde hair straight and blowing in the wind, a denim short, a silky white off the shoulder top and white high heels, came walking up to him and he smiled. He looked over at Shannon, with a short white skirt, a green top and light brown cowboy boots, and shook his head. What's with this girl and her cowboy boots?

It's summer in New York City for crying out loud! Emilie grinned when she saw him standing by the steps, wearing a light grey t-shirt and a pair of light blue jeans. She did not expect to stare at him, as she had only seen him an hour ago, but he seemed to take her breath away everytime she saw him. The two girls walked up to them and Shannon started running towards Zac. Emilie giggled and shook her head and walked up to Nathan.

"Hey." Emilie smiled at him.

"Hey pretty girl." He took her hand, pulled her close to him and kissed her softly on the lips.

"We can see you, so can the rest of New York." Zac chanted behind them.

Nathan grinned and pressed his cheek against her forehead. "I don't care." He chanted back.

"You don't?" Emilie frowned.

"Nope. Not today." He laughed. "Today, all that matters, is you and me." He brushed a strand of blonde hair out of her face and she smiled.

"And me!" Shannon called out to them. "And Zac!"

Emilie and Nathan looked over at Shannon and Zac. Zac was on the bottom step, bent over forward and Shannon was on his back, reading the names of the people who lost their lives. Emilie laughed at them and Zac looked up. "Check this out!"

Emilie and Nathan walked down the steps and joined Zac and Shannon.

"Isn't this amazing, Em?" Zac smiled. "This was where is all happened."

Emilie looked around her at the memorial site and shivered. She looked up at the sky, where the towers used to be, and all she saw was empty sky. She closed her eyes and heard tyres screeching and a loud bashing sound. She opened her eyes and it felt like the world around her was spinning.

"Em, are you okay?" Nathan touched her arm.

She looked over, across the road, at the concrete wall and she felt a cold shiver run down her spine. She could see the silver Escalade, on it's roof, with Jeremy's arm hanging out of the broken window. Slowly, she walked back through the trees, to the sidewalk, but she stopped a few feet from it.

"Nate, can we chat a second?" Shannon slid off Zac's back, ran up to Nathan and pulled him aside.

"Sure." He frowned.

Shannon and Nathan walked over to Zac.

"What's going on?" Nathan asked.

"You see that wall there?" Shannon pointed to a concrete wall on the opposite side of the road.

"Yes." Nathan and Zac looked at where Shannon was pointing.

"That's where it happened." Shannon said simply.

"Where what happened?" Zac frowned.

"The accident." Nathan said, shocked. He looked at Shannon and shook his head. "I'm sorry, I didn't know, Shannon, I..."

"It's fine, Nathan." Shannon touched his arm.

Nathan looked over at Emilie, still standing on the sidewalk, staring across the street. "Is this her first time back here?"

"Yes." Shannon nodded, crossing her arms.

"Can I go to her?" Nathan asked and Shannon nodded.

Nathan smiled grimly and made his way over to Emilie. He stopped next to her and touched her arm. "Em.."

Emilie turned her head and looked at him. "They say that the first time is the hardest."

"It doesn't have to be." He smiled at her and took her hand.

Emilie smiled softly and looked across the street.

"Come on." Nathan pulled her hand and

they crossed the road. Emilie took a deep breath as she stepped onto the sidewalk and turned to her right, with Nathan, still holding her hand. She would have never made it this far on her own. She stopped a couple of feet from the wall and stared at it. Nathan looked at her and squeezed her hand. She looked at him and could feel a tear run down her cheek. She looked at the wall again and sighed. She let go of Nathan's hand and felt a calmness wash over her. She closed her eyes and felt the uncontrollable hurt in her heart slowly fade away. "Lee, it's okay." She heard her brother's voice in her ears and she quickly opened her eyes. A sudden wave of nausea spilled over her and she swallowed loudly. "That's not possible." She whispered, but she had no voice. "Lee...." She heard his voice again and took a few shallow breaths. She turned around abruptly and stared out in front of her, her eyes wide.

"Em, are you okay?" Nathan looked at her, taking her hand again.

"No." She whispered to herself and looked at Nathan. "Please get me out of here."

Emilie took a large sip of water and tucked some hair behind her ear. She looked up from the table and directly at Shannon. "I'm fine."

She gave a small smile.

"Sure you are." Shannon rolled her eyes.

"I am. I promise." Emilie looked at Shannon and leaned towards her. "I need to tell you something."

"What is it?" Shannon frowned. Emilie looked around her and looked back at Shannon.

"I know this is going to sound completely insane, but I heard his voice." Emilie whispered.

"Em..." Shannon shook her head.

"Shan, I'm serious. I heard him." Emilie said.

Shannon looked at Emilie, a cynical expression on her face. When Shannon and Emilie were little, Spencer and Jeremy would take the girls camping and Spencer would tell them ghost stories. Emilie would be terrified, but Shannon would just sit there, looking at him. "There's no such thing." She used to say and would fold her arms. So Emilie was not surprized that Shannon had that same expression on her face now.

"You're just stressed and now your mind is playing tricks on you." Shannon frowned. "There's no such thing."

Emilie sighed heavily and put her glass down on the table. "I am not stressed, Shannon. I heard him. He was there."

"Em, look, I understand that it was hard for you, being back there for the first time, but honestly, you want to tell me that Jeremy was there?" Shannon lifted an eyebrow.

"I think so, yes." Emilie nodded.

"So then why didn't the rest of us hear him?" Shannon asked.

"I don't know. Maybe I'm still grieving over him." Emilie traced the rim of her glass with her fingertip.

"Maybe. You kind of scared me a bit. All of us actually. Nathan did not know what to do." Shannon shrugged.

"What do you mean I scared you?" Emilie asked at Shannon.

"You were spaced out for a few minutes. We were talking to you, but you didn't respond." Shannon placed her hand over her friend's.

"I don't remember you talking to me." Emilie frowned. "Is Nathan freaked out?"

"I think he's more worried than freaked out, really." Shannon tilted her head.

"I should apologize." Emilie shook her head.

"He'll be fine." Shannon shrugged. "It's you that I am worried about."

"I'm fine, Shan. Really." Emilie gave her a small smile.

Shannon narrowed her eyes at Emilie and

shook her head. "We should really teach you another word."

"Look who's talking." Emilie smiled.

There was a brief moment of silence, when Emilie looked at Shannon. "I just remembered something." Emilie said, grimly.

"What?" Shannon asked hesitantly.

"Something Jer said to me earlier that day." Emilie nodded.

"And what was that?" Shannon frowned.

"That life is short, and I should do what makes me happy, not what people expect me to do." Emilie traced the rim of her glass and looked at Shannon.

Shannon felt tears in her eyes, but blinked them away, and simply nodded. For the first time in Shannon's life, she had no words.

Nathan washed his hands and looked at himself in the restroom mirror. He shook his head at himself, disapprovingly and ripped some paper towels from the dispenser. He was angry at himself, firstly for suggesting to meet at the Memorial site, and secondly for making Emilie cry. Even though Shannon and Zac, and Emilie for that matter, told him it was alright, he still felt horrible. Guilty. Emilie's heartbroken expression was stuck in his head and he let out a frustrated growl.

"Stop being so hard on yourself, Nate. You didn't know." Zac said, suddenly next to him.

"I feel like a dick!" Nathan exclaimed.

"You are a dick, man." Zac laughed.

"I'm serious, Zac. This is not how I wanted to spend the day with her." Nathan shook his head.

"Dude, it doesn't matter. It happened, just get over it." Zac shrugged.

Nathan looked at him and frowned. "Your profoundness isn't useful."

"You're welcome." Zac laughed and opened the door.

"This is so great!" Shannon exclaimed as she felt the wind in her hair. She leaned over the railing of the ferry and her camera flashed like crazy. Zac grabbed hold of her waist and pulled her back.

"You Texas girls are out of control!" Zac laughed.

"Let's hear it for New York!" Shannon sang loudly.

Emilie sighed and felt Nathan's arms tighten around her shoulders. She lowered her face and the faint smell of his deodorant filled her nostrils. She looked out onto the water as the ferry moved surely towards Liberty Island. The Statue of Liberty came into full view and the four of them stared at the magnificent statue in front of them. Shannon aimed her camera at Nathan and Emilie and waved at them. "Smile guys!"

Emilie and Nathan looked over at her and smiled. "She's always like this." Emilie whispered to Nathan and Nathan laughed.

"You two make a very hot couple!" Shannon grinned. "Now give us a kiss."

Emilie turned her face towards the water and Nathan kissed her on the cheek. Shannon rolled her eyes and shook her head, but took the photo anyway. "I'll get you two eventually."

"Do it and die, physio!" Emilie pointed at her with a laugh and looked out onto the water again.

Jennifer walked into the bar of the Four Seasons Hotel and spotted Brandon at the counter. She walked over to him and sat down next to him. "Lonely much?"

He looked at her and frowned.

"How's your eye?" She smiled.

"Why do you care?" Brandon took a sip of his drink.

"Clearly this is a bad time..." She slid off the barstool, but her grabbed her wrist.

"What do you want, Jen?" He glared at her.

"I was just wondering if you know where my brother is?" Jennifer sighed. "I can't seem to find him anywhere, and he is not answering his mobile."

"Maybe he is avoiding you." Brandon smiled smugly.

"And why would he do that?" Jennifer raised an eyebrow at him.

"Oh, I don't know, Jen. You're not a very pleasant person to be around." Brandon shook his head.

"As opposed to someone who gets beat up in an elevator?" Jennifer smirked and pulled herself free.

"Better a coward than a bitch." Brandon said.

"In your case, they're the same thing." Jennifer said over her shoulder and walked out of the bar.

Emilie watched as Shannon took a gigantic bite of her hotdog and laughed. "You know you can eat that in more than one bite, Shan."

"I know, it's just so good." Shannon closed her eyes and rested her head on Zac's shoulder.

Emilie took a bite of hers and smiled at Nathan.

"Are you having fun?" Nathan wiped relish

off the corner of her mouth and she giggled.

"Yes, thank you. This is the best day ever." She rested her head on his shoulder and gave the rest of her hotdog to him. "Here, I'm stuffed."

"Thanks." Nathan smiled at her and took a bite.

"So where to next?" Shannon asked.

"Well, we seem to have missed the sunset." Zac pointed to the dark blue sky and laughed.

"Look at that!" Emilie exclaimed, pointing up at two bright blue vertical lights in the sky. She sat up in amazement and the others looked as well.

"Uhm, those are the Twin Towers lights." Shannon said, carefully.

Emilie shifted forward in her seat and rested her arms on her knees. Shannon, Zac and Nathan seemed to be holding their breaths, waiting for a response from Emilie. After a long pause, Emilie grinned and tilted her head. "It's beautiful." She smiled softly and met Nathan's gaze. "Listen, I want to apologize. About earlier. It was way too much for you..."

"Hey." Nathan leaned forward and looked at her. "It's okay, Em. You don't ever have to apologize to me, okay."

Emilie smiled at him and kissed him on the

lips. He cupped her face and pulled her in for another kiss.

"Oh, get a room." Shannon laughed, pretending to be utterly repulsed. "Some of us are trying to eat over here."

Emilie giggled and rested her head against Nathan's chest.

"Are you sure you're okay?" Nathan whispered in her ear.

"Yes, I'm with you, so I'm perfect." Emilie said and he could feel her smiling.

A sudden flash of light caught Nathan's eye and he looked over to his left. It was relatively dark, so he narrowed his eyes and looked again. He recognised the guy, crouching behind a park bench, holding a camera. It was a photographer! Nathan turned his head to Emilie and rubbed her back. "Photographer, three o clock." He whispered to Emilie.

Emilie looked up slowly and saw the guy, now pretending to be taking photographs of the skyline. "Time to go, guys."

"Just don't make it too obvious." Nathan whispered and Emilie gave a small nod.

Shannon stood up and pulled Zac up from the bench. "Come on! It's almost time!"

Zac grinned, stood up and threw his arm around Shannon's shoulders. Zac turned to Emilie and Nathan, still sitting. "Are you coming?"

"Yeah, I suppose." Emilie laughed and she and Nathan stood up.

The four of them walked in the opposite direction and the photographer followed them to the entrance of Central Park.

"So how are we going to lose him?" Nathan asked.

"My dad is going to kill me..." Emilie mumbled. "Shannon, I told you...."

"Hush up! I'm trying to think." Shannon shook her head and looked behind her. The photographer was still following them and Shannon cringed. "Just don't look behind you."

Emilie nodded and grabbed Nathan's hand.

"Let's just go to Amnesia, he'll lose us in there." Zac suggested.

"Sounds like a good idea." Emilie nodded. "So where is it?"

"Uhm, twenty blocks from here..." Zac muttered.

"What?" Emilie shrieked.

"Em, calm down, we'll just get a cab." Nathan took her hand

Shannon ran to the edge of the sidewalk and whistled loudly. A yellow cab stopped right in front of her and they quickly climbed into the cab. "Six-oh-nine West twenty-nineth street please. Step on it." Zac said to the cabdriver and they sped off.

CHAPTER 8

Emilie walked out onto the court the next morning, happy and ready for practice. A slight bit tired from dancing last night, but she was happy. That was all that counted. She put her bag down on the cement and knelt beside it. She unzipped her bag and took out her racquet.

"Look who finally decided to grace us with her presence." She heard behind her. She didn't have to look who it was, she already knew.

"Spencer." She said, standing up and walking up to him.

"Where were you yesterday?" Spencer asked.

"Shannon and I were sight-seeing." She said simply.

"Sight-seeing, hey." Spencer crossed his arms.

"Yes." She tilted her head in annoyance and glared at him.

"Is that what you call it, Em?" Spencer asked.

"Look, Spencer.." Emilie took a step towards him.

Spencer took out a newspaper and threw it

on the ground in front of her. Emilie scowled and bent down to pick it up. On the front page, there was a photograph of her and Nathan, sitting on the bench on the boardwalk. The headline read 'New Doubles partners?'

"Shit." Emilie muttered. The article caught her completely off-guard and she felt her arms drop to her side. She sighed and looked at Spencer. "Spence, I...."

"I can't believe this." He turned around and shook his head.

"Spence, wait...." Emilie walked to him.

"How could you lie to me?" Spencer looked hurt. "After everything that we have been through."

"I'm sorry, but you wouldn't have let me go anyway." Emilie defended.

"You're right, I wouldn't have!" Spencer exclaimed.

"Look, I know you and Nate..." Emilie said.

"Nate?" Spencer frowned and looked at her.

Emilie shifted her weight and looked at him. "Yes."

"Please don't tell me that there is something between you two?" Spencer frowned.

"I can't do that, because it won't be true." Emilie looked at him.

"I can't believe this!" Spencer closed his eyes and rubbed his temples.

"You don't have to believe it, just accept it." Emilie crossed her arms and raised an eyebrow at him.

"Don't come crying to me when you find out who he really is!" Spencer whirled around and marched off the court.

"Second headline, well done, Emilie." Emilie muttered and threw the newspaper onto the bench next to her. She knew her father would freak out if he saw it and she dreaded another lecture from him.

The next few days, Emilie and Nathan did not see much of each other, as quarters were on Tuesday, and they were training like crazy. After Emilie and Spencer's fight on Thursday, Spencer insisted on training with Emilie on court four instead of seventeen. He was extra hard on her, making her run laps and practicing her serves until it was dark out. Probably to make sure that she was so exhausted by the time she got to her room, that she did not have the energy to see or think about Nathan. At all. Emilie became more focused after the first day of intense training, and she exceeded Spencer's ridiculously high expectations. Nathan, who usually trained on court eighteen, was not impressed with Spencer's idea to move Emilie further away from him, but it made him focus more. His footwork improved by the hour and his serves were deadly. Even though he thought about Emilie every second, he knew that the sooner he could win this tournament, the sooner they could be together, without hiding from everybody. He saw her often, but only from a distance, and when they passed each other in the hotel, she merely smiled at him. Every cell in his body wanted to reach out to her, pull her close and kiss her, but he had to keep himself under control. Emily spent her days thinking of him secretly, and her nights dreaming of him. Her dad seemed oblivious to what was going on, keeping to himself most of the times. Every now and then, Jennifer would look at Emilie, as if she knew everything. It gave Emilie the creeps and she tried to stay as far away from Jennifer as she could. Shannon was more infatuated with Zac, but it seemed as if Zac was slowly losing interest in Shannon. "Maybe I'm just paranoid." Shannon would say and that would be the end of the conversation.

    Tuesday was a blur of interviews, press conferences and more interviews. Emilie's game was scheduled at two o' clock on court three and Nathan's was scheduled at three o' clock on court four. Spencer was not happy when he read the schedule, but there was nothing he could do about it. Emilie's opponent was twenty year old Eileen Truman, from Florida. She was tall, blonde and tanned, a very unfair combination in Emilie's eyes. Emilie, being only five-three, never liked tall blondes, and probably never will either.

Nathan's opponent was twenty-three year old Colin Harvey from Great Britain. He was confident enough not to think of Harvey as last year's Wimbledon winner. Colin was just another opponent in just another game.

By three fifteen, Emilie was thrashing the Floridian, by winning straight sets. The crowd seemed to love her drive and determination and cheered her on. Even Spencer cracked, a long overdue, smile when Emilie hit a perfect volley shot past Truman, missing her racquet by a mile. She loved the sound of the cheering and she thought about Jeremy. He would have been proud of that volley. 'Just like I showed you, Lee.' he would always say. She missed him so much, but she knew that he was with her, every day. She could feel him when Nathan walked with her to the wall last week. That's why she let go of Nathan's hand. Nathan. She knew she was in love with this guy, and she wished the tournament was over already. Even though she had the power to end her tournament, she did not want to disappoint her brother. She just had to stick it out for a few more days. The Charity games would be tomorrow, and the Charity cocktail party afterwards, made her look forward to seeing him. If only she could get rid of Spencer. She had the perfect dress picked out for the cocktail party, with help from Shannon, and couldn't wait to see Nathan's reaction when he saw her in it. She chuckled to herself and grabbed the ball from the ball boy.

"Don't you ever tell me that running laps does not improve your game." Spencer smiled at her and she wiped her face. "You kicked Floridian ass!"

Emilie looked up from her feet and sat back against the wall of the locker room. She breathed heavily, looked at Spencer and tilted her head.

"Don't give me that look." Spencer laughed.
"What look?" She asked.
"That look." He pulled his face at her.
She laughed again and closed her eyes. "I'm tired."
"You can have the rest of the day off." Spencer smiled at her.
Emilie's eyes flew open and she raised an

eyebrow. "I can?"

"Yes." Spencer laughed. "You ran enough this month."

Emilie groaned and wiped her face again with her towel. Spencer stood up and walked to the door. "There's someone here to see you."

Emilie frowned and shook her head. "Very funny, Spence."

"I'm serious." He opened the door and Brandon walked in. "I'll be outside if you need me." Spencer left and she could see him standing by the door.

She shifted her gaze from the door to Brandon. "Hey."

"Great game, Emilie." He smiled.

Emilie felt herself grin and she shook her head. "Thanks." She looked at Brandon and frowned. He was a good looking guy, his dark hair spiked up, his chocolatey eyes, a dimple in his right cheek, but he was not Nathan. He seemed more arrogant and pretentious. "Uhm, Brandon, do you want something else?"

"Rumor has it we have been paired up for the charity game." Brandon sat down across from her.

"Where did you hear that?" She wiped her face with her towel again.

"I have my sources." Brandon smiled.

Emilie tilted her head and pulled her face. "Well, I haven't heard anything yet."

"They're making the announcement at tomorrow's breakfast." Brandon grinned.

"Yeah, I know." Emilie nodded.

"Do you wanna sit with me tomorrow?" Brandon asked.

"Why?" Emilie frowned.

"Come on, Emilie, it's not like you are seeing anyone." Brandon grinned.

"I...uhm..." Emilie stuttered.

"Am I wrong?" Brandon asked.

"Very wrong." Emilie frowned.

"I don't bite." Brandon smirked.

"I just remembered, Samantha asked me to sit with her." Emilie looked at him.

"Bullshit." Brandon raised his eyebrows and looked at her. "It's Connor, isn't it?"

Emilie looked at him and pursed her lips. "No, it's not."

"You sure about that, Emilie?" Brandon smiled.

"Yes." She nodded.

"Well, if you change your mind..." Brandon stood up.

"I won't." She snapped.

"Suit yourself then." He grinned and walked out of the locker room.

Emilie growled and threw her towel on the

tiles. "Whoever let that jackass in here, is dead..."

Nathan sat in the locker room, by himself, his towel over his head when he heard the door open. "Not now, Jen."

"Connor." The voice said to him.

Nathan lifted the towel from his head and stared blankly at Spencer. "What do you want?"

"I want to know something." Spencer said crossing his arms.

Nathan looked at him and frowned. "Okay." Nathan stood up and also crossed his arms.

"Don't mock me, Connor." Spencer scowled.

"What's your deal, Spencer?" Nathan frowned.

"I don't like you." Spencer said flatly.

"I've noticed." Nathan laughed.

"Emilie seems to like you, and for some strange reason, she thinks that you like her." Spencer said.

"Look, Spencer, the fact that you don't like me is obvious. I'm not particularly fond of you either, but I like her. I am not the type of guy that hooks up with random girls that don't mean anything to me. I used to be like that, but I've changed." Nathan said.

"Dude, don't mess with me." Spencer

growled. "People don't just change over-night."

"I'm not messing with you, dude. Honestly, Emilie is a terrific girl, you know that, and I know that. The feelings I have for her are real, and nothing you say, or do, is going to change them. You say you know guys like me, but you're wrong. " Nathan's arms dropped to his sides. "Brigitte.."

"Don't go there, Connor!" Spencer exclaimed.

"Brigitte is a liar. She is a shallow, vindictive person that does not feel anything for anyone." Nathan crossed his arms.

"Connor..." Spencer growled.

"Think about it, Spencer. She was never interested in you, or me for that matter, as a person. The only thing she was interested in was our fame and our money. Those were the only things that mattered to her and to the rest of them. And as soon as someone better, richer and younger came along, she kicked us to the curb. We meant nothing to them." Nathan explained. "And I don't know about you, but I am sick of being treated like that. I deserve someone much better than that, and so do you."

Spencer looked at him and frowned. Nathan was right, Brigitte only used him, but he would never admit it. "So what do you want from Emilie?" Spencer asked.

"I don't want anything from her, I just want her to want me for who I am on the inside, not for what I am, or how famous I am, or for how much money I have." Nathan grabbed his bag and slung it over his shoulder.

"You of all people should know what that feels like." Nathan slammed through the doors and left Spencer alone in the locker room. Spencer ran his fingers through his hair and sighed. Seems like he had been wrong about Nathan all along.

Emilie sat on her couch, an icepack on her knee, and grabbed the remore control, feeling the anger boil up inside her. Not only did she have an ache in her knee, but she was also developing a headache from walking around with a lightning bolt above her head. Shannon would freak if she knew. "You don't want to look like an old woman, do you, Em?" Shannon would ask. Emilie rolled her eyes and growled angrily. She was getting angrier by the second as she flicked through the channels, every channel more nauseating that the previous one.

"Is there nothing good on TV today?" She snarled, threw the remote down next to her and she closed her eyes. She missed Nathan, but with Spencer keeping her on such a short leash, she did not dare go anywhere near fourteen twenty-three. Suddenly, her eyes opened, she sat up and laughed out loud. She still had the keycard for his room! She shifted forward and put the ice pack on the table. She stood up and walked to her handbag with a slight limp, when there was a knock on her door. She frowned and wondered if it was Nathan. Hopefully it wasn't Jennifer, or Brandon! She groaned in frustration and opened the door. It was Spencer.

"Hey." Emilie frowned.

"Hey, Em." Spencer said. "Can I come in for a second?"

"You said there were no boys allowed in my room." Emilie pouted.

"I'm not a boy, I'm an old man." Spencer said, crossing his arms and leaned against the doorframe.

"Fine." Emilie pulled a face.

Emilie shoved the door open and let Spencer in. She closed the door and looked at him. Spencer dug his hands into his tracksuit pants and looked at Emilie. Emilie took a few steps, still limping and Spencer frowned at her. He looked at her knee, red from the icepack and raised his eyebrows at her. "Is your knee acting up again?"

"No, I, uhm, it's fine. It's just an ache." She lied and shook her head. "It felt a bit tight, and seeing as I am not allowed out of my room to go swim some laps, the icepack was my only other option." She sighed sarcastically.

Spencer nodded and looked around the room.

"Spencer, I..." Emilie sighed.

"Why do you like Connor?" Spencer looked directly at her, his blue eyes piercing right through her.

"Spence, please..." Emilie felt her shoulders slump. She was tired of this.

"Answer the question." Spencer sat down on the couch and looked at her.

"This is going to sound lame and stupid, but he makes me laugh, and feel good, no matter what mood I am in. He is considerate and..." Emilie stopped and looked at Spencer.

"And what?" Spencer frowned.

Emilie walked over to him and sat down next to him. "He makes me feel safe, Spence. Do you remember what that feels like?"

"Yes, Jeremy had same effect on me, as lame and stupid as that may sound." Spencer nodded.

"Not to mention a little gay." Emilie pulled a face.

Spencer laughed and shook his head. "I was wrong about him, Em." Spencer admitted.

"What?" Emilie's mouth fell open.

"I was wrong about him. He's not the type of person I thought he was." Spencer said.

"But you...." Emilie frowned and looked at Spencer. Spencer had a guilty face and she sighed. "You picked a fight with him, didn't you?"

"It started out like that, but he ended up telling me a few things..." Spencer admitted.

"What things?" Emilie asked.

"Guy things, Em." Spencer grinned. "He's not so bad, and he really does care about you."

"That's good to know." Emilie grinned. " like him too."

"I've noticed." Spencer nodded.

"What type of person did you think he was, Spence?" Emilie looked at him.

"It's a long story." Spencer sighed. "But it doesn't mean anything now, everything was just a big misunderstanding."

"So, I get to see him?" Emilie asked slowly.

"Yeah, Em....."

Emilie jumped up and hugged Spencer. "Oh my god! Oh my god! Thank you! Thank you so much!" She shrieked.

"Alright, alright, enough with the

shrieking!" Spencer scowled. "Just don't overdo it, you still have a couple of games to play."

"I won't overdo it, I promise!" Emilie laughed.

"I'm really sorry, Em." Spencer looked at her. "You know I was just looking out for you."

"Aaw, come here, you big marshmallow." Emilie smiled and hugged him. "You're the best."

"I'm really sorry, Em. Is there anything that I can do to make it up to you?" Nathan smiled and pulled away.

Emilie thought for a moment and smiled. "Well, now that you mention it..."

"Oh, no. Here we go." Spencer rolled his eyes at her.

CHAPTER 9

Nathan and Zac pushed the doors open and Nathan sighed. He was really not in the mood for this social gathering, he would much rather be out and about, keeping busy, so that this week can pass quickly. He tugged at the sleeve of his crisp white shirt and looked at Zac.

"I think I should bail." He whispered to Zac.

"Nonsense, it's good for your image." Zac grinned and slapped his on the shoulder. "Besides, Emilie is going to be here."

"I know, but I am sick of keeping my distance from her." Nathan sighed, and dug his hands into his pockets.

"It's almost over man, just another week." Zac said. "I'll be right back." Zac left his side.

"This is going to be the longest week of my whole life." Nathan muttered and turned his head, scanning the room for Spencer. Luckily he was not around and Nathan breathed a sigh of relief.

"Good morning." He heard a voice behind him. He slowly turned around and looked into Emilie's beautiful face. Her hair was curled and pinned out of her face. The soft, flowing blue empire dress made her look even more beautiful, not that Nathan thought that was possible. She smiled up at him and he felt his heart skip a beat.

"Good morning pretty girl." He grinned, scanning the room.

"It's good to see you, Nate." She tilted her head. She obviously knew that it drove him crazy.

"I couldn't agree with you more." He smiled at her. Hopefully she couldn't hear his heart pounding in his chest.

"Congratulations with your win yesterday, Spencer told me you are through to the semi's." She smiled.

Nathan frowned and crossed his arms. "Did he also tell you he came to see me in my locker room yesterday?"

"Yes, he did." Emilie grinned.

"He did?" Nathan looked at her.

"Yes. He told me what you said, and he thinks you're okay." Emilie smiled at him. "He thought he had you figured out, but he was wrong."

Nathan lifted his eyebrows and ran his fingers through his hair. "So, he's okay with us?"

"Yes." Emilie nodded, with a smile. "You seem surprized."

"Surprized is not quite the word I would

have used, but yes. I am quite surprized." Nathan grinned at her, another wave of relief washing over him.

"I know he can be a real pain sometimes, but he's just looking out for me. He promised Jeremy that he would." Emilie looked at him.

"I understand." Nathan nodded.

"I am just so glad to be here with you. I have missed you so much." Emilie took his hand.

Nathan looked at her hand in his and looked at her. "No more sneaking around?"

"Nope." She smiled at him.

"You just made my day." Nathan grinned.

"Hmm, and I didn't even give my number to you." Emilie giggled.

"Yeah, okay, I know I was a bit forward.." Nathan said apologetically.

"A bit?" Emilie raised her eyebrows at him.

Nathan laughed and looked at her. "Okay, I was very forward, I admit, but I had to. You captivated me."

"Was it my handgrenade subtlety, or my ability to call three big bags traveling light?" Emilie giggled.

"Both." Nathan grinned and touched her cheek.

"Hey Emilie." Zac said next to her.

"Hey, Zac!" She hugged him and giggled. "Good to see you. Where's Shannon?"

"How should I know?" Zac gave her a strange look and she frowned.

"Uhm, I..." Emilie shook her head lightly.

"They're going to start. We should find our seats." Zac said, like nothing was wrong. Nathan nodded and Zac walked through the tables.

"See you later, then." Nathan smiled, sadly.

"Nate, Emilie is over here with us." Zac said.

Emilie and Nathan looked over at him, and Nathan grinned. "What a coincidence.."

Emilie shrugged with a sly smile and walked with him to their table.

"So how did you do it?" Nathan looked at her, sitting with her hands on her lap, looking straight at him.

"I don't know what you mean." She simply smiled.

Nathan narrowed his eyes at her and laughed. "Yet, again, you have taken me completely by surprize."

Emilie giggled and touched his face. "You're welcome."

"Have I told you how gorgeous you look today?" Nathan smiled.

"Not lately." She shook her head and put her hand back onto her lap. "Tell me properly, later." She winked.

Nathan smirked to himself and looked at Zac. "You knew about this?"

"What are you talking about?" Zac whispered with a frown.

Nathan laughed and the room went quiet. He looked up and everyone in the room was looking at him.

"I am glad that you are as enthusiastic about today as we are, Mister Connor." Jack Huxley nodded at Nathan.

"Always, Jack." Nathan grinned. He could hear Emilie chuckle next to him and shook his head.

"You're totally blushing." She whispered with a giggle.

After breakfast was served, Jack explained the details of the day's proceedings, Nathan leaned his head closer to Emilie's. "What are you doing later?" He whispered.

"There's this boring cocktail party that I have to go to." She said softly. "Do you want to be my date?"

"I was going to ask you that same question." He grinned. "But I was talking about afterwards."

Emilie looked him in the eyes and smiled slyly. "I still have your room key."

"You're not going to need it." He smiled and

sat back in his chair.

"What did you have in mind?" Emilie whispered with a smile.

"You will just have to wait and see, pretty girl." Nathan gently touched her knee under the table. Emilie smiled to herself and could feel her heart pounding wildly.

There was a knock on the door and Tom stood up from the couch to open it.

"Spencer, nice to see you." Tom smiled and gave him a hug. "Aren't you supposed to be at Emmy's game?"

"Emilie can handle herself quite well without me. Why aren't you there?" Spencer asked, closing the door behind him.

"You ask me the same question every time she plays." Tom frowned.

"Yeah, and every time you have the same answer." Spencer crossed his arms.

"Spencer, you know exactly why...." Tom muttered.

"Can we talk for a minute?" Spencer frowned.

"Sure." Tom motioned to the couch and sat down on the opposite couch. Spencer nodded and sat down.

"Tom, it seems that Emilie and Nathan Connor has taken an interest in each other."

Spencer smiled.

"Nathan Connor. Talented kid." Tom nodded.

"Yeah, so they say." Spencer nodded.

"What kind of interest, exactly?" Tom asked.

"They seem to be crazy about each other." Spencer leaned forward and rested his hands on his knees.

"You don't say." Tom frowned.

"I had a word with Nathan and his intentions are perfectly honorable." Spencer nodded.

"That's good to hear." Tom nodded.

"There may be a few more headlines...." Spencer said.

"Headlines." Tom mumbled. "I hate headlines."

"I know. So do I, but some things are unavoidable sometimes." Spencer frowned.

"Yes, they are." Tom nodded and looked at Spencer.

"Have you ever talked to her about it?" Spencer asked.

"No. I have never had the courage." Tom shook his head.

"She deserves to know the truth, Tom." Spencer said. "And it would mean a lot to her if you were there at her game tomorrow."

Tom lifted his head and looked at Spencer. "No, I can't."

"She thinks you hate her, Tom." Spencer said.

Tom looked at him and shrugged. "Maybe I do."

Spencer looked at Tom in disbelief and shook his head. "That's not fair."

"Don't talk to me about fair! I lost my wife and my son!" Tom exclaimed.

"And you're going to lose Emilie as well if you carry on like this." Spencer shook his head in disapproval and stood up.

"You can't lose something that was never yours to begin with, Spencer." Tom scowled.

"Keep telling yourself that, Tom." Spencer growled and walked to the door. He opened the door and slammed it behind him. "You're a real coward, you know that. You don't deserve someone like Em in your life!"

Tom stared at the door and rested his head in his hands. He thought back to the day when he met Paige in 1977. He was nineteen and working in a vineyard just west of Marseille. The sun was setting and there were no clouds in the sky. He was walking home from the vineyard and he saw a beautiful blonde, sitting by the river, her feet in the water. He walked closer and she turned her head towards him.

He had never seen a more beautiful woman in his life. She smiled at him, tucking a strand of hair behind her ear, just like Emilie does. Tom could feel the tears well up in his eyes and he cried, for the first time in years.

"Come on, baby." She heard Brandon say next to her.

She stood up straight and glared at him. "I have asked you repeatedly not to call me baby."

"Whatever." Brandon smiled, tugging at his cap. "You know you like it!"

Emilie tilted her head to the side and narrowed her eyes at him. Emilie could not believe that she got stuck with Brandon, and Nathan and Kelly were paired up. She felt a wave of jealousy consume her and she growled at herself.

"Hayes to serve." The voice over the speakers sounded.

"One more point." Brandon slapped his hand against his racquet. He lifted his racquet up and motioned to the crowd. "Some support, please!" He yelled and the crowd started clapping and cheering.

Emilie looked over her shoulder at Brandon and shook her head. The guy can get a crowd going, that's for sure. No pressure Emilie. She bounced the ball three times, as she always did, and hit it over the net, making it bounce right at Samantha's feet. Samantha swung her racquet and the ball flew towards Emilie again. It also bounced right at her feet and she easily knocked the ball over the net to Ronnie. Ronnie hit a powerful forehand shot to Brandon and Brandon volleyed the ball over Samantha's head. Samantha did not even try to reach the ball and she closed her eyes. Ronnie threw his racquet on the ground and stomped on it. Emilie and Brandon exchanged glances and she raised her hands in the air and clapped. The crowd went wild and Brandon laughed. "Yeah, that's better!" He shouted towards them. Emilie glanced over to the electronic score sheet where her total was flashing in red. It flashed $175-000. She smiled to herself and raised her racquet in the air, extremely proud that she raised so much money in just over an hour. She lowered her racquet and made her way to the net, where an unimpressed Ronnie and an upset Samantha, stood, waiting by the net. Emilie spotted Nathan in the crowd, clapping and smiling at her. She pointed to him with a smile and then blew a kiss at him.

"Forty, thirty."

"Come on, Campbell." Emilie said to herself, watching as he served. The ball flew over the net and Nathan ran forward, hitting it to the middle of the court. She ran towards it, the same time as Brandon ran to the ball and she slammed into him. They fell onto the cement and the crowd was instantly silent. Nathan ran towards the net and looked at Emilie, on the ground. "Emilie?" He called.

"I'm so sorry." Brandon started apologizing.

"Shut up and just get Shannon." Emilie frowned, touching her head and groaned. Brandon nodded at her, stood up slowly and waved to Shannon. Shannon came running down the steps and onto the court. She knelt next to Emilie and touched her head.

"Emmy, my friend, are you alive?" Shannon asked.

"It feels like it." Emilie frowned.

"Where does it hurt, Em?" Shannon asked.

"My head. Brandon's stupid racquet nearly knocked me unconscious." Emilie groaned.

Shannon laughed and shook her head. "Come on superstar, you're fine, you got some Connor-ass to kick." Shannon helped Emilie up from the cement and the crowd cheered.

"She's okay!" Brandon yelled and the crowd roared.

Emilie smiled at Shannon and Shannon

walked back off the court and to her seat.

"You sure you're okay?" Brandon looked at her.

"Yeah, I'll live." She nodded with a smile.

"Look I'm sorry, really..." Brandon explained.

"It's fine, just watch where you swing that racquet of yours." Emilie smirked, gently touching her head.

"Yeah, my bad." He tugged at her visor and she pushed him away.

"Deuce." The umpire's voice sounded.

Two points Emilie. Two points. You can do this. FOCUS!

"Campbell to serve. Quiet please."

Brandon served and hit it straight to Nathan. Nathan strained to reach the ball, and hit it back to Brandon. Brandon hit it hard and deep, making Kelly miss the ball.

"Advantage. Campbell and Hayes."

Emilie let out an excited laugh and grinned at Nathan, who did not look exhausted at all. She tilted her head at him and smiled. She looked at Kelly and was surprized to see a small smile on her face. Nathan saw her gently touching her knee and wondered if she had hurt it when she fell. Emilie watched as Brandon hit the ball to Nathan and Nathan swung the ball towards her at an incredible speed. It hit the cement by her feet and she hit it back to him, with impressive skill. Nathan hit it towards Brandon, but the ball flew high, instead of far. Brandon ran forward and hit the ball back to Nathan with ease. Nathan stepped back and Kelly jumped in front of him, hitting the ball to Emilie. The shot was short and slow and it made Emilie run for her life. She let out a startlingly loud growl as she hit the ball towards Kelly. Kelly, expecting the ball to be short and slow as well, ran forward.

"Back!" Nathan called, but it was too late. The ball flew over Kelly's head, bounced just in front of the line and eventually hit the back wall.

"Game, set, match. Campbell and Hayes."

The crowd rose to their feet and cheered wildly.

"Oh my god! You did it!" Brandon exclaimed and hugged her. She let out a shriek and put her arms around Brandon. Emilie pulled back quickly and shook her head.

"No, we did it." She grinned, holding out her hands.

Brandon grinned and high-fived her with both hands. Emilie took a few steps back and waved at the crowd. She looked at Shannon, cheering wildly, and laughed. She spotted Spencer in the crowd, cheering and clapping, and an empty space next to him, where her dad was supposed to be. That is what he has always been in her life, an empty space. She smiled miserably at Spencer and turned away, her heart aching, filled with the same emptiness she felt most of her life. Emptiness caused by a father that hated his daughter.

Nathan's blood boiled as she watched Brandon hug Emilie. He wanted to march across the court and beat him to a pulp. He looked at Kelly, picking up her racquet from the cement and ran his fingers through his damp hair.

"Good game, Kel." He said to her.

"I'll say. The girl's got skills." Kelly laughed.

Nathan nodded with a smile and looked at Emilie again. She had her back to him and she was laughing at something Brandon was saying. He could look at her forever. Her long, blonde hair was tied up, out of her face and her white visor on her head. Her light blue top was the same color as her eyes and the short black skirt fit her hips perfectly. He stared at her for a moment and grinned. She put her hands on her hips and turned to him, with a grin. She raised her eyebrows and gave him a cocky look. Yes, she had beaten him, and yes, she had every right to be cocky, but to look like that and not expect him to be able to resist kissing her in front of all these people, was not fair. He looked around him at the crowd and nodded to himself. He was going to do it. Why? Because he wanted to! Would it complicate things? Yes! Would it disrupt their lives? Quite possibly. Would she be embarrassed? Maybe. Did he care? Not at all!

He took a deep breath, threw his racquet down onto the cement and walked to the net. He jumped over it with ease and marched up to her. She narrowed her eyes at him and opened her mouth to say something cocky to him. Before she could do or say anything, he was right in front of her and she felt her knees go weak. Nathan grabbed hold of her waist, pulled her close and he kissed her. Not a congratulations-on-beating-my-ass kiss on the cheek, it was an I-want-you-every-minute-of-every-day kiss, full on the mouth, tongue and all. In front of everyone! He was the first to pull away, and Emilie opened her eyes.

"What was that for?" She said, breathless.

"I just wanted to congratulate you, you blew my winning streak to pieces." Nathan brushed her cheek with the back of his hand.

Emilie smiled and nodded. "Oops." She whispered.

Nathan nodded and they turned their heads to look at the crowd, still going wild and cheering. Shannon was grinning and gave them a thumbs-up. Emilie looked at Nathan and they laughed out loud.

"I think I'm getting fat." Shannon sighed as she and Emilie and stared at themselves in the full-length mirror in Emilie's bedroom.

"Don't be ridiculous, Shan." Emilie frowned, looking at Shannon.

"I'm serious, this dress fit better last week." Shannon poked Emilie's stomach. "Yours is so flat. Maybe I should also start playing this barbaric sport of yours."

"Stop that." Emilie giggled and shoved Shannon's hands away from her stomach. "There's nothing wrong with your stomach. You look great. Zac's going to love it."

"I hope so. He's been really off lately." Shannon frowned.

"He's playing Nathan tomorrow, so he has a right to be." Emilie pulled at her dress.

"No wonder." Shannon mumbled.

After a moment of silence, Shannon looked at Emilie. "You look better in black."

"You think?" Emilie asked, a little unsure if that was true.

"Would I lie to you?" Shannon looked at her.

Shannon's dark hair was curled and pinned

up, a few curls framing her face, and she wore a long red halterneck dress with an open back and silver high heels. Shannon pulled her face when she looked at the shoes, Emilie locked her boots away! Emilie grinned and straightened herself in the mirror. Her hair was also curled, but taken to the side and was draped over her one shoulder. She was wearing a black and silver strapless dress with a dropped waist and black high heels. Shannon turned to her friend and smiled.

"Personally, I wouldn't have chosen the black, I'm more of a white person." Emilie looked at Shannon and grinned. "But the black is growing on me."

"White is for your wedding day.   Come on, admit it, you look hot. Nathan won't be able to keep his hands off you tonight." Shannon winked.

The moment Emilie saw Nathan standing next to Zac, her heart flipped and she started breathing heavily. Nathan wore a dark suit, and looked absolutely gorgeous. She could feel her lips burning from their kiss on court and she felt dizzy all over again.

"Em, relax and breathe." Shannon squeezed her hand.

Emilie nodded and she made her way over

to Nathan. Nathan looked at her and he was blown away.

"Wow, you look beautiful!" Nathan was in awe and could not take his eyes off of her.

"You look pretty beautiful yourself, mister Connor." She tilted her head and smiled.

"How can I not kiss you right now?" Nathan grinned, cupped her chin with his hand and kissed her tenderly.

Their kiss was interupted by a couple of journalists talking at once and a couple of cameras flashed.

"Hey, take the party elsewhere!" Spencer exclaimed and chased the journalists and their cameras away.

"Thank you, Spencer." Nathan extended his hand towards Spencer.

"It's just good to see Emilie in such a good mood all the time." Spencer took his hand and shook his. "I'm sorry I was such a dick before. You turned out to be an alright guy."

Nathan raised his eyebrows at Spencer and Emilie smiled, putting her hand on Nathan's upper arm.

"I'll see you guys later, then. Enjoy the party." Spencer smiled at them and walked to the other side of the room.

"This party drags, you want to go rendezvous in my room?" Nathan whispered to her.

"We just got here." She looked at him and he pulled a sad face at her. "I promise we'll rendezvous..." She whispered.

"Miss Hayes, Mister Connor, good evening." A journalist walked over to them.

Nathan grinned. "Can I help you, sir?"

"Peter, Peter O'Reilly, sir. May I ask a few questions, please?" Peter asked.

"Sure, but you see that big guy in the black tux standing by the door over there, Peter?" Nathan pointed to Spencer standing by the door on their left, and Peter nodded. "If, for any reason, you ask anything that we don't like, then I am going to call that guy over there, and he'll pummel you so hard, you won't ever be able to write, again. Got it?" Nathan grinned.

Emilie giggled nervously and shook her head at Nathan. "What he means is, that there are certain things we don't discuss in interviews." Emilie smiled at Peter and touched his arm.

"Got it, Miss Hayes." Peter's face flushed a bit and he took out his voice recorder. "Miss Hayes, you raised over five hundred thousand dollars for your charity, The Tennis Rehab Center in Washington DC. Was it through your injury that you particularly chose this charity?"

Peter asked.

"Yes. The Tennis Rehab Center in DC was where I had my rehabilitation for my knee. The people there did an absolutely amazing job. Without them I would not be here today, and I owe it to them." Emilie smiled.

"Mister Connor, what was your charity and why did you choose it?" Peter asked.

"Well, my charity was the Future Tennis Players of America. It is a program that helps under-priviledged kids learn the wonderful game of tennis, and helps them achieve their dreams of one day also standing here one day and doing what they love. I have spent a lot of time with those kids and they all show great potential. Someone once told me, that do what you love, the rest doesn't matter. Those kids matter to me and that is why I raised four hundred and twenty thousand dollars for them." Nathan answered and Emilie looked at him. She smiled and touched his arm lightly.

"Are you two a couple now?" Peter looked at them.

"Yes." Emilie answered, reluctantly. Nathan looked at her and grinned at himself. "Yes, we are."

"Is the pressure more now since you are both through to the semi finals tomorrow afternoon?" Peter asked.

"We keep our personal lives and our professional lives separate. Or we try to. We focus on our games and keep our heads clear." Emilie nodded.

"Balance is the key." Nathan nodded in agreement.

"Miss Hayes, how did you feel being back in New York for the first time after your accident?" Peter asked.

Emilie glanced at Nathan and he gave her a subtle nod. "It was overwhelming, to say the least."

"Have you been back to the scene...." Peter started asking, but Nathan interupted him by raising his hand.

"Alright, buddy, that's quite enough." Nathan growled.

"Okay, sorry, sir." Peter apologized. "Thank you so much, Miss Hayes." Peter smiled at them and bolted for the door.

"Oh my god." Emilie shrugged, put her arms around Nathan's waist and rested her head on his shoulder. Nathan laughed and ran his fingers through her hair. She pulled back and looked at him.

"What?" Nathan asked, frowning.

"You're right, this party drags." She grinned at him. "You want to go for a walk?"

Nathan lifted his elbow and she slipped her

hand through, letting it rest on his arm. "I would love to."

They walked through the large gallery of the hotel and stopped in front of the elevator.

"Where to, pretty girl?" Nathan asked as they stepped into the elevator.

Emilie drew some of the shades back and looked out of the window of the empty top floor suite. "There are the lights again." She smiled and pressed her fingertip against the glass.

Nathan walked over to her, stood behind her and slid his arms around her waist. "I'm sorry about that, Em. I really did not know that was where it happened."

She leaned her head against his chest and smiled, still looking at the lights. "Don't apologise, Nate. It was good that I was there. Thank you for being there and holding my hand."

"You're welcome." He kissed her cheek and she turned around.

"This is going to sound completely insane, but I felt him, when I was there." Emilie looked at him.

Nathan looked at her, not knowing what to say, or to think for that matter. Emilie studied his expression and shook her head.

"You think I am insane, don't you?" Emilie

looked out of the window. "That's what I thought too, but I definitely felt him."

Nathan raised his eyebrows and dug his hands into his pockets. "You made him proud today."

"I hope so." Emilie looked up at him and grinned. "That was a pretty impressive speech you gave that journo downstairs."

Nathan looked at her and smiled shyly.

"No, really. It was so heartfelt, you're really passionate about those kids, aren't you?" She smiled.

"Yeah, everyone deserves a fair chance to live their dreams." Nathan nodded.

"So who told you to 'do what you love, the rest doesn't matter'?" Emilie smiled.

"There's this kid, Reilly, at the FTPA. He had the most amazing footwork, for a twelve-year old, but he had trouble with his temper. I always told him to keep his mind clear, and not let his anger get in the way of his game. Then he watched me play against Spencer in Boston two years ago and I sort of lost my temper and threw my racquet at the net. The next weekend, he came up to me and told me he watched my game, and I could see the dissapointment in his eyes. He asked me how can something that makes me so happy, make me so mad. I had no words and I felt like a real hypocrite. There I was, trying to teach him to control his temper, but I couldn't even control my own. He looked up at me and said to me, 'Do what you love, Nate, the rest doesn't matter.'. He completely changed my life." Nathan felt his throat go dry and looked away.

Emilie touched his cheek and smiled softly. "He sounds like a great kid."

"He is." Nathan cleared his throat and looked at Emilie. "I can take you to meet him when we get back."

"I would love that." Emilie smiled at him. He looked at her for a moment and lowered his face. Their lips met and Nathan cupped her face with his hands. Emilie felt like she was floating away again, so she put her arms around his shoulders, feeling the warmth of his body against hers. Seeing another side of him made her fall deeper in love with him.

Nathan pulled back and stared at her for a second. She smiled shyly and tugged the collar of his jacket.

"Tell me what you are thinking?" He said, almost whispering.

"I am thinking that we should check out the view from your room." Emilie dropped her chin, but still looked at Nathan.

"The skyline isn't that great...." He frowned at her.

"Who said anything about the skyline?" She raised an eyebrow at him and grinned.

CHAPTER 10

Nathan opened his door and held the door open for Emilie. She smiled at him and walked into his room. The room, even though it was not as big as hers, was beautiful. It had black and white modern decor and it smelled just like Nathan. She breathed in the air and put her clutch down on the white leather couch. Nathan closed the door and smiled at her.

"It's beautiful." She looked around her.

Nathan walked over to her and took her hands in his. "You are beautiful."

She tilted her head and looked at him. He ran his hands up her arms and shoulders. He gently touched her hair and cupped her face. He stared at her for another few moments and smiled, dreamily. "I'll be right back." He smiled.

"Okay." Emilie nodded and watched as he walked to the bedroom. She sat down on the couch, clasped her hands together and brought them up to her face. She closed her eyes and took a few deep breaths. "Okay, so this was happening now. Wait! Do I smell of sweat? Do I need a breathmint? Oh my god, my lips are all cracked. Okay, relax, Emilie, just breathe, everything is going to be perfectly fine." She opened her eyes and grabbed her clutch. She scratched around in it and dumped the contents of it on to the couch. She took out a couple of breathmints and chewed them quickly. She lightly misted herself with some perfume and put some lipbalm on. She threw everything back in her bag and swallowed the last of the chewed mints in her mouth. She closed her bag and put it back on the couch.

    After a few minutes, Nathan came out of the bedroom and held out his hand to her. She smiled, stood up and took his hand with a giggle. She followed him into his dimly lit bedroom and smiled. There were candles all over the room, the shades were drawn and in the background there was soft music playing. Emilie felt her heart pounding against her ribcage and she took a deep breath. Nathan looked at her, leaned his head in closer to hers and kissed her. He felt her lips part and he gently licked her bottom lip. She moaned softly and caressed his tongue with hers. She was the first to pull back and she looked at him.   She gently pulled his jacket off and it dropped to the floor. She reached for his tie and pulled it loose, a little more forceful now. He looked at her and brushed her cheek with the back of his hand. She grabbed the back of his neck and pulled him closer to her. She lifted her chin and kissed him again. His hands slid around her waist and he felt for the zipper of her dress. He unzipped the top of her dress and felt the soft skin of her back with his fingertips. She unbuttoned his white shirt and threw it onto the couch behind her. She traced the muscles of his shoulders and his chest with her fingers and looked at him.

"Nate." She breathed as he kissed her neck. He pulled back and looked at her. She looked at him with those beautiful eyes and Nathan pulled her dress off. It fell to the floor, she stepped out of it and kicked it aside. Nathan picked her up and gently put her down on his bed.

Emilie wiped a bead of sweat from Nathan's brow and smiled at him. Emilie was sitting with her back against the wooden headboard, and Nathan's head was resting on Emilie's stomach. She closed her eyes and gave a satisfied sigh. Nathan turned his head to her and sat up. He shifted closer to her and brushed a damp strand of hair out of her face. Emilie lifted her hand up to his face and touched his cheek. "Nate.." She whispered.

"Em..." Nathan whispered back.

Emilie sat forward and adjusted the sheet, so that her chest was covered. Nathan took her hand from his face and held it in both of his hands.

"Emilie, I love you." He whispered to her.

Emilie felt like her heart was about to burst out of her chest and she smiled, relieved.

"I love you too, Nathan." She smiled and took a few deep breaths.

Nathan moved his face closer to hers and kissed her.

Shannon looked over at Zac and crossed her arms over her breasts. "Are you serious?"

Zac turned around to face her and he pulled his shorts on. "Do I need to repeat myself?"

"That's bullshit, Zac." Shannon said, flatly.

"Whatever, Shannon. What else do you want me to say?" Zac put his hands on his hips.

Shannon reached for her grey t-shirt and pulled it over her head. "The truth would be nice." She mumbled.

"Did you honestly think that this was something?" Zac looked at her. "You can't be serious, Shannon. Besides, guys like me and girls like you...."

"Girls like me?" Shannon exclaimed.

"You know what I mean." Zac scowled.

"So I was just another fuck to you? Another notch on you arrogant-ass belt?" Shannon exclaimed.

"Yeah." Zac looked at her blankly.

"Well, that's a first." Shannon muttered sarcastically and she sighed.

Zac turned around and looked at her. "Are you still here?"

Shannon narrowed her eyes at Zac and shook her head. "You're a piece of shit!" Shannon stood up and pulled on some black hotpants. Shannon grabbed her jeans and her shoes from the floor and marched out of Zac's room. Shannon closed the door behind her and she stood in the hall, breathing heavily. She dialled Emilie's number, but it went straiht to voicemail. "Em, please come to my room, I need you." Shannon said and tears ran down her cheeks. She let out a frustrated growl and walked back to her room.

Kelly opened her door and walked down the corridor. She stopped abruptly and ran her fingers through her hair. She shook her head and continued down the corridor. She spotted Shannon marching towards her and frowned. Shannon was wearing only a t-shirt and held her shoes and her jeans in her hand. Her hair was mussed and she looked like she had been crying. Kelly saw dark mascara lines running down her cheeks as Shannon looked at her.

"Hey." Kelly said. "Are you okay?"

"Yeah, I'm perfect. How are you?" Shannon scowled.

"What happened?" Kelly reached for her arm.

Shannon bit her lip and looked at the floor. "Nothing."

"You wouldn't be this upset over nothing, would you?" Kelly asked.

"I guess not." Shannon shook her head.

"Do you want me to call Emilie?" Kelly asked.

"She'll only be back later. She's with Nate." Shannon sniffed.

"I could sit with you until she's back." Kelly said and wiped a tear off Shannon's cheek.

"Okay, sure." Shannon frowned.

Kelly smiled at Shannon and the two girls stood in the corridor for a few moments, looking at each other.

Nathan brushed Emilie's hair outof her face and she blinked. "Hey." She smiled and rolled onto her side.

"I thought you were asleep." He smiled and caressed her cheek.

"Nope." She shook her head.

"Well, I don't know about you, but I'm exhausted." He pulled her closer and held her tight. "You wear me out."

"Really?" Emilie giggled.

"Just a bit. Give me another twenty minutes." Nathan gave her a crooked, cocky smile.

Emilie laughed and shook her head. "I think I should let you get to bed." Emilie sat up and tucked loose strands of hair behind her ear. "We have a big day tomorrow. I also want to get in some practice after breakfast."

Nathan grinned and sat up as well. "I think you got enough practice for a week."

Emilie giggled and touched his hand. "I had a wonderful night."

"So did I." Nathan nodded.

"Thank you." Emilie whispered and kissed him softly on the lips.

Emilie stood up from the bed and Nathan helped her back into her dress. While she was putting her shoes back on, he quickly got dressed as well. She looked at her phone and saw that Shannon tried to call her.

"Shannon tried to call me." Emilie said and listened to Shannon's message.

"Anything serious?" Nathan asked as they walked to his door and he opened it for her.

"She sounds upset. I think I should go check on her." Emilie ran her hands through her hair.

"You need an escort?" Nathan asked.

"As tempting as that sounds, I think this is a

girls only party." Emilie frowned.

"Yeah, I better get some sleep." Nathan chuckled.

"Good idea." Emilie giggled. "I will see you tomorrow then, at eleven thirty. Then after your game, we will have the rest of the day to ourselves."

"I can't wait." Nathan smiled and kissed her.

"Good luck for tomorrow." She winked at him. "You'll be great!"

"So will you." Nathan brought her hand up to his mouth and kissed it.

"Shan, I am so sorry, are you okay?" Emilie burst into Shannon's room and found Kelly sitting on the couch. "Kelly?"

"Hey, Emilie." Kelly stood up from the couch.

"What are you doing here?" Emilie asked and looked around the room. "And where's Shannon?"

"She's asleep. She was pretty upset." Kelly said.

"What are you doing here?" Emilie crossed her arms.

"Well, I was out in the corridor and bumped into Shannon. She was pretty upset about something. She said that you would only be back later. So, I offered to sit with her until you got back." Kelly said.

"That was nice of you." Emilie frowned.

"Don't look so shocked. I'm not such a big bitch as everyone makes me out to be." Kelly said.

"I never said..." Emilie shook her head.

"You didn't have to." Kelly smiled. "Being Jennifer's best friend does not exactly get you on the most popular list."

"Right." Emilie nodded.

"Look, I want to apologize." Kelly took a step forward.

"For what?" Emilie frowned.

"I haven't been very nice to you since the press. You sound like a really nice person, Shannon speaks highly of you." Kelly said.

Emilie tilted her head and smiled shyly. "Well, I haven't exactly been very nice to you either."

"It's okay. I would really like it if we can atleast try to be friends." Kelly said sincerely.

"That would be nice." Emilie smiled. "And I'm sorry for being a bitch towards you as well."

"Don't worry about it." Kelly laughed and Emilie smiled.

"I better be going, then." Kelly said.

"You don't have to." Emilie shook her head.

"I think I do. I have the early game

tomorrow." Kelly nodded.

"Ouch. Well, good luck, Kelly." Emilie smiled.

"Thanks, you too." Kelly walked to the door.

"Kelly." Emilie said and Kelly looked over her shoulder at Emilie. "Thank you, for Shannon."

"No problem." Kelly smiled and opened the door.

"So what happened then?" Emilie sat down next to Shannon on her bed, putting her arm around Shannon's shoulders.

"Basically, he just used me when no-one else was available!" Shannon exclaimed. "How could I be so stupid?" Shannon wiped a tear from her cheek.

"You're not stupid, Shan. He is." Emilie shook her head.

"When it comes to guys I am." Shannon looked at her friend. "It's proven. Look back at every relationship I ever had, and tell me that there was one worthwhile guy."

Emilie thought for a second and frowned.

"Let me list them all for you, Em." Shannon started counting on her fingers. "Barry was too arrogant. Andrew was jealous and possessive. Mark was a control-freak. Robert was a liar. Justin was a cheater. Donald was aggressive. Vaughan was obnoxious. Wayne was gay. And now Zac just used me for sex!"

Emilie gave Shannon an encouraging smile and hugged her. "I'm sorry, Shan. You deserve so much better."

Shannon sniffed and looked at her. "Does Nathan have a brother?"

"Nope, sorry Shan. He's got two cousins in Malibu though." Emilie smiled.

"That's too far. I think I am done with men anyway." Shannon shook her head.

"Come here." Emilie held out her arms at Shannon and Shannon rested her head on Emilie's shoulder. "Everything is going to be okay, Shan."

"Yeah, I know." Shannon nodded and wiped another tear away. Zac was not worth crying over anyway.

"I'm sorry that I wasn't here when you needed me." Emilie said.

"It's okay." Shannon sniffed. "Kelly was really nice though."

"What's up with that?" Emilie asked.

"I don't know." Shannon shook her head. "Maybe she is sick of that psycho friend of hers."

"Well, that would definitely be a first." Emilie shrugged.

CHAPTER 11

Nathan rolled over onto his back and stretched out. He stared at the empty space next to him and smiled. He could still see Emilie next to him, wrapped in the sheets. He grinned to himself and reached for his phone, dialing a number. He sat up and rested his head against the headboard.

"Good morning, Mom." He smiled.

"Good morning honey! How are you?"

"I am great, and you?" Nathan asked.

"Well thank you!" Zoe, laughed. "You sound good."

"Yeah, I would say so." Nathan laughed.

"Could it have anything to do with a certain young blonde you kissed on the court yesterday?" Zoe smiled.

"Maybe." Nathan grinned.

"Maybe?" Zoe asked.

"Mom, I can't tell you how amazing she is. She's perfect. There's no other way to describe her!" Nathan smiled.

"It sounds good to hear you so happy, honey." Zoe smiled. "So, when do I get to meet her?"

"I will ask her. I've told her all about you, and she thinks you are great!" Nathan said.

"Don't go telling any lies about me." Zoe said. "How are you feeling about today, Nathan?"

"I feel good. Zac's being a bit of a dick though." Nathan shrugged.

"Nathan..." Zoe's voice growled.

"Sorry, Mom, but it's the truth. He's not the person that I thought he was, you know. It's like he had a personality change, or something." Nathan frowned.

"You just concentrate on your games, forget about all those things. You don't need them. You're going to do great. " Zoe said.

"You're right. Thanks Mom." Nathan smiled.

"You're welcome, honey. I'm just sorry that I can't be there." Zoe said sadly.

"It's okay, I understand." Nathan's jaw clenched. "Is he there?"

"No, he's in Phoenix." Zoe said.

"Big surprize. He gets to go screw around and you have to stay home." Nathan felt the anger in his veins.

"Nathan, he's your father." Zoe said.

"Sometimes I wonder." Nathan grumbled.

"Nathan, you don't mean that..."

"No, Mom, he's a dick and we both know it. Just because we share the same DNA, does not make him a father. He's an ass." Nathan frowned.

"Yes, alright, you've made your point, many times." Zoe sighed.

"Look, Mom, I have to go. Emilie's game is in an hour and I need to get ready. I'll speak to you soon." Nathan sat up and looked at the clock against the wall.

"Thank you for the call, my baby." Zoe smiled. "Have a great day, Honey. Good luck with your game."

"Thanks Mom, you too." Nathan grinned.

"I love you baby." Zoe said.

"Love you too, Mom." Nathan shook his head and closed his phone.

Emilie stared at herself in the mirror of her locker room and tied up her hair. She knelt down to get her trainers out of her bag and sat down on the bench. As she was putting on her trainers, she closed her eyes and took a few deep breaths. "Right, Emilie. Breathe, girl breathe. Keep yourself focused, no distractions, no pressure, no stress." Emilie opened her eyes and saw Spencer standing in the door.

"Ten minutes until game time. You almost ready?" Spencer smiled at her.

"Almost, yeah." Emilie nodded.

"How's the knee?" Spencer asked.

"It's fine." Emilie nodded. "Is my dad out

there?" Emilie asked and adjusted her sweatband on her left wrist.

"No, he's not up for it." Spencer shook his head and grimaced.

"Why does that not surprize me?" Emilie closed her eyes and shook her head. She could feel hot tears stinging her eyes and covered her face with her hands.

"Hey, Em. Don't cry, please." Spencer walked to her and put his arms around her.

"I just wish he didn't hate me, or this game so much." Emilie sobbed.

"Just give him some time. It's been hard for him too." Spencer said, running his fingers through Emilie's blonde hair.

"He wasn't the only one that lost Jer. I did too, Spence and so did you." Emilie pulled away and looked at him.

Spencer looked at her and wiped a tear from her cheek. "You don't have to tell me that, Em."

Emilie nodded and wiped her face. "Yeah."

"What's with all the tears today, Em?" Spencer frowned.

"Everything and nothing." Emilie shook her head.

"Is it Connor? I'll kick his ass if..." Spencer growled.

"No, it's not Nathan, it's Shannon." Emilie

interrupted him.

"Why? What happened?" Spencer asked, looking at her.

"Let's just say Zac Gilmore is the biggest ass in the world." Emilie looked at Spencer.

"Is she okay?" Spencer asked, concerned.

"You know how Shannon is. She says she's fine, but I know she's not." Emilie tilted her head.

"Why do you girls do that?" Spencer looked at Emilie and she frowned at him. "Why do you say that you're fine, when you're not?"

Emilie looked at Spencer for a few seconds and grimaced. "That's a good question."

"It's not a crime to be upset or hurt about something." Spencer said.

"Tell that to Shannon." Emilie said.

"Maybe I will." Spencer grinned and stared at Emilie's knee. "So is your knee really fine, or are you just saying that to shut me up?"

Emilie bit her lip and looked away.

"Emilie." Spencer said firmly.

"I dont know. It's okay sometimes and then it's not." Emilie shook her head.

"Do you want me to call Shannon?" Spencer shifted around uncomfortably.

"No, it's okay. She's got enough to deal with." Emilie looked up and smiled. "I've got a game to win."

Spencer nodded with a smile and he watched Emilie walk passed him and out the doors.

"Thirty, love, Hayes to serve."
Emilie glared at Samantha, standing on the other side of the court, ready. Emilie took a few deep breaths and bounced the ball by her feet. Once, twice, three times. It had always been a habit of hers. It had to be three. Three was the number of months she couldn't walk after the accident, it was the number of roses she put on her brother's coffin, it was the number of surgeries she had, it was the number of times her heart had been broken, it was the number of years Shannon was older than her, it was the number of times she had fallen in love. Third time lucky, as Jeremy always said. Emilie threw the ball in the air and felt her racquet automatically lift and hit the ball over the net. For seventeen years, tennis was all she knew, and her mother had been part of that for three years. If she did not still have a picture of her mother, she would not remember her at all. At least Jeremy knew her a little bit more than she did, he had the pleasure to have had her at his games. Emilie watched as the ball flew towards her and hit it back to Samantha. Samantha's dirty blonde

hair blew in the wind as she ran to get to the ball, but it was out of her reach.

"Forty, fifteen."

Emilie walked back to the baseline and spotted Nathan in the crowd, clapping for her. She gave him a shy smile and felt her face flushing. She turned around and a ball boy threw two balls at her. She looked at Samantha again and spotted Spencer just above Samantha's head. He was alone, yet again. She gave a frustrated growl and bounced the ball. She served, but the ball flew straight into the net and the crowd groaned. Emilie closed her eyes and took out the other ball. She served again, the ball clipped the top of the net and bounced back to Emilie's side of the court. Emilie groaned and felt her anger rise.

"Forty, thirty."

The ball boy threw a ball at her and she caught it, giving him a slight nod. She took a deep breath and exhaled slowly. She bounced the ball three times and sent a killer shot to Samantha. Samantha ducked out of the way and the ball bounced on the line.

"Out!" The umpire said and the crowd groaned.

"What?" Emilie exclaimed. "That was on the line!"

"Out." The umpire repeated.

"Are you fucking kidding me?" Emilie yelled, throwing her racquet onto the deco-turf.

"Deuce."

"What are you doing, pretty girl?" Nathan said to himself, looking at Emilie on the court. Her racquet was next to her on the ground and she was tapping her foot irately. Her hands were shaking and she breathing was very shallow. "You're upset, and now you're letting the umpire get the better of you. Just calm yourself, Em. Clear your mind." Nathan crossed his arms and looked over at Shannon.

"Calm down, Em." Shannon frowned to herself and covered her mouth with her hands. She looked over at Nathan, looking at her, his arms crossed. She lifted her hands, her palms facing to the sky, and Nathan lifted his shoulders. "Please, Emmy, just calm yourself. Just breath. Deep breaths." Shannon wished that Emilie could hear her. She looked over at Spencer, who looks like he is about to pull his hair from his skull.

"Em, what are you so worked up about? Just focus, please. So you hit the net, twice, so what? So the umpire is blind, so what? Learn from it and move on." Spencer growled to himself and looked over at Shannon. She looked as worried as he felt. He gave her a small smile and shook his head.

"Oh, for god's sake! What is wrong with you? First you can't hit the stupid ball over the net! Then the umpire is blind and gives you a bad call! Even the people in the back row could see that the ball was in! Idiot!" Emilie's blood was boiling and she tugged at her visor. She did not dare look at the crowd, Spencer and Shannon was most probably pulling their hair out at this moment, and would just frustrate her even more. Looking at Nathan would not help either, she had to calm herself and fast. She could never serve when she was upset. She remembered the story Nathan told her about twelve year old Reilly and she felt ashamed. She closed her eyes and took a few deep breaths. She heard her brother's voice in her head. "Calm down, Lee. Deep breaths. You can do this. Just do everything I taught you." His voice rang in her ears and she felt the anger melt away. "That's better, Lee, now pick up that expensive racquet you just threw onto the ground and kick that girl's ass. Two more points, Lee, two more points." She opened her eyes and smiled to herself. She walked to her racquet and picked it up, tracing her fingers along the smooth edge of the frame. "Sorry about that." She smiled and walked to the baseline. She caught two more balls from the ballboy and she smiled at him. She bounced the ball three times at her feet, threw it in the air and hit it hard with her racquet. The ball went over the net, bounced close to Samantha, but she missed it.

"Advantage Hayes."

Emilie felt relief wash over her and she nodded to herself. She walked back to the line and served, hopefully for the last time today. The ball flew over the net, bounced at Samantha's feet and she hit it back to Emilie. Emilie ran forward and hit it to the centre of the court. Samantha ran to the middle and hit the ball, high and shallow. Emilie jumped, raising her racquet and hit the ball back to Samantha. Emilie ran back to the middle of her baseline and took a deep breath. Samantha hit the ball and it flew towards Emilie. She hit it, with relative ease, back to Samantha. Samantha changed her angle and sent the ball flying to Emilie left side. The side that Samantha, and everyone that knows Emilie, knows is Emilie's weaker side. Emilie ran to the ball, and strained to reach it, but she did. She hit it back to Samantha, groaning loudly. Samantha, knowing Emilie is not as fast as she is, hit the ball to the other side, hoping it will pass by Emilie to level the scores. Emilie ran to the other side and hit the ball back to an unsuspecting Samantha. As Emilie hit the ball, she felt herself fall forward and let out a shriek. The ball flew passed Samantha and the crowd rose to their feet, just as Emilie hit the deco-turf.

"Game, set, match, Hayes."

The crowd cheered for a few seconds, but then died down, as they looked at Emilie, on the ground, motionless. Emilie, too scared to move, felt the familiar, burning pain her in knee and the world blurred around her. The smell of iron and gravel filled her nostrils and she heard muffled voices above her.

"Emmy?" She heard Shannon's voice and felt herself being turned over onto her back.

"Emmy?" Shannon repeated.

"Em, are you okay?" She heard Spencer's voice and felt his hand on her shoulder. "How badly is she hurt?"

Emilie felt a fire explode from her knee and felt tears run down her cheeks. Suddenly, a bloodcurdling scream filled the air and she realized that it was coming from inside her. The world started spinning and she felt that familiar wave of nausea wash over her.

Nathan's face flickered in her mind and the last thing she heard before everything went black was Spencer's voice saying, "It's okay,

Em. It's okay."

Nathan paced around Emilie's lounge and crossed his arms.

"Hey, man." Spencer opened the bedroom door.

Nathan's hands dropped to his sides and he walked over to Spencer. "How is she?"

"Shannon can't seem to get her to sleep, Emilie is fighting it like a toddler. Shannon gave her some morphine. So atleast she'll be out of pain for a couple of hours." Spencer said.

"And her knee?" Nathan asked.

"There's a lot of inflammation, so Shannon and the doctor don't really know how extensive it is. And Em won't exactly tell them how much it's hurting." Spencer rolled his eyes.

"Sounds like her." Nathan grinned. "Thanks man."

"No problem, Connor." Spencer shook Nathan's hand.

The two guys looked over to the door just as Shannon came out and looked at them.

"Shannon.." Nathan said, but not sure how to finish his sentence.

"Go on in." She held the door for him. Nathan smiled and walked through the door.

He closed the door behind him and looked at Emilie, on the bed, her knee strapped up.

"Hey pretty girl." He smiled, sat down next to her and took her hand.

"Hey." She whispered, giving him a smal smile.

"You gave me one hell of a scare." Nathan brushed a strand of hair off her face and kissed the top of her head. She was slightly paler than usual and there were beads of sweat on her forehead.

"Sorry." She said softly.

"How are you doing?" He asked. "And don't you dare say that you are fine."

Emily smiled weakly and shook her head. "Not so good. It hurts, a lot."

"You'll be okay." Nathan smiled. "You just take it one day at a time." Nathan kissed her hand and she smiled.

"How come I always feel better when you're with me?" Emilie rested her head against her pillow.

"Because that is what I am here for." Nathan grinned. "I'll always be here for you, Emilie."

"I know. Thank you." Emilie nodded.

"You're welcome, pretty girl." Nathan smiled.

"I'm still coming to your game later." Emilie

said, serious.

"Em, I don't think that is a good idea." Nathan frowned.

"I promised I'll be there." Emilie frowned.

"I know, but you need to get better. Besides, you can watch me on T.V." Nathan frowned.

"But I don't want to. I want to be there, cheer for you." Emilie sighed.

"I know, and I appreciate that." Nathan smiled.

"I don't ever break my promises, Nathan." Emilie said.

"I know, honey, but your well-being is more important than anything else. If something were to happen to you...." Nathan looked at her, his voice trailing.

"You worry too much." Emilie grinned.

"I am supposed to worry, you're my girl." Nathan smiled.

Emilie smiled and took Nathan's hand, brought it up to her face and kissed it. "Yes I am."

Shannon looked at Spencer, sitting on the couch and sat down next to him.

"I think I need some morphine. She gave me one hell of a scare." Shannon sighed.

"She'll be okay." Spencer looked at her. "It's you that I'm worried about."

"Me? Why?" Shannon frowned.

"You look like you have a lot on your mind." Spencer crossed his arms.

"I have, actually." Shannon looked at him.

"You want to share?" Spencer asked. "I'm a good listener."

"Thanks, Spencer. That's nice of you." Shannon smiled.

"I'm heading down to the bar later. you're welcome to join me." Spencer said.

"Maybe. I'll see how Em is feeling. I might have to babysit." Shannon looked at him.

"Why is that?" Spencer asked.

"Emilie refuses to miss Nathan's game later today." Shannon said.

"I don't think Em should go anywhere." Spencer shook his head.

"Try telling her that." Shannon frowned.

"We'll have to tie her to the bed and keep watch." Spencer grinned.

"That doesn't sound like too bad an idea." Shannon smiled at him.

"It would be really great to actually have intellectually stimulating conversations for a change." Spencer nodded.

Shannon felt herself flush slightly and she smiled at him. "I guess so."

The door opened and Shannon jumped up from the couch. Spencer chuckled and looked over his shoulder at Nathan. Nathan shut the door behind him and looked at Shannon.

"Emilie wants you." He said to Shannon.

"Okay, cool." Shannon nodded.

"Listen, I have to go warm up. I'll see you there?" Nathan frowned.

"We'll try our best. Good luck, man." Spencer shook Nathan's hand.

Shannon walked over to Nathan and hugged him. "Good luck, Nate. Kick his ass." She whispered.

"I plan to." Nathan laughed.

"Thank you. For being here. For Em." Shannon said as she pulled away.

"She's my girl, how can I not?" Nathan smiled and headed out the door.

"He's so sweet with her." Shannon smiled sadly. "Why can't guys be so sweet with me?"

"Maybe you just never noticed." Spencer grinned and looked at Shannon.

Shannon looked at Spencer with a slight frown and heard Emilie calling her name from the bedroom. She grinned at Spencer and whirled around and went into Emilie's bedroom.

Shannon sat down in her seat and looked at Emilie, sitting next to her, looking rather pleased with herself. Emilie's right knee was still heavily strapped, but that did not seem to bother her at the moment. What did bother her was if she did not feel better by Saturday, she had to forfeit her final. Emilie was convinced she would be fine, like she would let Kelly, or anyone for that matter, get a free pass at the championship. That will be the day!

Shannon handed Emilie a bottle of water and two muscle relaxers and frowned.

"Thanks, Shan." Emilie said and took the tablets from Shannon. "Are you sure you are okay with being here?" Emilie asked.

"Of course. You're supporting your boy and I'm supporting you." Shannon grinned and watched as Emilie swallowed her tablets. Emilie screwed the cap back on the bottle and looked out onto the court.

Shannon looked over at Emilie. "Are you not in pain or anything?"

"You did dose me with morphine. I'm not a rhino, you know." Emilie shrugged. "It feels good, but Spencer thinks I should have stayed in bed."

"I actually agree with Spencer." Shannon nodded.

Emilie looked amazed and looked at Shannon. "Since when do you agree with Spencer?"

"We should let Doctor Gilbert take a look at it when he gets back, before Saturday." Shannon ignored her question and frowned.

"Answer my question, Shannon Moore!" Emilie playfully smacked her on the arm.

"Since he knows about your injury, that's all." Shannon blushed slightly.

"Shy much, Shan?" Emilie teased her.

"What ever." Shannon rolled her eyes. "Like I said, we should let Doc take a look at it tomorrow."

"Yeah, okay. You're the boss." Emilie looked out onto the court and saw Nathan and Zac walking out onto the court. She stood up from her chair and heard a soft cracking sound.

"That didn't sound good, Em." Shannon looked at her and frowned.

There was a sharp pain in Emilie's knee and she closed her eyes. "Shit, that hurts." Emilie exclaimed.

"Oh, for god's sake, Em!" Shannon stood up, rolled her eyes and let her sit down. She flipped open her phone and dialed Spencer's number. "Spence, it's Shannon. It's Em's knee. I think I just heard cartilege move. Yeah, I'm taking her to the clinic. Okay, see you there." Shannon shoved her phone back in her pocket and took Emilie's hand. "Come on, I'm taking you to the clinic."

"No, Shannon!" Emilie exclaimed.

"Em..."

"I promised, Shannon!" Emilie shook her head.

"He'll understand! Now get your ass of that chair. You can watch the game at the clinic." Shannon threw Emilie's arm over her shoulder and helped her up the steps.

Nathan frowned as she watched Shannon helped Emilie up the stairs. Emilie seemed as if she was still in a lot of pain and he sighed. He ran his hands through his hair and turned to Zac. Zac scowled at him and walked to the baseline.

Emilie smiled when she saw Nathan come running into the clinic on the overhead screen, obviously straight from the court. He burst through the door and stood there, looking at her. His hair was damp and his face was slightly flushed, but he looked as gorgeous as ever. He put his bag on the floor walked over to her, sitting on the bed, her right leg on the bed, stretched out.

"Congratulations! You were great!" Emilie smiled as he put his arms around her and held her.

Nathan pulled away and cupped her cheek with his hand. "Thanks, pretty girl."

"You had me worried there for a while." Emilie pointed to the overhead television, showing highlights of the game.

Nathan looked at the screen and scowled. "So did I." He turned to her and smiled. "It's your fault. You had me worried."

"I'm sorry I couldn't be there." Emilie smiled sadly.

"Don't you ever do that to me again." Nathan took her hand and kissed it. "I was ready to forfeit when I saw Shannon drag you out."

"I'm sorry." Emilie frowned and put her hand over his.

"You're forgiven, but only if I can take you out tonight." Nathan's voice had that velvet tone again.

"That won't be possible, Mister Connor." A nurse said behind him.

Nathan whirled around and looked at the nurse. She was a short, stumpy woman with dark curly hair and a button nose. She wore a pair of dark-rimmed glasses and waddled like a duck.

"Mister Byrne and Miss Moore won't allow Miss Hayes to go anywhere." The nurse said, checking Emilie's vitals. "Neither will Doctor Gilbert, or myself for that matter."

"But I'm fine, Liz." Emilie rolled her eyes.

"Yes, you're fine! That's why you're all strapped and high on morphine, because you're fine!" Liz exclaimed.

Nathan chuckled and Liz glared at him, so he took a step back, to avoid being in her way.

"You!" Liz pointed her finger at him. "You were on the television just now."

"Yes, there he is." Emilie pointed to the screen.

Liz looked at the screen and narrowed her eyes. She looked back at Nathan and grinned. "You made me a lot of money today, Mister Connor." She smiled.

"I'm glad I could help, Liz." Nathan smiled.

"It's Nurse Rodriguez to you, buddy." She scowled, putting one hand on her hip.

Emilie laughed and covered her mouth with her hands.

"You just press the button if you want me to throw him out, honey." Liz grinned and walked out the door.

"Thanks Liz." Emilie laughed.

"She's evil, that one." Nathan laughed.

Emilie giggled and smiled at him. "Come here."

Nathan walked over to her and put his arms around her, kissing her tenderly. "So how are we going to get you out of here tonight?"

"Not gonna happen Nate." Shannon said

behind them.

Nathan turned around and smiled at her. "Shannon, so good to see you!"

Shannon smiled at him and hugged him. "Congratulations, champ! You kicked ass. Well, the last three sets atleast."

"Hey, I was worried about this gorgeous girl of mine. Do you blame me?" Nathan grinned.

"Not at all." Shannon smiled. "Thanks for sending him home."

"Any time." He turned back to Emilie and smiled. "And on Sunday, I'll send Brandon home for you, my love."

Emilie smiled at him and rested her head against her pillow.

"Are you sure she can't leave the clinic tonight, Shan?" Nathan asked and Emilie looked at Shannon, hopefully.

"Come on you guys. You know Em is not allowed to leave. Doctor Gilbert would have me killed." Shannon said.

"You could always just stay here with me, Nate." Emilie said.

"Okay. I'll get us dinner, then we can dine on some hospital sheets." Nathan smiled and kissed her.

"That's so sweet." Shannon grinned at Nathan and Emilie smiling at each other.

CHAPTER 12

"Okay, so you're not going anywhere, right?" Spencer asked.

"Nowhere, I promise." Nathan nodded.

"Don't make me regret trusting you, Connor." Spencer narrowed his eyes at him.

"I won't let you down, sir." Nathan smiled.

"You better not." Spencer crossed his arms.

"Come on, Spence. I'll take you out for a beer." Shannon rolled her eyes.

"You drink beer?" Spencer asked.

"Yeah, sure, why not?" Shannon shrugged and looked at Spencer.

"Okay, sure." Spencer nodded, but still stood in front of Nathan.

"She'll be fine, Spence. Come on." Shannon pulled his arm.

"Have a good time." Nathan smiled at them.

"So where's the best place to go for a beer?" Shannon asked as they walked through the clinic.

"I know the perfect place." Spencer grinned at her and touched the small of her back.

Spencer and Shannon exited the sliding doors and walked over to his black Camaro. They got in the car and Spencer sped off.

"I told my mom about you." Nathan said as Emilie rested her head on his shoulder.

"You did? What did you say?" Emilie smiled and touched his hand on his lap. Emilie looked at the drip on her right hand and sighed.

"Just how great you are, and pretty and smart." Nathan smiled.

"So you lied?" Emilie laughed.

"She wants to meet you." Nathan said.

"She does?" Emilie frowned and Nathan nodded. "I'd like that."

"You're going to love her." Nathan nodded. "She already thinks very highly of you."

"I am not too sure if your dad is going to feel the same though." Emilie rested her head on his shoulder.

"If he can't see what an amazing person you are, then he is a bigger asshole than I thought. Besides, I don't care what he thinks anyway." Nathan shrugged.

"As long as you're happy." Emilie nodded.

"Exactly." Nathan kissed her forehead and pulled her closer to him. "So tell me, pretty girl, was it your mom that made you start playing?" Nathan asked.

"Yes, she was the one that made us fall in love with tennis. She loved it, so it was only natural for us to love it as well. When I was a little kid, my mom and Jer would teach me how to hold a racquet and hit the ball. My mom loved the game and she was there whenever Jer had a game at school. My dad would also go along. After my mom died, he stopped coming. Apparently it was too painful for him to watch his children play the game that she loved so much. So it was always just me, Jer and Spencer." Emilie felt her eyes burn and she blinked a couple of times.

"How did she die?" Nathan rubbed her shoulder.

"She was driving to work and another car jumped a red light. Drove straight into her. She died seven hours later in the hospital. My dad couldn't look at me for months afterwards. He still can't." A tear ran down Emilie's cheek and she wiped it away.

"Why is that?" Nathan frowned.

"Probably because I remind him too much of her. According to my grandparents, I look just like her." Emilie sighed.

"I'm so sorry." Nathan took her hand and she looked at him.

"It's okay. I don't really remember her, I was only seven." Emilie gave him a small smile and put her hand over his. "Most people think that I'm sad because she died when I was so young and that I had to grow up without a mother, but that's not true at all. The truth is, I'm sad because when my mother died, so did my dad." Emilie said.

"Well, well, well, it may seem that beer is not at all as bad as it smells, and it sure beats absinthe." Shannon took another sip of beer from her glass and Spencer frowned.
"Absinthe?" He asked.
"Long story." Shannon giggled. "I can't believe I have never tried this before."
"For someone who's never had beer before, you sure can put them away." Spencer laughed and looked at Shannon, sitting opposite him on a barstool, gulping her mug of beer.
"I'm from Texas. There, when we do something, we do it right!" Shannon exclaimed, in a proper Texan accent.
"You sure do." Spencer grinned.
"Tell me, Spencey, why do you think they call it a pint in Europe?" Shannon frowned at the glass. "It looks like a mug to me."
"They don't just call it that in Europe, Texas girl. A pint is a unit of measurement for liquid, or something like that." Spencer shook his head.
"I like mug better." Shannon said to herself.
"Absolutely!" Spencer laughed. "Barman, two more mugs please!"
A few moments later, the barman put two mugs of beer in front of them and Shannon cheered.
"To Beer!" Shannon lifted her glass. "And to great company!"
"To great company!" Spencer agreed and looked at her.

"I wasn't sure if being back here would be okay, but it's fine." Emilie said. "I'm fine."

"You know, I really hate that word." Nathan said. "Fine."

"I use it a lot, don't I?" Emilie grinned.

"Yes. You do." Nathan pulled her closer. "Tell me how you really feel."

"Well, right now I am happy, because I met you, and can sit here with you in one of the most beautiful cities in the world, even though it is in a hospital bed. Just being with you makes me happy. Just thinking about you makes me happy." Emilie smiled at him and he kissed her. "But then at the same time, I feel sad. I feel abandoned by my dad, I feel like I'm not good enough for him, that I can't make him happy with whatever it is that I do. Everything I do seems to upset him more and more. Then I'm disappointed in myself for not healing properly. That my knee is giving me problems again, that I fell on court, the...." Emilie sobbed so hard, the last three words did not even want to come out. She felt the lump in her throat and closed her eyes.

"Em, it's alright. Listen to me. None of those are your fault. Your father doesn't know what he's missing, having a daughter like you. He should be the happiest and proudest father in the world. Your injury is just a temporary setback, and falling wasn't your fault, and neither was the accident."

Emilie opened her eyes and whimpered.

"Em?" Nathan asked.

"Actually, there's something I should tell you." Emilie sighed.

"What is it?" Nathan frowned and looked at her.

"It's pretty bad, Nate." Emilie shook her head and tears ran down her cheeks.

"Em, you can tell me anything." Nathan turned to her.

"Nobody knows this, not even my dad, or Shannon. Spencer is the only other person that knows." Emilie said slowly.

"Then it will be me and you and Spencer. That's how it will stay." Nathan said.

Emilie took a deep breath and nodded at him. "The night of the accident, Jer wasn't the one that was driving the Escalade. I was."

"But the paper said..." Nathan frowned.

"It's not true. None of it." Emilie shook her head. "I wanted to get a cab, but Jer wouldn't let me. He gave me his keys, even though I told him that I didn't want to. According to me, I was too drunk to drive. He insisted, because he did not want to leave his car in Brooklyn." Emilie paused for a moment and took a deep breath. "We were close to the Twin Towers site when Spencer dropped his drink and he was swearing loudly on the backseat. I swear I only looked away for a second, just a second. When I looked back on the road, the car was heading straight for a metal barrier. I tried to swerve, but my reflexes weren't up to scratch, and the car hit the barrier on the left hand side. The car flipped over and hit against the wall. There was blood and glass everywhere. I called out to Jer, but he didn't answer. I heard Spencer groan and I called his name. He said that he was okay. We unbuckled our seatbelts and tried to get Jer out of the car, but we couldn't. Spencer got out and called nine-one-one, and my dad. I was lying next to Jer inside the over-turned car, on the roof and he mumbled something to me. He told me to tell the police that he was driving. I took his hand and told him that he could tell them himself and that the ambulance was going to be there soon. He looked at me, told me that he loved me and then he died... " Emilie's voice cracked and Nathan put his arm around her.

"It's okay, love." He ran his fingers through her hair as she cried in his arms.

"Oh my god! I killed my brother!" Emilie sobbed into Nathan's shirt, holding him.

"No, you didn't. It was an accident." Nathan tried to console her the best he could.

"I'm so sorry I didn't tell you." She lifted her face and looked at him

"Hey, listen to me." Nathan cupped her face with both his hands. "You don't have to apologize to me. It takes a really brave person to do what you did. Everything you went through. You're the bravest person I have ever met. And I love that you trust me enough to tell me this. And I promise you, that this will stay between you and me."

"Thank you, Nate." Emilie nodded and Nathan wiped the tears from her face.

"You're welcome, pretty girl." Nathan looked at her and kissed her lips.

Jennifer's phone rang and she scurried to answer it. "I told you not to call me...."

"I was busy with my rounds and I overheard something that might be of interest to you."

"What?" Jennifer asked, grabbing her notepad and a pen.

"Jeremy was not the driver of the car, Emilie was."

"What? Are you serious?" Jennifer exclaimed, writing frantically. "So she lied to the police?"

"Yes."

"Oh my god! This is the best news ever!" Jennifer laughed.

"I hope you know that this is a very serious....."

"Sure, sure, whatever." Jennifer shrugged and closed her phone. Jennifer opened her laptop and laughed wickedly. "You're going down, Emilie Hayes."

"I got it!" Jennifer burst into Kelly's room and Kelly let out a high-pitched scream.

"Paranoid much, Kel?" Jennifer grimaced.

"Holy shit, Jen!" Kelly yelled from the couch, spilling her glass of wine. "Look what you made me do!"

"Sorry." Jennifer pulled a face.

"I can't believe this." Kelly frowned and ran to the kitchen, grabbing a few paper towels. Kelly got on her hands and knees and blotted the carpet with the towels. "This is never going to come out!"

"Kelly!" Jennifer exclaimed and Kelly looked up at her. "I got it."

"You got what, Jen?" Kelly sighed.

"The story that is going to ruin Emilie and Nathan's puppy love, and bring both of them down!" Jennifer said, excitedly.

Kelly threw the towels down and glared at Jennifer. "Look, I told you, give it up. I don't understand what the big deal is?"

"I'll tell you what the big deal is. That girl comes in here, out of nowhere, acting like she owns the place, with her wonderful coach and her soppy story about how she survived a tragic accident, how she lost her brother, and still managed to get into the finals. She's trying to make everyone else look bad, including you. Then she dismisses me when I try to get her to do an interview, she distracts my brother at the most crucial time in the tournament, and you want me to give it up?"

Jennifer exclaimed.

Kelly stood up and walked to Jennifer, looking like she was going to hit her. "I can't believe that I am actually friends with you, Jen. You are a selfish, vindictive person that only thinks of yourself."

"What's your point?" Jennifer tilted her head and grinned.

"Forget it. I can't do this anymore, Jen." Kelly threw her hands up in defeat.

"So anyway, about the story...." Jennifer continued.

"Jen, for god's sake, get out!" Kelly yelled.

Jennifer put her hand on her hip, looking at Kelly. "Excuse me?"

"You heard me. Get out. I never want to see you ever again." Kelly exclaimed.

"You can't talk to me like that!" Jennifer exclaimed. "I'm Jennifer Grayson!"

"No, you're not. You're Jenny Connor from DC, with a fake name, a fake personality and a fake nose!" Kelly shook her head and crossed her arms. "Now get out!"

"I really had fun, Spencey." Shannon grinned as they stopped in front of her door.

"Yeah, me too, Texas girl." Spencer smiled.

"You know I have a name, right?" She frowned.

Spencer nodded with a smile and looked at her.

"You wanna come in?" Shannon asked, opening the door.

"No, I'd better go. That would be more appropriate." Spencer looked at her.

"Yeah, that would be the appropriate thing to do." Shannon leaned her head against the frame.

Spencer nodded and turned away. Shannon looked at his butt as he turned and smiled. Spencer stopped and turned around again. Shannon met his gaze and frowned.

"Actually, I'm done being appropriate with you, Shannon." Spencer shook his head and pushed her into her room, and closing the door behind them. He pushed her against the wall and kissed her. She put her arms around his neck and kissed him back. She pulled back and frowned at him. "What are we doing?" She asked.

He looked at her and frowned. "Uhm, we're kissing."

"I can see that, but why?" Shannon asked.

"For a drunk person, you ask too many questions." Spencer grabbed hold of her butt, lifting her off the ground and kissed her again. She wrapped her legs around his waist and moaned softly.

Nathan threw his wallet onto the desk and ran his hands through his hair. He was developing a really bad headache and his eyes burned. He took of his jacket and threw it on the bed. As he was walking to the bathroom, his phone rang. He frowned and answered it.

"Nathan."

"Who is this?" He rubbed his eyes.

"It's Kelly. Listen, I'm sorry to bother you so late, but Jen was just here."

"And?" He grumbled.

"She's up to something."

"Jen is always up to something, Kel. You know how she is." Nathan sat down on his bed.

"It's serious this time. She's done something bad. Really bad." Kelly sounded scared.

"What did she do?" Nathan asked.

"I'm not sure, something about a front page story that involves Emilie." Kelly said.

"Emilie?" Nathan exclaimed.

"Yes, Emilie. Jennifer is set out to ruin her. And apparently she found the perfect story to make that happen. I asked her not to, but she wouldn't listen." Kelly said.

"I thought you were the one that wanted Emilie ruined?" Nathan sat up.

"Me? Why would I want to do that?" Kelly

frowned.

"That's what Jen told me." Nathan said.

"No, Nate! It's been Jen all along. She has taken this way too far, and I don't know what to do." Kelly said.

"Thanks for letting me know, Kel. I'll deal with her in the morning." Nathan nodded.

"No problem, Nate. I just hope it's not too late by then."

Nathan heard Kelly hang up and he growled.

CHAPTER 13

Emilie opened her door the next morning and walked into her empty hotel room, with a slight limp. She sent Shannon and Spencer back to their rooms, she just wanted some peace and quiet, without them constantly hovering over her. She put her bag down on the floor and noticed a rolled up newspaper on the floor, and a white envelope on top of it. She reached down and picked it up. Her name was written on the front of the envelope in a handwriting that she did not recognize. She frowned, forgetting to close the door behind her and put her key on the table next to the couch. She tore open the envelope and looked inside. There was a handwritten note inside and she took it out.

Thanks for sharing....
Soon, everyone will know...

Emilie frowned and unrolled the newspaper. She gasped as she looked at the front page and brought her hand up to her face. In big black letters it read 'Hayes: Legend or Liar?'. There was a picture of her getting into the driver's seat of the Escalade, and a picture of

Jeremy. She felt a wave of nausea hit her and the pain in her knee intensified. She swallowed and took a few deep breaths. She started reading the article and felt hot tears stinging her eyes. It was about the accident, how she was responsible for Jeremy's death and how she lied about it to the police. How she lied to everyone, including her father. Her vision became blurry and she could feel her heartbeat in her throat. She felt the room spinning and she tucked a strand of hair behind her ear. How could he do this to her? He promised not to tell anyone! She reached her hand out towards the couch for support and closed her eyes.

Nathan looked at the front page of the newspaper and his heart stopped. He looked at the photograph and started reading, feeling his blood boil with every word. He growled angrily and marched to the door. He pulled the door open and Jennifer stood in his doorway, with a smile.
"What the fuck is this?" He exclaimed, waving the newspaper at her.
"It's my story. Do you like it?" Jennifer entered his room.
"This is bullshit, Jen!" Nathan shook his head.

"I disagree, I think it's a masterpiece!" Jennifer smiled.

Nathan grabbed her by the shoulders and shoved her against the wall. "How could you do this?" Nathan glared at her.

"She's a liar, Nate, she had to be exposed." Jennifer said simply.

"You're the one that needs to be exposed!" Nathan growled.

"Did I make my little brother mad?" She gave him a satisfied smile.

"I can't believe you did this! Do you realize what you have done?" Nathan snarled.

"Yes, I created an award-winning front page story." Jennifer crossed her arms.

"No, you just destroyed a bunch of people's lives." Nathan exclaimed.

"That too." Jennifer grinned.

"Fuck you, Jen!" Nathan let out an angry growl, pushed Jennifer away, and ran down the corridor to Emilie's door.

The door was half open and he slowly pushed the door open all the way. He walked into the room and saw Emilie leaning against the couch, with the newspaper in her hands.

"Em." Nathan whispered.

She looked up and he saw the hurt in her eyes, the tears on her cheeks and the anger on her face. She stared at him for a second and took a deep breath.

"Did you do this?" Emilie looked at him, without blinking, or moving.

"Em, let me explain." He took a few steps forward.

"How could you?" She yelled.

Nathan was a little surprized to hear her yelling at him for the first time and held out his hands. "Em..."

"You promised me...." She cried.

"Em, it wasn't me, I swear!" Nathan said. He felt his hands tremble, all he wanted to do was hold her.

"You were the only one that knew! Who else could it be?" She exclaimed.

Nathan looked at her and shook his head. "I swear to you, I did not tell anyone, let alone Jennifer."

"Then how did she know all this? And the picture?" Emilie asked.

"I don't know..." Nathan said.

"That's not a good enough answer." Emilie crossed her arms and looked at him.

"That's the best answer I have right now." Nathan ran his hands through his hair. "Jen has ways of getting information......"

"Yes, like her brother." Emilie scowled.

"Emilie, I did not tell her." Nathan looked at her.

"And I am supposed to believe that?" Emilie tilted her head.

"Yes, you should." Nathan frowned. "Because it's true. I would never lie to you. Emilie, I love you....." Nathan took a step towards her.

"Don't...." Emilie wiped her cheek with the back of her hand and the newspaper fell to the floor. "Just leave, Nathan."

"Emilie, please..."

"Nathan, please, just go." Emilie shook her head and ran her fingers through her hair.

Nathan felt his shoulders slump and frowned. He looked at her for a second, but she avoided his eyes. He turned around and walked out the door. Emilie let out a couple of shallow breaths, threw a pillow onto the floor and felt a deep pain in her heart. She felt her knees give in and slowly fell to the floor. She grabbed the pillow on the floor, held it close to her and cried.

"That son of a bitch, I'm going to fucking kill him!" Spencer marched out of Emilie's room and slammed the door behind him.

"Spencer, wait!" Shannon called after him, but he was already out the door. Spencer stood in the hallway, his pulse racing and adrenaline pumping through his veins. He closed his eyes, to calm himself down a bit, otherwise if he had to see Nathan at this very moment, he would literally kill him! He opened his eyes, feeling a slight bit better and heard loud footsteps coming from the elevator. Nathan came marching around the corner and Spencer could feel his rage take over his mind.

"You son of a bitch!" Spencer balled his fist and punched Nathan in the ribcage.

Nathan slammed against the wall from the force of Spencer's hit and he frowned. "What the fuck, man?"

"You lying piece of shit!" Spencer spat and punched him in the face.

Nathan winced and threw a punch against Spencer's shoulder, but Spencer shoved him against the wall. Nathan growled and grabbed him, pulling him down onto the floor.

"How dare you?" Spencer spat, pushing Nathan away from him.

"Dude, it's all a big misunderstanding!" Nathan grabbed the front of his t-shirt and balled his fist.

"You're a liar!" Spencer snarled, pushing Nathan off him and punched him against the chest. Nathan fell backwards, onto the carpet and Spencer grabbed the front of his shirt. Just then, Shannon came running out of the room and towards Spencer and Nathan. "Nathan! Spencer! For god's sake, stop it!" Shannon exclaimed. "You're going to kill each other!"

"That's fine with me!" Spencer growled.

Emilie came out of her room and took a few steps towards them. Nathan was on the floor, with Spencer crouching over him. Spencer's one hand gripping the front of Nathan's t-shirt, and the other one trying to hold him down. There was blood coming from both their mouths and there was a bruise forming just below Nathan's left eye. Nathan turned his head and looked straight at Emilie. Emilie stood there, looking at him, a shocked expression on her face, with her arms hanging from her sides. Her eyes were red and he could see her hands were shaking. "Spence...." Emilie whispered.

"Em, get inside!" Shannon touched her shoulder, but Emilie shrug her off.

"Spence..." Emilie whispered again, a tear running down her cheek.

Spencer let go of Nathan's shirt and stepped away from him. Nathan stood up slowly and wiped his mouth, still looking at Emilie. "Are you okay?" Shannon touched Spencer's arm and he looked at her.

"Yeah, I'm good." He winced, his lip

bleeding. He turned to Nathan and sneered. "You stay the hell away from us!"

"Spencer...." Nathan sat up, but Spencer shook his head.

"I mean it, Connor!" Spencer pointed at him and turned around.

Nathan watched as Shannon and Spencer walked to Emilie's door. Emilie was still standing there, her arms at her sides, looking at him. "Em..." Nathan took a step towards her. "Please...."

"I'm sorry..." Emilie blinked and shook her head at him. "I can't..." She choked and slowly walked back into her room. Nathan stood in the corridor for a few seconds, feeling his eye throb. He turned and walked back to his room, running his fingers angrily through his hair. He opened his hotel room door and stepped inside, slamming the door behind him. He wiped his face with his hands and looked at the blood on his palms. He sighed and walked to the bathroom. He stood over the basin, and frowned heavily. He had a splitting headache, but it did not compare to the pain he was feeling in his heart. He spat some blood into the basin and watched as the water from the faucet mixed with the blood and swirl down the drain. He closed the faucet and stared at himself in the mirror. There were tears in his eyes and he sat down on the edge of the bath. He closed his eyes, covered his face with his hands, slid down onto the tiles and cried his heart out.

Emilie paced the room, running her fingers through her hair. "I should just own up."

"No, Em." Spencer shook his head and stood up.

"Own up? Em, what are you talking about?" Shannon frowned and looked at Emilie.

"It's true. I was driving the Escalade." Emilie nodded and crossed her arms.

"No, Em! That's impossible. Everybody knows it was Jeremy." Shannon frowned. "Tell her Spencer."

"Spencer knows that I was driving." Emilie looked at Shannon.

"What?" Shannon exclaimed and looked at Spencer. "Of course. You were there."

"I killed my brother, okay! It was my fault!" Emilie exclaimed.

"Em, you didn't kill him, it wasn't your fault." Spencer stood up and walked to her. "It was my fault."

"What?" Shannon exclaimed.

Spencer nodded. "Yes. I spilled my drink on the backseat, and Em looked over her shoulder for a second. If I didn't spill my drink, it would never have happened."

"No, I was the one driving, I should never have looked away."

"Em, why did you tell the police, and everyone else, that Jeremy was driving?" Shannon asked.

"Because Jeremy told me to." Emilie said, feeling the tears in her eyes.

"Jeremy told you to lie to the police?" Shannon asked. "Why would he do that?"

"He was protecting her." Spencer said softly and Emilie nodded.

Shannon looked over at Emilie and then at Spencer, frowning.

"He knew that if he died, Emilie would be charged with driving under the influence and manslaughter." Spencer nodded. "He was protecting her, as he always did."

"Why didn't you tell me?" Shannon glared at Spencer.

"Because I was doing the same." Spencer looked apologetically at Shannon.

"I can't believe you never told me." Shannon looked at Emilie and crossed her arms.

Emilie wiped the tears off her face and looked at Shannon. "I'm sorry, Shan."

Shannon looked at Emilie and closed her eyes for a second, trying to make sense of everything.

"I don't know what to do." Emilie sobbed.

Spencer stood up and walked over to Emilie. He put his arms around Emilie and held her tight. "We'll figure it out, Emmy."

Shannon looked over at them and stood up. She felt her own eyes well up, walked over to them and put her arms around them.

Kelly stepped into the elevator, where Samantha and Maria stood.

"Did you hear, Kelly?" Maria whispered.

"Did I hear about what?" Kelly frowned.

"The fight on the fourteenth floor." Samantha said.

"What fight? When?" Kelly asked.

"Nathan and Spencer decked each other in the hall." Maria said.

"About an hour ago." Samantha nodded.

"Nathan and Spencer?" Kelly exclaimed, panic in her voice.

Maria and Samantha nodded and Kelly sighed.

"Do you know why?" Kelly asked, pressing '14' on the panel.

Maria handed Kelly the newspaper and Kelly stared at it, her eyes wide. "Oh my god."

"Is it true, Kelly?" Samantha asked.

"No, of course not! It's bullshit! Jennifer

made the whole thing up!" Kelly growled.

"But the picture..." Maria said, but Kelly cut her off.

"Where are they?" Kelly asked.

"Spencer disappeared and Nathan locked himself in his room. Apparently he's not talking to anybody." Maria said.

"And Emilie?" Kelly frowned.

"We're not sure, but..." Samantha said.

The doors opened and Kelly ran out before Samantha could could finish her sentence. Samantha and Maria looked at Kelly running down the corridor and exchanged worried looks. Kelly ran as fast as she could, and stopped in front of Nathan's door. She caught her breath for a second and banged her fist against his door. There was no answer.

"Nathan, open up, it's Kelly." She called out. Still no answer. "Nathan, I know you're in there!" She banged on the door again.

After a few seconds, the door opened. Kelly walked inside and looked at Nathan. "Oh my god! You look terrible!" She exclaimed.

Nathan's eyes were red and just below his left eye there was a dark purple bruise. His hair was sticking in all directions and his hands were shaking. Kelly walked over to him and hugged him. "I heard what happened."

"You were right about Jen." Nathan said,

pulling away, looking at her.

"God, I wish I wasn't." Kelly sighed.

"Can you believe she wrote that?" Nathan said pointing to the newspaper on the floor.

"Nothing surprizes me anymore." Kelly looked at Nathan and shook her head.

"Emilie doesn't want to talk to me, she can't even look at me." Nathan sat down on the couch, his face in his hands. "I don't know what to do."

"Have you told her the truth?" Kelly sat down next to him.

"I tried to, but she doesn't believe me." Nathan felt a tear run down his cheek.

Kelly bit her lip and looked at Nathan. In the eleven years that she has known him, she had never seen him so upset before, in fact, she has never even seen him cry. He was always the happy go lucky guy, that everybody loved. The type of guy that every girl wished they could have, and what every guy wanted to be like, at least that's how it seemed to Kelly. She leaned forward and put her hand on his shoulder. "I'm going to go talk to her."

Nathan lifted his head and looked at her. "It won't make a difference, Kel. She wants nothing to do with me."

"I refuse to believe that." Kelly stood up and walked to the door. She paused and looked over her shoulder at Nathan. "Don't give up, Nate." She whispered and left.

Shannon closed Emilie's bedroom door and walked to Spencer, sitting on the couch, a big white bowl of potato chips on his lap.

"Is she asleep?" Spencer looked at her.

Shannon nodded and crossed her arms. "Yes, the morphine knocked her right out."

"Good." Spencer smiled sadly. "Chip?"

"No, thanks. How's your face?" Shannon sat down next to him and gently touched his cheek.

"Bruised. Connor's swing has definitely improved." Spencer winced.

"You want some ice?" Shannon asked.

"No, but there's some vodka in the cupboard too." Spencer grinned.

There was a long pause, as Shannon took the bottle out of the cupboard and walked over to Spencer. "Spence, why do you think he did it?"

"Because he's an arrogant son of a bitch that...." Spencer growled.

"Okay, okay, now put your own opinion of him aside, and then answer my question again." Shannon said.

"I don't know." Spencer said. "I don't understand why he would tell Jennifer anything. He can't stand her."

"What? Really?" Shannon asked.

"Yeah, if there's one person on this earth that Nathan hates more than his dad, it's Jennifer." Spencer nodded.

"Then why would he tell her all that stuff about Emilie, so she can write a story?" Shannon frowned.

"Some people never change..." Spencer's voice trailed and he took a sip from the bottle.

"Is it possible that she might have blackmailed

him?" Shannon asked.

"Quite possible. Jennifer is the most deceitful person that I know." Spencer said.

"God, what's with his family?" Shannon frowned. "They make our families seem normal."

Spencer raised his eyebrows and nodded.

"So what's the deal with his dad?" Shannon asked.

"I'm not sure, Nathan is a very private person where his family is concerned. There are only a few people know that Jennifer is his sister." Spencer said.

"Well, I don't blame him, then." Shannon shook her head and sat forward, resting her chin on her hands, her elbows on her knees. There was a long pause and Shannon looked at Spencer. "Spence..."

"Yeah, I know." Spencer nodded and took Shannon's hand. "You're sorry."

"That's not what I was going to say." Shannon shook her head.

Spencer looked at her and frowned.

"You were right." Shannon said to him.

"I usually am, but what was I right about this time?" Spencer grinned.

"Don't get cocky." Shannon smiled softly. "You were right about last night. It wasn't a mistake."

Spencer smiled and raised his eyebrows.

"It did mean something to me." Shannon said.

"And what would that be?" Spencer smiled.

"Sometimes I can't stand you, but I can't stand being away from you either." Shannon frowned.

Spencer laughed and brushed a strand of hair out of her face. He touched her cheek and smiled. "I can't stand to be away from you either." He leaned in and kissed her. Shannon pulled away and giggled.

There was a soft knock on the door and Shannon

stood up from the couch and went to open it. It was Kelly.

"Hey Kelly." Shannon frowned.

"Is she okay?" Kelly asked, as she entered the room.

"Not really. Where did you hear?" Spencer stood up, defensively.

"I just came from Nate. He's in pretty bad shape." Kelly said.

"Well, so is Emilie." Spencer snapped.

"Look, I'm not choosing sides here and I'm not here to fight with you guys. I want to help......" Kelly said.

"You want to help? Haven't you done enough?" Spencer exclaimed.

"Spence, enough. Let Kelly talk." Shannon looked at him and shook her head.

"It wasn't Nathan that told Jennifer. Jennifer bribed a nurse at the clinic to feed her inside information." Kelly said.

"And you know this how?" Shannon exclaimed.

"She told me." Kelly shrugged and grabbed a potato chip from the bowl, looking over at Shannon on the floor.

"She told you?" Spencer shook his head in disbelief.

"Yes, Jen openly brags about everything." Kelly nodded.

"But what self respected person does a thing like that?" Shannon asked.

"Shan, it's Jennifer we are talking about. She's anything but self-respected." Spencer said.

"True, but that's bad." Shannon shook her head. "Does Nathan know?"

"He knows what Jen is capable of, but he doesn't

know all the details." Kelly said.

"Kel, do you have any pictures?" Spencer asked.

"She has them on her laptop. She stashes everything in that thing." Kelly nodded.

"We have to get it." Shannon said.

"Uhm, problem, it's probably locked in her room." Spencer sighed.

"Problem solved." Kelly waved a keycard in the air. "We always make copies for each other."

"Smart!" Shannon nodded and turned to Spencer. "We should do that."

Spencer smiled at Shannon and shook his head.

"Being friends with the enemy has it's perks!" Kelly smiled.

"So all that's left is to get the laptop." Shannon said.

"Correction, we have to get the data from the laptop." Spencer said. "We can't take it, then she'll know it was Kelly."

"And that won't go down well." Kelly looked at her watch and nodded. "She's probably at the bar right now, but is usually back in her room by twelve, so we have an hour to get into her room and decrypt her files, transfer the data from the laptop to the memory stick and get the hell out of there!"

"Will that be enough time?" Shannon asked.

"Yeah, piece of cake." Kelly smiled.

Kelly stood with her back against the wall, peeking around the corner. "Do you have a visual?" Kelly asked, raising a walkie-talkie up to her face.

"Affirmative, the snake is at the watering hole." Spencer replied on the radio. Kelly grinned at Spencer's response and motioned to Shannon to hurry up. The two of them walked briskly to Jennifer's door.

"What the hell are you wearing?" Kelly frowned, looking at Shannon, wearing a black cat-suit with a black ski mask.

"What does it look like? I'm blending in with my surroundings." Shannon frowned.

"Your surroundings are beige and white." Kelly shook her head and whispered as she opened Jennifer's door. "Come on, Harriet."

Once inside, Kelly switched on Jennifer's laptop and Shannon slowly paced the room. Kelly decrypted all the passwords and started copying everything onto the memory stick.

"This is fun." Shannon giggled nervously.

"I'm glad one of us is enjoying ourselves." Kelly muttered, watching the screen. Fifty-five percent complete.

Shannon smiled and put her hands on her hips. "How long?"

"Just a few more minutes." Kelly looked over at Shannon. "Don't touch anything. Jen is very particular."

"Okay." Shannon frowned and walked back to Kelly.

"Come on. Come on." Kelly whispered and bit into her knuckles, still staring at the screen.

Shannon stood next to Kelly and looked at the screen. "Ninety eight."

"Ninety-nine. Done!" Kelly nodded and ejected the memory stick. She buried it in her pocket and gave a satisfied sigh. She turned the laptop off and switched on the desk lamp.

"Come on." Kelly stood up and walked to the door. "Are the hinged oiled?" She said into the walkie-talkie.

"Dripping." Spencer's voice sounded over the radio.

"Awesome." Shannon smiled and opened the door. Kelly switched the lights off and they left the room. They checked the hallway and ran to the elevator. When the elevator stopped on the fourteenth floor, Kelly and Shannon bolted down the corridor and quietly entered Emilie's room.

"The panther is safely in it's cage." Kelly said into the walkie-talkie as they closed the door behind them.

"Great, get some room service." Spencer said. "This panther is starving."

Kelly laughed and leaned against the wall. She took the stick from her pocket and stared at it.

"Right, let's take a look at what we've got!" Shannon grabbed the memory stick and ran to the laptop.

Shannon started up her laptop and inserted the memory stick. She opened a file marked 'Sins' and stared at the screen.

"Oh my god!" Shannon gasped.

"I told you she was bad." Kelly dug her hands into her pants pockets and looked at Shannon.

CHAPTER 14

It was 03:45 and still dark outside, as Emilie turned onto her side on the bed. The shades were open and the two bright lights lit up the sky, giving her room an eerie glow. She could feel a heaviness in her heart as she rubbed her burning eyes. It was completely quiet in the room as she slid off the bed. She put on her black coat and buttoned it up all the way to the top. She opened the door and saw Shannon and Spencer, fast asleep on the couch. Spencer had his arm around

Shannon's shoulder and her head was resting on Spencer's chest. Kelly was on the opposite couch, also asleep. Emilie ran her fingers through her hair and took a deep breath, before tiptoeing through the room to the door. She looked back over her shoulder at Spencer, Shannon and Kelly, and quietly left the room, closing the door behind her. She had a sudden urge to look in the direction of Nathan's room, but she fought against it. She walked briskly to the elevator and dug her hands into her jacket pockets.

Nathan was on his bed, staring at the ceiling, in the dark. He glanced over at the watch next to him and sighed. The bright red numbers glowed eerily, it was 03:50. He stared back at the ceiling again and closed his eyes. He rolled over onto his side and grabbed the pillow next to him. He could still smell Emilie on his pillow, on his clothes, on himself. He did not know what he was going to do. He could try to talk to her again, but after the way she shook her head after his fight with Spencer in the corridor, he knew that he blew his chances. Besides, Spencer and Shannon would never allow him to see her, and Nathan did not feel like fighting anymore. He could not imagine his life without Emilie in it, but the chances of her believing him, were slim to none. He frowned heavily as Kelly's words ran through his mind. "Don't give up, Nate." Don't give up. He sat up and frowned. That was exactly what he was doing, giving up on Emilie. By doing nothing, by letting Emilie slip through his fingers, he's allowing Jennifer to win!

"That'll be the day!" He stood up and ran out the door, down the corridor and stopped a few steps from Emilie's door. He stared at the door, he couldn't move.

Shannon woke up with a start from a horrible nightmare and looked around the room. She felt her heart beating in her throat and she looked over at Spencer. His head was bent backwards, his lips parted slightly and he was snoring. Shannon sat up and looked at the bedroom door. She clearly remembered that she closed it the last time. Or did she? Puzzled, and still half-asleep, she stood up and walked to the open door. Her eyes widened when she saw the empty bed.

"Em?" She walked to the bathroom and checked inside. Empty.

"Spencer! Kelly!" Panic ran through her veins as she ran out to the living room.

"Spence!" She tugged at his arm.

His head fell forward and he muttered something.

"Spence, wake up." Shannon shook her head and looked at Kelly. "Wake up, you guys."

"Hmmm, what time is it?" He mumbled.

Shannon looked over her shoulder at the clock on the wall. "It's ten to four."

Spencer nodded and closed his eyes again.

"Spencer, wake up. It's Em!" She tugged at his arm again.

His eyes opened and he looked at her.

"What's going on?" Kelly sat up on the couch and yawned.

"She's gone!" Shannon shrieked.

"What do you mean she's gone?" Spencer's eyes widened and he stood up.

"She's gone! There's no sign of her!" Shannon shrieked. "Oh my god! She's been kidnapped!"

"Shannon, relax, she's not kidnapped. She probably just went for a walk!" Kelly frowned.

"At four in the morning?" Shannon exclaimed.

"She's fine, Shannon." Spencer rubbed his eyes.

"Oh my god! We lost her!" Shannon shrieked again.

"Shannon, relax, we didn't lose her. I'm sure she's safe, you know Em, she's always responsible." Spencer walked out of the bedroom and put his hands on his hips, looking at Shannon. He walked over to the kitchen and put his hands on the cool marble.

"At the risk of sounding completely insane, I think I know where she might be." Shannon frowned.

"Where?" Kelly looked at her.

"The lights." Shannon said.

"What lights?" Kelly asked, puzzled.

"The lights? As in the Memorial lights?" Spencer looked at her and frowned. "Why on earth would she go there?"

"To see him." Shannon said.

"Who?" Kelly asked.

"Jeremy. She heard him talk to her. I didn't believe her when she told me...." Shannon turned to Kelly.

"What are you..." Spencer frowned and his voice trailed. "No, that's not possible."

"That's exactly what I said." Shannon said and looked at Spencer.

"Why didn't she just come to us?" Spencer asked.

"Spencer, who was the one person that Emilie always used to go to when she felt alone and scared?" Shannon smiled sadly.

"Wel, let's go then." Spencer nodded and opened the door.

Nathan was standing outside the door and Spencer looked at him. Nathan took a step backwards because

Spencer looked like he was about to punch him again.

"Connor, get the hell out of my way!" Spencer growled.

"No, not until you let me talk to Emilie...." Nathan said, and frowned as Shannon pushed passed him.

"Emilie is not here." Spencer snapped.

"Where is she?" Nathan frowned.

"Come on guys, please don't fight again." Kelly rolled her eyes at the guys and stood in the corridor, her hands on her hips.

"What are you doing here?" Nathan looked at Kelly and frowned. She shrugged and he shook his head. "Never mind. I'm not here to fight, I just need to talk to Emilie. Please."

"She's not here, Nate." Shannon said.

"Well where is she?" Nathan exclaimed.

"Connor, just go back to your room. We can handle this." Spencer said to him.

"You don't know where she is, do you?" Nathan exclaimed and looked at Shannon.

"Of course we do. She's at the lights." Kelly said.

Nathan stared at them for a second and nodded. "I'm coming with you." Nathan said firmly.

"No, you're not." Spencer glared at him and he balled his fists.

"Okay, cool it guys." Kelly rolled her eyes at them.

"But..." Nathan frowned.

"Stay here, Nathan. We'll let you know when we find her. Come on, Spence. Come on, Kel. Let's go." Shannon said, pulled Spencer to her and the three of them walked down the corridor. "I thought I told you, no more fighting, Rocky." Shannon shook her head at Spencer and slapped his arm.

Emilie stepped onto the sidewalk, two blocks from the memorial site and felt her knee aching again. "Just quit aching, for god's sake. You already cost me so much." She growled, fed up with her knee, her life and herself. She dug her hands into the pockets of her jacket and slowly walked towards the lights. Surprizingly, the streets were still semi-alive, with people passing her, some walking, some stumbling. Emilie watched as they passed her by and sighed. There was a cold edge in the air as she slowly approached the lights and her heart started to race. The lights came into full view and Emilie stood on the sidewalk, looking at the sky. She felt a tear run down her cheek and she frowned. Was it even worth crying over what happened? Maybe Spencer was right.

She frowned heavily and shook her head. She looked over her shoulder at the wall across the road. She carefully crossed the road, stopping in the middle, where the barrier was. Is. That's strange, they should have fixed it by now. She knelt next to the barrier and traced the spot where the car had hit it with her fingertips. She closed her eyes and felt herself sitting behind the steering wheel, trying to turn. She felt the dented metal under her fingers and gasped as she felt the impact of the car against the barrier. She opened her eyes and stood up. The dull ache in her knee that constantly reminded her of that night, when she had lost her brother, frustrated her with every passing second. It was her fault, she had killed her brother. She wished that she had died instead of him, nobody would miss her. Her dad would be happier if she had died instead of Jeremy. Then there would be nothing that reminded him of Paige anymore. She was dead to him anyway, so it didn't matter. She crossed the road and stood a few feet from the wall. The hairs on the back of her neck rose and she took a few steps forward. She carefully touched the wall and closed her eyes. She felt the rough concrete against her fingers and heard the smash of the car as it hit the wall. A rush of emotions washed over her and she felt the world spinning around her. A sudden burst of nausea hit her and she felt light-headed. She heard herself screaming and Jeremy's voice rang in her ears. "Lee..." She felt a tear run down her cheek and opened her eyes. She turned her head and saw Jeremy standing next to her, leaning against the wall, smiling at her. She jumped, partly from shock and partly from surprize.

"Oh my god, I really am crazy." She rubbed her eyes and let out a laugh.

"You're not crazy, Lee." Jeremy laughed.

"You'd be surprized." Emilie raised her eyebrows. "Am I dreaming?"

"No, Lee. You're completely awake." Jeremy grinned.

"So, you're not real." Emilie shook her head with a frown.

"Nope." Jeremy laughed. "You should really tell Shannon not to overdo it with the morphine."

"Great, I'm hallucinating!" Emilie muttered. "God, I am crazy."

"It comes with being a Hayes, Lee." Jeremy smiled.

Emilie tucked a strand of hair behind her ear and looked at Jeremy. She felt tears stinging her eyes and looked away.

"What's wrong, sis?" Jeremy tilted his head at her.

"It was my fault." Emilie frowned. "I killed you."

"Lee, it's not your fault, you know that, and I know

that." Jeremy frowned.

"It's true..."

"Lee..." Jeremy walked over to her and brushed her cheek with the back of his hand.

"If I wasn't the one driving, you'd still be here..." Emilie shook her head.

Jeremy smiled sadly and took her hands. "Lee, if you weren't driving, none of us would be here."

"But it's so unfair." Emilie sighed.

"I know, Lee." Jeremy nodded.

Emilie nodded and another tear ran down her cheek.

"What else, Lee?" Jeremy asked.

"What do you mean?" Emilie frowned.

"Come on, sis. I know there's something else." Jeremy tilted his head.

Emilie sighed and felt her heart breaking all over again. "Nathan lied to me." Emilie said simply.

"I don't believe that." Jeremy shook his head.

"Jer..." She said.

"Connor's an alright guy, Lee. He wouldn't lie to you." Jeremy crossed his arms.

"But he did." Emilie said. "I told him about the accident being my fault and he went and told his sister, who wrote this horrible article about me, how I lied to the police and tried to cover it up. It's all over New York." Emilie exclaimed and ran her fingers through her hair. "I might as well forfeit, because my career is over anyway." Emilie pointed to her knee.

"That's ridiculous, sis." Jeremy frowned. "I don't want you talking like that."

"But it's true. I have nothing anymore." Emilie looked at him. "I lost Dad, I lost you and now I have lost Nathan."

"He loves you, Lee." Jeremy shook his head. "And so does Connor."

"I don't know, Jer. How can you love someone and then do something like that to hurt them?" Emilie shook her head.

"I doubt that he told her." Jeremy crossed his arms.

"How else did Jennifer find out then?" Emilie sighed.

"Clearly you don't know Jennifer very well. Jennifer can get almost anyone to do exactly what she wants them to do." Jeremy frowned. "She is everything Connor isn't. Why do you think he hates her so much?"

"I just don't know if it's worth it anymore, Jer." Emilie tilted her head.

"Lee, life is about taking risks, and you'll never know if it was worth it if you didn't take the leap." Jeremy looked at her. "The what-if's will haunt you for the rest of your life. I don't want you living with regrets, Lee."

"Did you have any regrets?" Emilie asked after a long pause.

"A few, but I wouldn't change anything." Jeremy sighed sadly.

"I would." Emilie sniffed and looked at him. "You were the best brother I could ever have asked for! I miss you so much."

"I miss you too, Lee, but I'm always with you." Jeremy smiled. "And I am so proud of you."

"You are?" Emilie asked, feeling a lump in her throat.

"I always have been. No matter what you do." Jeremy nodded at her and smiled. "As long as you do what makes you happy, and not what people expect you to do."

"I wish it was so simple." Emilie felt her voice cracking.

"Everything will be okay, Lee." Jeremy put his arms around her and held her tight.

"I love you so much." Emilie sobbed.

"I love you too, baby sister." Jeremy smiled and stroked her hair.

"I wish you were real...." Emilie whispered and Jeremy pulled away and smiled at her.

"Lee, will you do something for me?" Jeremy asked.

"Anything." Emilie nodded.

"Please don't give up what makes you happy. And please don't be angry with dad." Jeremy said.

"What do you mean?" Emilie frowned.

"He loves you, Lee." Jeremy said.

"He has an odd way of showing it." Emilie pulled a face.

"It's not his fault, okay?" Jeremy frowned.

"Sure, but it's not mine either." Emilie said.

"Fair enough, baby sister. Just don't be too hard on him." Jeremy said.

"Okay." Emilie nodded, reluctantly and frowned as Jeremy took a step back. "Jer, please don't go...."

"I'm not going anywhere, I'll always be right here." Jeremy put his hand over his heart and smiled at Emilie. "When you feel lonely, just remember the lights. When it's darkest outside, that's when they shine the brightest."

Emilie looked over her shoulder at the lights, smiled and looked back at Jeremy, but he was gone. "Jer?" She felt two more tears running down her cheeks and she blinked. She took a couple of deep breaths and turned around. She walked back towards the lights, crossing the street. She stopped next to the barrier and stared at it for a few moments.

"Jer..." She whispered to herself, and felt the world spinning around her. Another wave of nausea hit her as she knelt down on the sidewalk and her legs gave in. "Don't leave me...." The world continued spinning, until everything around Emilie went dark.

"Did you find her?" Nathan walked into Spencer's room and looked at Spencer and Shannon on the couch and Kelly on the ottoman. "Is she okay?" Nathan asked, sitting on the couch opposite them.

"Yes, she's fine, she's just sleeping off the morphine." Shannon nodded.

"Good." Nathan nodded as well.

After a moment of silence, Spencer looked at Nathan. "Connor, listen man."

Nathan looked at Spencer and frowned.

"I'm sorry for earlier. Punching and calling you names. I was just angry, I completely lost it. I've known Em for a really long time, she's like a sister to me and..." Spencer said.

"It's okay, man." Nathan nodded and gave Spencer a small smile. "No need to explain. I would've done the same."

"So, we're cool?" Spencer asked.

"Absolutely." Nathan smiled and they pressed their fists together.

"Nate, there's something we need to talk about." Kelly took a deep breath and looked at Nathan.

"What?" Nathan frowned at her.

"Spencer, Shannon and I have been talking this over for a couple of hours and we want to know if you will help us." Kelly said.

"What are you talking about?" Nathan frowned.

"We want to get back at your sister." Shannon said. "Seeing as she ruins everybody else's lives, we want to give her a taste of her own medicine, by exposing her, for what she truly is."

"And how are you going to that, exactly?" Nathan asked.

"With this." Kelly held up the memory stick.

"A memory stick?" Nathan frowned.

"Not just any memory stick. This special memory stick contains everything we need to crush Jennifer and send her back into the hole she crept out from in the first place. Every scam she has ever pulled, every deal she has ever made, every person she has ever blackmailed, every wrong move, is on this stick." Kelly said.

Nathan frowned, then looked at Kelly with a smile. "Sure, that sounds good."

Kelly and Shannon stared at Nathan in disbelief. "Really?" Shannon asked.

"Yes. What do you want me to do?" Nathan nodded.

Kelly and Shannon exchanged glances. "That was easier than I thought it was going to be." Shannon whispered.

"Don't look so surprized, I hate her just as much as you do." Nathan smiled at Shannon.

Kelly looked at Nathan and hesitated for a moment.

"What is it, Kel?" Nathan frowned and looked at Kelly.

"We need Jen's birth certificate." Kelly said. "I was hoping you could get your mom to send it to you."

269

"Without it, we can't prove anything." Shannon begged.

"Guys, it's my Mom..." Nathan frowned.

"Nate, come on man." Spencer said.

Nathan sighed and looked at Shannon, Kelly and Spencer. He rubbed his eyes and nodded. "Fine. When do you want it?"

"As soon as you can get it." Kelly winced.

Nathan pursed his lips and looked at his watch. He nodded and took out his phone. "You owe me, big time." He dialed his mother's number and looked at Kelly, smiling, with a mouthful of chips. He grinned and shook his head. "Hey Mom."

"Good morning, honey." Zoe said.

"Mom, I need you to do something for me." Nathan said. "Is Jen's birth certificate still at the house?"

"Yes, I believe it is. Why?" Zoe asked.

"I can't explain right now, Mom. Can you mail it to me please?" Nathan frowned.

"Should I be worried?" Zoe asked.

"No, of course not. You should know me better than that." Nathan laughed.

"Alright, that was absurd of me to think you would do anything like that, Honey." Zoe said. "Do you need it right away?"

"Yes, please, it's urgent. I will explain everything later, I promise."

"That's alright, Honey. You do what you have to do." Nathan heard the uneasiness in his mother's voice.

"Mom, is everything okay?" Nathan frowned.

"Yes, Honey. It's nothing..."

"What did he do?" Nathan felt his blood boil in his

veins.

"Nothing, he..." Zoe's voice trailed.

"Is he there?" Nathan stood up and walked to the kitchen. "Put him on, please Mom."

"Nathan, this is unnecessary stress..." Zoe protested.

"Mom! Give him the phone!" Nathan gritted his teeth and rubbed his eyes. He took a deep breath and leaned against the kitchen counter.

"Nathan." He heard his father's voice. "The son every father wished he had."

"Screw you! What did you do to my mother?" Nathan asked.

"Oh, you know how your mother can exaggerate." Alastair laughed wickedly.

"What did you do?" Nathan exclaimed.

"Nothing she did not deserve." Alastair's cold tone sent a shiver down his spine.

"I swear to god, if you touch her, I will kill you!" Nathan growled.

"Your threats mean nothing to me, Nathan." Alastair snarled and Nathan heard the call disconnect. He took a few deep breaths and turned around.

"Everything okay?" Kelly asked behind him.

"Yeah." He looked at her and gave her a tight smile. "She'll send it right away."

Kelly nodded and looked at Nathan. "She's going to be okay, Nate."

"Em?" She heard Spencer ask.

Her head was pounding as she opened her eyes and she winced. "Ouch."

"Hey, Em. How are you feeling?" Spencer asked with a relieved smile.

"What time is it?" Emilie's head was spinning.

"Just after eleven, Emmy." Shannon answered.

"What the hell happened?" Emilie frowned.

"We found you in the middle of the street, next to the Memorial site. You passed out by the barrier." Shannon said, suddenly next to her.

"I though I had an hallucination." Emilie frowned and looked at Shannon.

"What do you mean?" Spencer asked.

"I was at the wall." Emilie frowned.

"Em......" Shannon said.

Emilie frowned. "Don't look at me as if I'm crazy, Shannon."

Shannon raised her eyebrows and crossed her arms. Shannon and Spencer exchanged worried looks and then looked at Emilie.

"I walked to the wall, I touched it. I saw Jer." Emilie looked at Shannon and Spencer.

"You saw Jeremy?" Spencer frowned.

"Yes! He told me that he misses me and that he is proud of me, and that I shouldn't be angry with my dad." Emilie said, with a frown.

"Shan, how much morphine did you give her?" Spencer looked at Shannon.

"The morphine I gave her doesn't cause hallucinations." Shannon walked to her, with a frown, and put her hand against Emilie's forehead. "Not even in very large doses. It's not possible."

"It felt so real." Emilie frowned and crossed her arms.

"Maybe it was." Spencer mumbled.

Emilie looked at Spencer and frowned. There was a strange look on his face, a look that she had never seen before. Did he believe her? Or was she just going completely and utterly insane? Spencer was standing by the window, staring outside. Emilie noticed the two blue lights and felt herself smile slightly. The two blue lights were the same color as Jeremy's eyes. Funny that she only realized it now. Maybe it was too late to assume she was going insane, maybe she already was.

"Detective Rollins please." Spencer said and looked over at Shannon, making coffee in the kitchen.
"Please hold."
Shannon looked over her shoulder and smiled at him.
"Detective Rollins, good morning."
"Good morning Detective. I believe you are the one to talk to about information of any illegal activities in the New York City area." Spencer said.
"Yes, that's correct. Who am I speaking to?"
"I would prefer to remain anonymous, if that is alright." Spencer said.
"Of course, of course." Detective Rollins said.
"I would like to report acts of fraud and blackmail, illegal smuggling, arson and attempted murder." Spencer said.
"Those are a lot of activities. Is this from a single person?" Detective Rollins asked.
"Yes sir." Spencer nodded.
"And do you have the name of this person?"
"I have her name, as well as her alias." Spencer nodded. "Jennifer Grayson, formerly known as Jenny Connor."
"Why does that name sound so familiar?" Detective Rollins mumbled.
"She is a journalist for the telegraph, sir." Spencer said.

"And do you have the current location of this person?" He asked.

"She is staying at the Four Season's Hotel, New York City, suite 1506." Spencer said.

"You do realize that these are very serious accusations and that you may face prosecution if this is not the truth?" Detective Rollins said.

"Detective, I have all the proof in the world to prove that this is indeed true. Should I fax it over to you? Or should I have my assistant deliver it to the station?" Spencer asked.

"The latter would suffice." He answered.

"Excellent, I will have my assistant sent right over. Thank you for your help, Detective Rollins." Spencer grinned. "Good-bye."

"Good-bye then."

Spencer put the phone back on the receiver and smiled at Shannon.

"Wow, you're all sexy when you are serious." Shannon pouted and walked over to him. She sat on his lap and put her arms around his shoulders. She leaned her face towards him and kissed him. Spencer pulled away and smiled at her.

"What?" Shannon frowned.

"You're going for a ride." Spencer took his keys out of his pocket and dangled it in front of Shannon.

"I get to drive the Camaro?" Shannon asked in disbelief.

"Don't crash it." Spencer nodded. "And wear those big sunglasses of yours. And no boots."

"Why?" Shannon frowned, but then her eyes widened. "No, wait a minute! Spencer!"

Spencer nodded and handed her a large brown envelope, filled with all of Jennifer's antics. "All yours, honey."

Shannon tilted her head and sighed. "Oh my god! I can't believe this." Shannon mumbled and stood up. She dragged her feet to the bedroom, closing the door behind her.

Spencer grinned at himself and turned on the television. ESPN Live's Allison Thomas was on and talking about last year's Men's final. Spencer shrugged and changed the channel to Nickelodeon.

"Is this better?" He heard Shannon ask after a few minutes. He looked up and stared at Shannon. She was wearing a tight black skirt and a fitted black jacket, a white shirt underneath, a pair of grey high heels and her hair was out of her face rolled into a bun.

"Wow." Spencer said. "You look...so...professional."

"Didn't you think I could dress professional?" Shannon asked and put her hand on her hip.

"It's not that, Shan. It's just so different." Spencer shook his head.

"I know. These suits are a bitch to get into." Shannon laughed. "Right, where're those keys of yours?" She held out her hand towards him. Spencer smiled and handed her his keys. "Don't let Sting find out I'm driving something else." Shannon mumbled and Spencer laughed. "Envelope." Shannon held out her other hand.

Spencer handed her the envelope and smiled at her.

"I'll be right back, boss." Shannon winked.

"Right, and when you get back we can talk about your raise." Spencer smiled and Shannon laughed.

"Em, I can't just leave him outside!" Shannon exclaimed.

"I don't want to talk to him, Shannon!" Emilie shook her head and stared at Shannon.

"Em, be reasonable." Shannon said softly.

"Why now?" Emilie asked.

"Just listen to what he has to say, Em." Spencer smiled softly.

"Fine." Emilie shrugged.

Shannon and Spencer left the room and Emilie shook her head. She looked at the door and saw her dad standing on the door.

"Hey." Emilie crossed her arms.

"I'm glad you're okay." Tom looked very uncomfortable and fiddled with his sleeve.

"Yeah, well." Emilie muttered.

"You shouldn't run off like that." Tom said.

"Like you would have noticed if I was gone..." Emilie snapped.

Her father looked at her and frowned. "Emilie, about the article....."

"I don't want to talk about it." Emilie shook her head.

"All I want to know is, is it true?" Tom looked at her. "Did you drive?"

Emilie felt tears in her eyes and swallowed the lump in her throat. "Yes."

Tom closed his eyes and shook his head. "Why didn't you tell me?"

"Why didn't I tell you?" Emilie exclaimed. "Are you fucking serious?"

Tom's eyes popped open and glared at Emilie.

"You are not the easiest person to talk to, you know. How the hell was I supposed to tell you that it was me driving? That I'm the one that killed your son? I knew that he meant everything to you!" Emilie screamed. "Maybe I did not want you to hate me even more than you already do!"

"Emilie..." Tom shook his head.

"If you didn't hate me, then why have you never watched me practice, why have you never been to one of my games, why have you never told me that you are proud of me? Tell me!" Emilie sobbed.

"Because you're not my daughter!" Tom exclaimed and looked at her.

"What?" Emilie's eyes widened.

"The morning of your mother's accident, she told me that seven years ago, she had an affair with a guy from the school she was teaching at. It completely crushed me and I wanted to know who the guy was, but she wouldn't tell me. She said that it did not matter. She also told me, that...." Tom's voice cracked and closed his eyes.

"I wasn't your daughter...." Emilie felt the blood drain from her face and shook her head.

"Yes..." Tom said.

"Who's the guy?" Emilie asked.

"I don't know. Your mother wouldn't tell me.' Tom said.

Emilie sat forward and rested her hands on the bed next to her. She shook her head and looked at him. "Is that why Mom had the accident? She was upset, and she ran a red light?"

"Yes." Tom said, closing his eyes.

"Oh my god." Emilie sobbed. "No wonder you hate me." Emilie lifted her face and glared at him through her tears. "I killed your wife and I killed your son."

CHAPTER 15

"I can't believe I fell. Again. What the hell is the matter with me, Spence?" Emilie exclaimed as she sat on the bench in her locker room.

"There's nothing with you, Em. It's those vultures out there. They're enough to make anyone fall." Spencer looked at her and took her hand.

"The crowd's not really helping either." Shannon mumbled at the door.

"I don't really blame them." Emilie shrugged.

"I'm just glad Huxley allowed you to still play." Shannon muttered.

"Never mind any of that, Em. You just focus on your game, nothing else matters." Spencer frowned at Shannon.

"I'm such an idiot!" Emilie closed her eyes and pulled a face. Her whole body was tensed up, awaiting yet another painful injection.

"It's alright, Em, just relax." Spencer smiled as Emilie started squeezing his hand.

Emilie opened her eyes and glared at Spencer. She looked over at Shannon standing by the door, looking out on to the court. Out of the corner of her eye, she saw the needle Aiden was holding. "Oh my god! Look at that thing!" She exclaimed, horrified.

Aiden frowned and stuck the needle into a small bottle, filling up the syringe with a clear liquid. "It will be fine."

"Let me stick that in your knee, Doc!" Emilie groaned and Aiden gave her a tight smile.

"Okay, Em. Take a deep breath." Spencer said.

"Just do it." Emilie growled.

Emilie felt the sharp needle enter her skin just below her kneecap and she held her breath. She felt the burning liquid in her leg and she cried out in pain. She squeezed Spencer's hand so hard, that it actually made him wince. Shannon looked over her shoulder at Spencer with a grin and crossed her arms.

Aiden slowly pulled the needle out and gently rubbed her kneecap. "All done, honey." He screwed the needle off the syringe.

Emilie bit her lip and opened her eyes. "Is it supposed to burn like that?"

"How bad?" Aiden asked.

"Inferno bad." Emilie opened her eyes and winced.

"Just wiggle your toes a bit." Aiden rubbed Emilie's leg.

Shannon looked over her shoulder at Aiden and crossed her arms again. "It's still raining."

Emilie leaned her head against the wall, wiggling her toes, waiting for the burning to stop.

"How is it feeling, Emilie?"

"It's better." She looked at Aiden and nodded. "How long will it last?"

"Three hours, at most." Aiden looked at her. "If you feel that it starts wearing off, let me know immediately."

"I will do." Emilie nodded and sat forward. "Thank you, Doc."

"You're welcome." Aiden smiled and stood up.

"Spence?" Emilie looked over at him. "Can I talk to you?"

"Sure, Em." Spencer nodded. "Shan, can you leave us alone for a minute?"

"Of course." Shannon smiled and left the room.

"Are you okay, Em?" Spencer sat down next to her.

"Did you know? About my dad not being my real dad?" Emilie asked.

"Yes." Spencer nodded.

"How long have you known?" Emilie asked.

"For a while." Spencer said. "Jer..."

"Jer knew?" Emilie's jaw dropped and she stared at Spencer.

"Yeah." Spencer looked at her.

"Why didn't you tell me, Spence?" Emilie frowned. "Why didn't he tell me?"

"Would it have mattered?" Spencer frowned at her. "Jer was still your brother, and he would always be, no matter what any bloodtest said."

Emilie looked at him and sighed. "It would have been nice to know."

"Look, your brother loved you, and that's all that matters. Jer didn't tell you, because he was just protecting you, doing what he has always done. Your real dad obviously didn't want you, and Tom still raised you as his daughter."

"Yeah, but he never treated me like his daughter." Emilie frowned.

"Okay, here's a hypothetical situation for you. Let's say you and I get married..." Spencer said.

Emilie looked at him with a puzzled look and shook her head.

"Just humor me, okay." Spencer laughed. "Besides, you're not my type."

Emilie laughed and crossed her arms.

"So, anyway, we're married and you find out that I had a kid with some other woman. The woman dies and you and I get the kid. Would you treat it like it was your own?" Spencer asked.

"I guess I would try." Emilie nodded.

"Okay, let's say that I die and you are left with the kid. How would you feel then?" Spencer asked.

"I would not take it out on the kid, it's not his fault." Emilie frowned.

"That's not what I asked." Spencer said.

"I'd be happy. At least I'd have something of you after you were gone. Even if it's not mine." Emilie felt a tear run down her cheek and looked at Spencer.

Spencer stared at her for a few seconds, not knowing what to say.

"What?" Emilie asked.

"You know what? You're right." Spencer said. "It wasn't your fault, none of it, but remember, not everyone is as strong, or as nice, as you are."

"It's not about being strong, or nice, Spencer. It's about doing what is right." Emilie looked at him.

"Look at you, little miss profound." Spencer looked at her and put his arm over her shoulders. "When did you get so smart?"

"I had two really great rolemodels." Emilie smiled.

"You mean friends." Spencer frowned.

"That too." Emilie nodded and rubbed her eyes.

"Did you really see him?" Spencer asked after a long pause.

"I thought so, but now I'm not so sure." Emilie frowned and looked at Spencer. "Are you sure that morphine can't make you hallucinate?"

"Usually it's only supposed to make you feel light-headed and dizzy, and obviously takes away the pain."

"Not all the pain." Emilie ran her fingers through her hair and sighed.

Spencer laughed. "Maybe it did take away your pain and that's why you saw him."

"Could be, I don't know, Spence. Maybe I am insane. This whole situation has made me doubt everything, even my sanity." Emilie nodded and looked at him. "Even if I am insane, it was good to see him, Spence. I really wish you could have seen him too."

Spencer pulled her close and she rested her head on his shoulder. "Me too, honey."

Shannon held the doors open for Emilie and Spencer. The moment Emilie walked out onto the court, the crowd started making a noise, not a good noise. Emilie took deep breaths as she walked to her seat and put her bag on the ground. She looked around her at the crowd and knew she would never win this crowd over. The story had spread faster than a wild fire and everyone was looking at her, like she was a criminal. Deep inside, she felt like one, it was her fault her mother was dead, and it was her fault her brother was dead. The overwhelming pain in her heart was so intense, that when she sat down, she struggled to breathe. Amazingly, her limp was gone, and she did not feel any pain, not even an ache, in her knee. She was also amazed at how quickly the injection worked, she has not walked this comfortably in a long time.

"You'll be fine, Em." Spencer smiled and took his seat next to Shannon and Doctor Gilbert.

Emilie nodded with a slight smile and sat down. She unzipped her bag and took out her racquet, gently tugging at the strings. She looked up and saw Kelly walking back out onto the court and Emilie smiled. Kelly looked at her, with a worried smile and walked over to her.

"Are you okay?" Kelly asked.

"Actually, yes." Emilie nodded and gripped the handle of her racquet. "No pain."

"I've decided something." Kelly said, her face difficult to read.

"What?" Emilie frowned.

"Please don't be angry with me, Emilie, but I have to do this." Kelly said, turned around and walked to the umpire's chair.

Emilie frowned and watched as Kelly and the umpire exchanged a few words. The umpire frowned at Kelly and she nodded. Emilie looked over her shoulder at Spencer and Shannon and frowned. Spencer stood up and walked to where Kelly and the umpire was standing. After a short conversation, Kelly nodded, looked over at Emilie and gave her a small smile. Kelly walked to her bag, swung it over her shoulder and walked off the court.

"Kelly!" Emilie called after her.

"What just happened?" Shannon touched Emilie's shoulder and Emilie jumped.

"I have no idea." Emilie frowned.

Spencer walked back from the umpire and dug his hands into his pockets.

"What's going on, Spence?" Emilie asked.

"Kelly just forfeited." Spencer frowned.

"What?" Emilie exclaimed. "Why?"

"She wouldn't say." Spencer raised his shoulders and looked at Emilie.

"Oh my god. I need to talk to her." Emilie said and ran after Kelly.

"Emilie, wait!" Shannon yelled and Spencer and Shannon ran after her.

Nathan rested his chin on his knuckles and stared

at the television screen above him. He frowned as he watched Emilie's fall on court and shook his head, wishing he could be there. He looked around the hotel lounge and sighed. There were a couple of people, scattered on the couches, most of them from the bar. The lounge was relatively quiet, except for Diane's voice coming from the televisions. He had vowed to himself that he was going to talk to Emilie, but that would only be possible after tomorrow. He just had to wait it out, for now. Nathan growled as he felt his phone vibrate in his pocket. He took his phone from his pocket while he walked briskly through the lobby.

"Hey Mom." He smiled.

"Nathan Connor! It's been three days! Do you have any idea how..."

"Whoa, it's only been two days." He rolled his eyes.

"Well it feels like a month, honey." His mother said. "I miss you!"

"I miss you too, Mom." Nathan sighed with a smile. "I'm sorry I haven't called, these past two days were a bit..."

"A bit what?"

"Difficult." Nathan rubbed his eyes and stepped into the elevator.

"Why? Is everything alright?" Zoe asked.

"Well..." Nathan frowned.

"Nathan...." Zoe said.

"I don't really want to talk about it." Nathan pushed the rotating doors forward and stepped outside.

"How was your game?" Zoe asked.

"It was good! I won Zac and I'm playing finals tomorrow evening." Nathan smiled.

"That's wonderful, darling!" He heard his mother

say proudly. "How is Kelly doing?"

"Kelly?" Nathan frowned. "What do you mean?"

"Have you not been watching ESPN, Nathan? Kelly just forfeited." Zoe said.

"What?" Nathan exclaimed.

"Didn't Emilie tell you?" Zoe said and Nathan felt his knees go weak.

"No, we uhm....." Nathan stuttered.

"Does this have anything to do with your sister, and her birth certificate?" Zoe asked.

"Mom, I have to go, I'll call you tonight, I promise. Okay?" Nathan said.

"Okay, Honey. Speak to you later then."

"Bye, Mom."

Nathan looked up and saw Kelly crossing her street and run up the steps towards him. She ran straight passed him and through the doors. Nathan frowned and followed her inside.

"Kelly!"

Kelly spun around and stared at him with wide eyes.

"What happened?" Nathan walked to her. "Why did you forfeit?"

"I didn't know what else to do..." Kelly stuttered.

"Tell me what happened." Nathan touched her shoulder.

Kelly took a deep breath and looked at Nathan. "I couldn't...."

"What are you talking about?" Nathan frowned.

"Kelly!" Shannon and Spencer came running through ther doors, and Nathan and Kelly looked at them.

"What the hell happened?" Spencer asked as he and Shannon walked closer to them, worried expressions on their faces.

"I don't want to be here anymore...." Kelly shook her head and frowned.

Suddenly Kelly's eyes widened and she stared at the door. Nathan, Spencer and Shannon looked at the door.

Emilie felt her heart pound in her chest as she saw Kelly, Nathan, Shannon and Spencer staring at her as she came through the doors of the hotel. Her legs were tired and her chest hurt from running all the way from the arena.

"Kelly...." Emilie breathed.

Kelly looked at her and shook her head. Emilie took a step forward and met Nathan's eyes, but only for a second. She looked away almost immediately and clasped her hands together. Shannon and Kelly walked towards her and stopped in front of her.

"Kelly, what...." Emilie started, but was interupted by a commotion coming from the elevators. Guests from the lounge entered the lobby to see what the commotion was.

"What's going on?" Emilie asked.

"The shit is about to hit the fan." Kelly sighed.

"What do you mean?" Emilie frowned and looked at Kelly and Shannon.

The two girls exchanged glances, not saying a word.

"Shannon?" Emilie glared at her, but she just raised her shoulders.

Suddenly, three police officers and a dark-haired woman stepped out of the elevator.

"Oh my god. Is that..." Emilie asked.

"Yip." Kelly nodded.

"It can't be..." Emilie shook her head.

As the officers came closer, she could see that it was Jennifer, handcuffed and being escorted across the lobby, towards the doors.

"Oh my god." Emilie gasped.

Jennifer lifted her head and looked at Emilie. "This is your fault, isn't it? I knew it was you!" Jennifer yelled at Emilie.

"What is she talking about?" Emilie asked Shannon, but Shannon did not say anything, she just took Emilie's hand.

Emilie was so shocked to actually see her handcuffed, she just stared at her. She gently squeezed Shannon's hand and held it tight. Jennifer scowled as she looked at Nathan. Nathan saw his sister look at him and he shook his head in disapproval, as he always had, his entire life. He never approved of anything that Jennifer did, which made him think that nothing she ever did was good. He felt his hands started to shake and he dug them into his pockets. He watched as Jen walked passed and he took a deep breath. He almost felt sorry for her, that her past had finally caught up to her. He blinked as all the emotions from his childhood came rushing back and he remembered everything that Jen had done to him. As he watched the three officers and Jennifer exit the hotel doors, the brief moment of sympathy for his sister was replaced with a feeling of relief. Justice!

"Okay, before you start flipping out, let me just explain." Shannon raised her hands in the air.

"You better." Emilie folded her arms and glared at Shannon.

Shannon took a deep breath and looked at Emilie.

"I'm waiting." Emilie tilted her head.

"We wanted Jennifer to get a taste of her own medicine. She practically destroyed your life, Emmy." Shannon said.

"My life wasn't perfect to begin with, Shan." Emilie shrugged.

"Emmy, please understand." Shannon pleaded.

"No, Shannon! By doing this, you are no better than Jennifer!" Emilie shook her head.

"That's not true and you know it!" Shannon exclaimed and her eyes filled with tears. "All that I have ever wanted was to have you happy! You deserve to be happy! I thought..."

"I doubt that you thought at all, Shannon." Emilie muttered.

"Sure, that's the thanks I get! You're welcome, Emilie!" Shannon stood up and stormed out of the room.

"Shannon...." Emilie ran her hands through her hair and ran to the door. She looked out into the corridor but Shannon was nowhere to be found. Emilie ran to the elevator, and as she approached the corner, she saw Shannon. Emilie gave a sigh of relief and walked closer. Shannon had her hands up to her face and cried. Emilie jumped when the elevator doors opened and Spencer stepped out. Spencer put his arms around Shannon and held her. Emilie stopped dead in her tracks and frowned, pressing her back against the wall. "Spencer and Shannon? No. That's impossible." Emilie thought to herself and shook her head. She looked over to them and saw Spencer whispering something in Shannon's ear, Shannon nodded and Spencer tilted her chin up. Spencer and Shannon looked at each other for a second and Spencer leaned in and kissed Shannon. Emilie was still frowning as she slowly backed away from them, trying not to let them see her, but she accidentally bumped into someone and let out a sharp shriek. She looked up into Brandon's face and he gave her a crooked smile, his chocolate eyes twinkling.

"Emmy?" She heard Spencer's voice behind her.

"We should stop bumping into each other like this." Brandon grinned.

"I'm sorry, I should really watch where I'm going." Emilie said, breathlessly and tried to push passed him.

"Where are you going?" Brandon frowned.

"I'm late for something..." Emilie frowned.

"Emilie?" Spencer called out behind her.

"Get out of my way, Brandon!" Emilie pushed Brandon and he moved out of her way, laughing.

"Emilie, wait!" Spencer and Shannon called after Emilie.

"Dude, what's going on?" Brandon asked Spencer.

"We're in deep shit." Spencer tugged at his cap and looked at Emilie, marching back to her room. She paused at the door and glared at him for a second.

"Really deep shit." Shannon sighed.

Zoe walked up to the front desk and put her suitcase down on the ground next to her.

"Good evening. I'd like a suite please. Fourteenth floor, north facing." Zoe smiled.

"Of course. The name please?" Marilyn asked.

"Zoe Pearce-Connor." Zoe smiled and handed Marilyn a creditcard.

"Thank you." Marilyn took the card from Zoe and entered some data into the computer. She handed the credit card back to Zoe, as well as a room key card.

"There you are, Miss Pearce-Connor. Fourteen twenty-nine."

"Thank you so much, dear." Zoe smiled and took the cards. She picked up her suitcase and walked to the elevator. She stepped into the elevator and a few moments later, she walked down the corridor to her room. When she came around the corner, she saw Kelly walking towards her.

"Aunt Zoe." Kelly had a shocked expression on her face.

"Kelly, dear. How good to see you!" Zoe smiled and hugged her.

"Same here! What a surprise!" Kelly smiled. "What are you doing here?"

"I was hoping you could tell me what has been going on here the last couple of days." Zoe pursed her lips.

"What do you mean?" Kelly frowned.

"Nathan is in a horrible mood, he hasn't mentioned Emilie at all, and he used to talk about her all the time. You forfeited your match, and my daughter was arrested." Zoe crossed her arms.

"Oh, that." Kelly shifted her weight, uncomfortably.

"Well?" Zoe looked at her.

"Okay, I will tell you everything." Kelly nodded. "What number are you?"

"Twenty-nine." Zoe said.

"Okay, let's go." Kelly turned around and walked next to Zoe to her room.

"Mom! What are you doing here?" Nathan exclaimed as he stared blankly at his mother.

"It's good to see you too, Honey." Zoe tilted her head and looked at him.

Nathan smiled and hugged her. "It's always good to see you, Mom. Come on in."

Zoe smiled and walked into his room. Nathan closed the door and looked at his mother. "I can't believe you're here."

"Yes, well. I was worried." Zoe frowned.

"You should be." Nathan nodded. "Things are a mess. With Emilie and Jen and Kelly..."

"Kelly told me." Zoe sat down on the couch.

Nathan raised his eyebrows. "You're mad, aren't you?"

"Slightly." Zoe looked at him. "Why didn't you tell me, Nathan?"

"I didn't want to get you involved with all of this." Nathan sighed.

"You're my son, Nathan, and Jen is my daughter. I think I was already involved, whether I wanted to be or not." Zoe shook her head.

"We thought we could handle it, but it got way out of control." Nathan admitted.

"That's putting it mildly, Nathan." Zoe shrugged.

"Mom, I'm sorry...." Nathan looked at her, but stopped talking and sat down. "Actually, I am not sorry. Jen got exactly what she deserved. She's been doing this her whole life and never once did I, or anyone else, do anything about it."

"Nathan..." Zoe shifted forward on the couch.

"No, Mom. I am glad I helped Shannon and Kelly. If I had to do it again, I wouldn't change a thing." Nathan said.

"I know, baby." Zoe smiled.

"And Dad? Does he know?" Nathan scowled.

"Probably not. He's in New Orleans. Or Dallas. Or the Moon." Zoe shrugged. "I don't actually care."

Nathan tilted his head and frowned.

"Don't look so puzzled. I'm not your father's babysitter." Zoe frowned. "So tell me what happened with you and Emilie."

CHAPTER 16

"It's the afternoon of the big final in the men's U.S. Open, here in New York City. I'm Allison Thomas and you are watching ESPN Live. The final is only two hours away and this year should be an interesting one. The District of Columbia's very own wonderboy, twenty-three year old Nathan Connor faces up to twenty-one year old Brandon Campbell from Louisiana. Many of you will remember Connor's spectacular win last year in the U.S. Open, where he obliterated fellow Columbian, twenty-eight year old Spencer Byrne. Byrne has retired from playing, some time last year, and was seen coaching Emilie Hayes. Speaking of Emilie Hayes, last night's Women's final was something quite out of the ordinary. The game between twenty-one year old Hayes and twenty-two year old Kelly Shaw, was suspended due to bad weather. When the game resumed, Shaw walked up to the umpire and forfeited. Shaw simply walked off the court without a word, giving Hayes a free pass at the title. Hayes, however refused to accept the title and also ran off the court. Byrne was not available for commentary, but we can only imagine what this out-spoken Columbian would say....."

Emilie turned off the television and stared at the blank screen. She stretched her legs out onto the couch, rested her head against the armrest and frowned. She closed her eyes for a second, enjoying the silence around her. These moments were rare lately, so Emilie appreciated it. Suddenly, there was a loud banging on her door and her eyes snapped open.

She stood up and shook her head.

"Unbelievable..." She muttered as she walked to the door. She opened the door and Spencer and Shannon were standing there. Emilie stared at them for a second and Spencer crossed his arms.

"Can we come in?" Shannon asked.

"I suppose." Emilie frowned and crossed her arms.

Shannon opened her mouth to say something, but she wasn't quite sure what. She looked at Spencer and he shook his head. They stepped into her hotel room and Spencer sat down on the couch. Shannon, on the other hand, was still standing, nervously tugging at her clothes. Emilie sat down on the couch and leaned against the armrest, not saying a word, but still looking at them. Spencer clasped his hands together and looked at Shannon.

"What?" Emilie asked and looked at Shannon.

"Are you mad at us?" Shannon asked.

"What do you think?" Emilie looked at Spencer.

"We can explain." Spencer said and looked at Shannon.

"That would be great." Emilie looked at Shannon and then at Spencer. "I would love to hear how my two best friends were hooking up behind my back, and how it didn't even cross their minds to tell me about it. Or warn me, or something."

"Em, look, we wanted to tell you, but...." Spencer said, and Shannon sighed behind him, crossing her arms.

"But what?" Emilie frowned, looked at Spencer and then at Shannon.

"A lot of things were going on, and you had enough to deal with already." Spencer said.

"Plus we were scared that you would act this way,

Em." Shannon said.

"That's a pathetic excuse!" Emilie shook her head, stood up and started pacing the room. "The two people I trust more than anyone in the world, lied to me. How do you think that makes me feel, Shannon?"

"You lied to me too, Em!" Shannon exclaimed and pointed at her. "I have been your best friend for fourteen years, and you couldn't even tell me about the accident, and everything that happened. How do you think that makes me feel?"

Emilie felt like she had been punched in the chest and took a step back. She stared at Shannon and felt tears in her eyes.

"When did this happen?" Emilie whispered and looked at them.

"About two nights ago." Shannon said, her voice ready to break.

"I can't believe this is happening...." Emilie whispered, closed her eyes and shook her head. She paced around the room and put her hands on her hips. "Shannon and Spencer...." She paused and let out a laugh.

Shannon and Spencer exchanged glances and stared at Emilie.

"Actually I am not that surprized at all..." Emilie muttered to herself. "I think I knew that this was going to happen sooner or later." She stopped and looked at them. She let out another laugh and shook her head.

"I think she really is losing her mind." Spencer whispered to Shannon.

Emilie stopped and looked at them. "I can't believe I am about to say this, but you two are perfect for each other."

Spencer and Shannon frowned and exchanged

looks. "What?"

"I'm glad you agree." Spencer said, hesitantly.

"Yeah." Emilie nodded and shook her head in disbelief.

"Really?" Shannon asked.

"Yes. Why didn't I realize it sooner?" Emilie muttered to herself.

"Spence? She's worrying me. This is not like her. Talking to herself." Shannon whispered to Spencer.

"She'll be fine. She's just in shock." Spencer winked at her. "Em?"

Emilie stopped pacing and looked at Spencer. "Yes?"

"Are you okay with this?" Spencer asked. "With me and Shannon?"

"Yeah, I guess so." Emilie smiled.

"Well, that's a relief, isn't it?" Spencer asked Shannon.

"Obviously, Brainiac." Shannon rolled her eyes. "Em, you're not just saying that to be nice, are you?" Shannon looked at Emilie.

"What do you mean? I'm always nice." Emilie narrowed her eyes at her and Spencer laughed.

"Thanks, Em." Shannon smiled, stood up and hugged her.

"No problem." Emilie frowned. She pulled away and took a few steps back. She leaned against the wall and looked at Spencer and Shannon. It made her extremely happy to see Shannon and Spencer happy, but she couldn't help but feel a little depressed at the same time. Her heart still ached for Nathan. His smile, his laugh, his soft touch, his kisses. She felt a tear run down her cheek and she crossed her arms.

"Emmy?" Shannon walked over to her.

Emilie looked up and at Shannon, standing in front of her.

"Are you okay?" Shannon asked.

"Yes." Emilie nodded.

"Are you sure?" Spencer frowned.

"Of course." Emilie wiped the tear from her cheek and smiled. "I've got to go do something. Do you guys want to stay here?"

"No, that's okay." Shannon smiled and they walked to the door. "You go do what you got to do, Em."

"I wish it was that simple." Emilie sighed.

Kelly dropped her suitcases on the floor and looked around her hotel living room.

"Well, this was fun." She muttered to herself. There was a soft knock on her door and she sighed. "It's open."

"Kelly..."

She looked up and saw Emilie walking towards her, limping slightly.

"You're limping again." Kelly frowned.

"Oh, I hadn't noticed." Emilie frowned and looked at her knee. "You become used to it after a while."

"Are you okay?" Kelly asked.

"Can I sit down? I need to talk to you." Emilie asked.

"Of course." Kelly nodded and sat down on the couch.

"Thanks." Emilie smiled and sat next to her. She looked over at the suitcases on the ground and frowned at Kelly. "Are you leaving?"

"Yes, it's time." Kelly nodded.

"Kel, what happened last night? Why did you just forfeit?" Emilie asked.

"I looked back on my life, and realized, I don't deserve anything good. I've done horrible things, Em. You deserved that title more than anyone else." Kelly said.

"That's not true. You're a good person, Kel." Emilie frowned.

"A good person does not befriend someone like Jennifer, Em." Kelly shook her head. "She's deceitful and does not care about anyone other than herself. She got a kick out of ruining everyone's lives, especially Nathan's.

"Why? He's her brother." Emilie asked.

"Pure sibling rivalry. Nathan is more well-known and successful than she is and it eats at her, in a way you would not believe! She wanted to destroy him with a headline story so shameful that he quits professional tennis for good, so she can be the only famous Connor in the family." Kelly explained.

"That's so petty." Emilie shook her head.

"That's Jennifer." Kelly sighed. "It's a Connor thing. Jennifer is just like their dad."

"So he's like his mom?" Emilie asked.

"Yes, they even look alike. Nathan's mom, Zoe, is the most wonderful woman in the world. His dad, Alistair, on the other hand is a complete dick. He is cruel and abusive. He works all the time and has had so many affairs that we have lost count. When he's not at home, he cheats on his wife, and when he is at home, he screams and shouts at her. Their poor mom had to go through so much shit, but she still stays with him."

"Why?" Emilie asked.

"Maybe she loves the old bastard. Who knows?" Kelly frowned. "People do strange things, Emilie."

"I've noticed." Emilie nodded. "

"To uncle Alistair, nothing anyone ever does is good enough for him, unless it was what he wanted them to do. It was his way or no way. He's a very pushy man, not very approachable and very judgemental." Kelly rolled her eyes. "Being like her dad, Jennifer did what she wanted to, when she wanted to. Always drinking, partying, being reckless, where Nathan was the complete opposite. He was responsible, level-headed and he even helped his mom out in the house, which his dad hated more than anything in the world. Said it made him less of a man." Kelly said with a slight smile, looking at Emilie's expression softening. "He was an absolute sweetheart, he still is. A bit cocky sometimes, but the best of the best."

"He is." Emilie nodded.

"Nathan never got any support from his father, ever since he was a little boy. That's also why he volunteers at the FTPA. He wants those kids to have what he never had, what he still doesn't have." Kelly said.

Emilie felt a lump in her throat and rested her head against the wall next to her.

"Jennifer on the other hand, got whatever she wanted from her dad. Unlike Nathan, in Jennifer's mind, there was nothing that money couldn't buy. Uncle Alistair, being the person that he is, was more than willing to give her everything she desired, just so that he wouldn't have to spend time with her. Jennifer is just like her father, immoral, manipulative and deceptive, and she could make anyone do whatever she wanted, with the exception of Nathan and his mother. She has slept with so many people to get to where she is now, it's sad." Kelly said, sadly.

"No, it's pathetic." Emilie shook her head. "I can't understand how someone can do things like that."

"Jennifer was also one of the reasons why Nathan and Spencer couldn't stand each other." Kelly said.

"Really? How come?" Emilie asked.

"Jennifer introduced them to a girl called Brigitte, one of her friends, who is just as manipulative as she is. Brigitte pretended to like both Nathan and Spencer, and ended up just using them. She spread rumors about the two guys and they ended up having one hell of an argument. Tempers were flying and ego's got bruized and Nathan was the one that ended up heartbroken. Jennifer thought that by hurting Nathan, he would quit, but he didn't. He ended up beating Spencer in last year's Open final, and ever since then, they can't stand each other. Nathan had the upper hand on her and she didn't like it one bit." Kelly smirked.

"Major back-fire." Emilie nodded.

"You have no idea!" Kelly laughed. "Jennifer was my friend for eleven years, so I got to see all the destruction she caused, all the lives she ruined, all the relationships she destroyed. The night of the top floor party, she was being her normal charming self, trying to plan a course of action to ruin your life as well. I asked her to let it go but she's like a pitbull, she never lets anything go."

"Kelly, you've been friends with her for so long, but you barely knew me." Emilie frowned.

"And your point?" Kelly frowned.

"You went against your best friend. I guess I am just struggling to understand why." Emilie said.

"Jen uses people, and I am quite sick of being used.

I have had enough of her lies and her empty promises." Kelly said. "Going against her was the best thing I could have done. I feel liberated, to say the very least."

"Good for you, Kel." Emilie smiled.

"When I saw you and Nathan together, you both looked so happy. He was happier than I had ever seen him and it made me think. There's enough sadness in the world. You guys made me believe that life could be beautiful and I couldn't let anyone ruin that. Love like that does not come along every day." Kelly smiled.

Emilie looked at her and felt the lump in her throat again. "Kelly..."

"Two nights ago was the first time, in the eleven years that I've known Nathan, that I saw him cry. All those other times that he was hurt by his sister and her stupid friends seemed like nothing compared to losing you. It broke my heart, because I knew it was partly my fault, that I could have stopped it from happening." Kelly smiled sadly.

Emilie felt a tear run down her cheek and she frowned. "He didn't tell her, did he?"

"No, he would never break a promise." Kelly shook her head.

"Oh my god. It's all my fault, I didn't believe him." Emilie closed her eyes and tears ran down her cheeks.

"Don't cry." Kelly leaned over and put her arms around Emilie. "And it's not your fault, Em."

"It is. How could I think that of him, Kelly?" Emilie sobbed and put her arms around Kelly's shoulders. "He must hate me."

"He could never hate you, Em, he loves you." Kelly shook her head. "Very much."

Emilie felt another tear run down her cheek and

sighed.

Kelly pulled back and looked at her. "Listen to me, Em. I have known him for a long time, and I've never seen him look at anyone the way that he looks at you, and the way he talks about you, and the way he is when he was with you. You bring out the best in him. He's a better version of himself, because of you. He's so in love with you, it's beyond me." Kelly said.

"I feel exactly the same way." Emilie smiled.

"So go tell him that." Kelly said and Emilie looked at her hands on her lap.

After a long pause, Emilie lifted her head and sighed. "You can't leave." Emilie looked at her. "I need you here."

"I'll just be in the way." Kelly frowned.

"I want you to stay." Emilie smiled.

Kelly looked at her for a moment and smiled. "Okay, I'll stay. On one condition."

"Anything." Emilie smiled.

"You come with me to Nathan's game." Kelly smiled.

Emilie took a deep breath and looked at Kelly. Kelly raised her eyebrows and Emilie sighed. "Okay, but I have something to do first. I'll meet you there."

"Don't bail on me, Em." Kelly narrowed her eyes at Emilie.

"I won't, I promise." Emilie stood up and smiled at Kelly.

Nathan took a deep breath as he stepped out onto the deco-turf, and into the light. Center court was fully packed, which did not surprise him. It was a final after all. Even though his heart was heavy and he felt like breaking down, he held his head high and kept his jaw clenched. Right, this was it. The final game, the game that will determine if you are a winner or a loser. Whether you will be victorious, or if you will be a failure. He was used to being a failure to his father, but maybe that was why he loved the sport so much. Partly because it made him happy, and partly because it made his father unhappy. Nathan nodded to himself and ran his fingers through his hair. His heart was racing and his stomach felt like it was churning butter, but he was focused. He was wearing his lucky black t-shirt, so he was feeling confident. As he walked to his seat on the side of the court, he heard a few people cheering and he rolled his eyes. Probably another fan club, he thought. He looked over his shoulder and saw Spencer and Shannon, along with his mother and Kelly, standing and cheering. Nathan felt his heart sinking and his bag slid off his shoulder.

Brandon smirked at him and walked passed him. "I knew she wasn't going to show. She's probably on her way home already."

"Shut up, Brandon." Nathan frowned.

"Or what? What are you going to do, Connor?" Brandon laughed and Nathan glared at him. "That s what I thought. Unlike you, I'm not a pussy. I'm going to wipe you so far off the grid that if your name pops up somewhere, people will be asking "Nathan who?' You ready for that, Connor?"

Nathan tried his best to ignore Brandon's taunts, but it was extremely difficult. Nathan knew that if he was going to allow Brandon to get inside his head, he was going to lose his focus and beat him to a pulp. And that would not go down very well. He took a deep breath and took his racquet out of his bag.

"Campbell is trying to piss him off." Shannon whispered to Spencer.

"It looks like it's working. Nate had that same look on his face just before he gave me a black eye." Spencer said.

"Poor Nate." Shannon sighed and looked at Spencer. "Has there ever been a fight on court?"

"The only thing even remotely close to a fight was three years ago, when Wesley Harrison intentionally hit Travis Collier in the face. Fighting is not allowed, both players are instantly disqualified." Spencer said.

"Well, in that case, get ready for another eventful final." Kelly leaned forward and said to Spencer.

"Oh god." Shannon sighed.

"He looks like shit." Kelly shrugged.

"I think he looks rather handsome." Zoe looked at Kelly and frowned. "Troubled, but handsome."

"Where's Em?" Shannon asked.

"I don't know, she said she was going to meet us here." Kelly frowned.

"I think I should call her." Shannon said to Kelly.

"Give her a few minutes." Kelly smiled at Shannon nodded. "She'll be here."

"I need to talk to you." Emilie walked into Tom's room and looked at him.

Tom looked up from his book and frowned at her. "I'm not in the mood, Emilie."

"Well, I need to get this out, so you're going to listen, whether you want to or not." Emilie said.

"Very well then." Tom nodded and looked at her.

"I can't believe that you didn't tell me about my mom!" Emilie frowned, crossed her arms and looked at him. "Even though I'm not your daughter, I'm still your wife's daughter, and that has to count for something. I'm the only thing you have left of her, but yet you pushed me away. You still push me away! Why?"

"Your mother ripped my heart out when she told me about her affair! Do you know what that feels like?" Tom exclaimed. "I hated her, I hated him and I hated you! Jeremy was the only true thing in my life at that moment!"

"You still had a responsibility..." Emilie growled.

"I had nothing of the sort! You weren't my daughter! Why should I claim responsibility for something's that's not even mine?" Tom yelled.

"Because I was a seven year old kid, for god's sake!" Emilie exclaimed. "Do you know how many nights I cried myself to sleep because I was convinced that you were going to send me away, because that's how much you hated me? Do you realise the irreparable damage you caused all these years! No wonder I have trust issues!"

"Irreparable damage? If it weren't for you, my wife and son would still be alive and not dead and buried!" Tom yelled.

Emilie looked at him in disbelief and shook her head. "I can't believe you just said that."

"It's the truth, isn't it?" Tom asked.

"My whole life I have tried to make you proud of me, I tried so hard to make you look at me the way you looked at Jeremy. I never understood why nothing I ever did was good enough for you." Emilie frowned. "But I've realized that I was wrong. I wasn't good enough for you, for your family, no matter what I did, no matter how hard I tried."

"If you're trying to make me feel guilty for my

actions, it's not going to work." Tom crossed his arms and frowned at her.

"Of course it won't." Emilie sighed.

"Does this conversation have a point, Emilie?" Tom asked.

"The days of seeking your approval in everything I do, are over. I'm done, because I don't need your approval! I have friends out there, that would do anything for me at the drop of a hat. Those people are more like family than you will ever be, because they love me for who I am and they don't care about the things that I have done, because that's what family does! You treated me like I was never good enough for you, but maybe you're the one that was never good enough for me!" Emilie exclaimed.

Tom stood in front of her, motionless, not saying a word.

Emilie's blood was boiling in her veins, but at the same time she felt incredibly happy. She frowned and turned around to the door.

"I will never be able to forgive you..." Tom softly growled.

She looked over her shoulder at him and paused. "You know what? That was never the issue. I came here, thinking I should not be too hard on you, because Jeremy always told me that maybe you have a good reason for being the way you are. So I gave you the benefit of the doubt, but as always, you gave me nothing. My mother would be ashamed of you right now, and so would Jeremy. So just go home, because you don't want to be here, and I don't want you here either." Emilie turned away from Tom and walked out the door.

Nathan wiped the sweat from his forehead and took a deep breath. Brandon was tougher than he had anticipated. The guy had drive and a strong backhand, that he used much too often, according to Nathan. Brandon made Nathan run around, trying to tire him out. Well, it was working, because Nathan was exhausted. His head was not in the game either and he was getting frustrated with himself. So, putting it bluntly, he was screwed. He thought about Emilie ever since he stepped out onto the court and couldn't get her out of his mind. As he walked back to the line, exhausted and ready to give up, visions of Emilie ran through his mind. The first time he saw her on the plane, all flushed and embarrassed. Her standing by the bar at the top floor party, smiling at him. Her playful laugh when she showed them his room key. The way she took his hand and the shy smile on her face as they walked to her room. Her sleeping next to him on the floor in her room. Her far-away look as the wind blew her hair back on the ferry to Liberty Island. The way she looked at him after he kissed her on the court. The way she was curled up next to him on the carpet in his room, covered in a sheet. The way she tilted her head at him when he was being too cocky. Nathan felt his heart pounding and grinned to himself.

    "The next time I see her, no matter when or where it is, I am going to go right up to her and kiss her, the way she deserved to be kissed." He vowed to himself. "You don't let a girl like that slip through your fingers!" He bounced the ball once, twice, threw it in the air and hit a powerful serve to Brandon. Brandon ducked out of the way and the ball rocketed passed him.

    "Ace."

"That's what I'm talking about!" Nathan balled his fist and nodded to himself.

Emilie checked her watch as she pushed through the doors of the center court building. She was late, but she felt better. Getting everything off her chest even made breathing easier. She felt invincible for the first time in over a year, and it felt great. As she ran up the stairs, her phone started to ring. She took it out and saw that it was Shannon. She opened her phone and smiled.

"Yes, Shannon." She said.

"Where the hell are you?" Shannon shrieked.

"I'm here, I'm here." Emilie rolled her eyes.

"Where's here?" Shannon asked.

"Do you see her?" She heard Kelly in the background.

"Why do you sound so out of breath? Are you okay?" Shannon asked.

"I'm running up seven flights of stairs, okay!" Emilie frowned. "How is he doing?"

"Not too good, he's behind. Campbell is really getting to him." Shannon said.

"Shit!" Emilie growled.

"Did you just say shit?" Shannon asked.

"Em said shit?" She heard Spencer say and she laughed.

"Yes, I did." Emilie said as she reached the top of the stairs and looked out onto center court. She caught her breath as she saw Nathan on the court. She took a couple of deep breaths and shook her head. "He's not that far behind."

"Where are you?" Shannon exclaimed.

"We're in section nine, row two." She heard

Spencer call out.

Emilie tried to count the sections, but she was distracted by Nathan's presence. She could feel her heart pounding against her ribs as Nathan turned towards her to walk back to the baseline. He lifted his face and his eyes met hers.

The moment Nathan looked up at the crowd, he froze and felt his heartrate accellerate. It was Emilie, standing by the railing, looking more beautiful than he had ever seen her look before. She wore a pair of light blue jeans, a white top and her hair was hanging down her shoulders. She held her phone in her hand, close to her face and she was staring at him. Nathan was paralyzed by the sight of her and couldn't tear his eyes away from her.

"Em, are you there?" Shannon shrieked.

"Yes, Shan. I'm here." Emilie breathed.

"Where?" Shannon asked into her phone and looked around her.

"What is Nathan looking at?" Spencer frowned and looked at the court.

"Over there!" Kelly exclaimed and pointed to the big screen.

Shannon, Spencer and Zoe looked at the screen and smiled.

"Never mind. I see you." Shannon said in disbelief.

"So does everyone else." Kelly laughed.

"What do you....." Emilie frowned, and gasped as she spotted herself on the screen to her left. "Oh god."

"Em?" Shannon asked.

"I'm hanging up now." Emilie muttered.

"Good idea." Shannon laughed and Emilie closed

309

her phone. She shoved it into her pocket and put her hands on the metal railing. She looked at Nathan and took a deep breath as he took a step towards her.

Nathan stared at her and felt his heart pound in his chest. He had to go to her, now! He turned to look at Brandon and tugged at his cap, with a slight nod.

"What the hell is he doing?" Brandon frowned at him and crossed his arms.

Nathan threw his racquet down on the ground and started walking off the court, but he was stopped by one of the line judges.

"Nathan, if you leave the court now, you'll forfeit the game." The blonde judge said.

"That's fine." Nathan shrugged.

"Nathan, are you sure you want to do that?"

"I have never been so sure of anything in my life." He grinned and walked off the court.

"Connor forfeit, game Campbell." The umpire said over the microphone.

The crowd went completely quiet and followed Nathan as he made his way to Emilie. He ran up the steps two at a time until he reached Emilie. He took a deep breath and looked at her, standing about six feet away from him.

"Emilie, you're here..." He whispered, breathlessly.

"Sorry I'm late. I had to take care of something." She smiled slightly.

"I have so much that I want to say to you." He looked at her.

"You don't have to say anything." Emilie shook her head. "On my way here, I was trying to figure out what to say to you. I had this whole long speech prepared, but when I saw you, I forgot everything."

"Just speak from your heart, Lee...." Jeremy's voice sang in her head.

"So I'm just going to speak from my heart, if that's alright." Emilie tilted her head.

"Of course." Nathan nodded and smiled slightly.

"You are one of the best people that I have ever known. You are sweet and funny and smart and most importantly, you are honest. Sometimes you can be a little cocky, but that's one of the reasons why I love you. With you, I feel safe, and I haven't felt safe in a very long time. No matter what kind of mood I am in, you always manage to make me smile, to make everything better, just by being there." Emilie said and she could feel the tears in her eyes. "I know you didn't break your promise to me, but yet I still accused you that you did. I knew it all along, but I was too scared to admit it. Being this close to someone is scary, it scares the hell out of me, but I want to be with you. I want to take the leap because I know that you're worth it. And I'm sorry that I didn't believe you, and if you want me to go, I will, but I just want you to know that I can't imagine not being with you and that I love you with everything that I have in me. I just hope that that's enough for you." A tear ran down her cheek and she looked at him.

"I just walked off the court in the middle of a final. I have never done that before, for anyone." Nathan looked at her. "There will be a lot more games for me to play, sure, but a girl like you only comes along once in my lifetime."

Emilie smiled and two more tears ran down her cheeks. "I'm so sorry, Nate...."

Before Emilie could finish her sentence, Nathan

walked up to her, cupped her face with both his hands and kissed her. The crowd rose to their feet and started cheering for them, but Emilie and Nathan was oblivious to anything going on around them. Nathan was the first to pull away, but only slightly. His hands still cupped her face and her hands still held on to his upper arms as they stared into each others' eyes.

"I love you so much." Emilie whispered.

"I love you too, pretty girl." Nathan smiled and tucked a strand of hair behind her ear.

"Sorry for crashing your game." Emilie tilted her head to the side.

"It's okay. You're more important." Nathan grinned. "Besides, there's always next year."

"This was definitely an Open to remember." Kelly laughed and looked at Zoe.

"Indeed, honey. Indeed." Zoe nodded and put her arm around Kelly's shoulders.

"I wonder what's going to happen next year." Kelly grinned.

"Please, Kelly. We've had enough drama to last us a lifetime." Shannon exclaimed.

"I completely agree with Shannon, Kelly." Zoe nodded.

"Speak for yourselves. I enjoyed every minute of it!" Kelly smiled. "Especially when Shannon wore that black catsuit and a ski mask, to blend into her surroundings!"

Spencer and Kelly laughed and Shannon frowned and crossed her arms.

"And when she drank beer with me for the first time and asked the barman for a cup of beer." Spencer grinned.

"Are you two done making fun of me?" Shannon raised her eyebrows.

"Oh, come on, Texas girl. You know you had fun." Spencer winked at her.

"Yes, I admit it, but we learned a lot of things too." Shannon nodded. "That nothing is impossible."

"That looks can be deceiving." Spencer nodded.

"That blood isn't always thicker than water." Zoe smiled and took Shannon and Kelly's hands.

"And most importantly..." Kelly looked over at Emilie and Nathan. "....that love does conquer all."

Shannon, Spencer and Zoe looked at them and they smiled. Shannon looked dreamily at Spencer and took his hand.

"What?" He looked at her with a frown.

"Nothing." Shannon shrugged.

"I know you by now. What?" Spencer grinned.

"Nothing, really." Shannon grinned.

"If you want me to move in with you, it's not going to happen." Spencer shook his head.

"Spence...." Shannon frowned at him.

"I have too much stuff to move." He said.

Shannon looked at him and he put his arm around her waist.

"Besides, my place is bigger." He whispered in her ear.

Shannon smiled slowly and nodded. "You're right. Plus it's a great apartment."

Spencer laughed and pulled her close.

"Socrates is going to love it!" Shannon laughed. "So will I."

EPILOGUE

It was a beautiful May evening in Washington and the sun was almost setting. Nathan parked his blue Shelby on the side of the street and looked over at Emilie in the passenger seat, wearing a rather ridiculous looking eyemask, completely covering her eyes.

"We're here." He smiled.

"And where is here?" Emilie shrugged.

"You'll see." Nathan laughed and got out the car. He ran to the other side of the car and opened her door. "Come on, pretty girl." He took her hand and helped her out the car.

"I can't believe you are making me wear this stupid thing." She sighed and touched the mask.

He chuckled and led her onto the sidewalk and along the wooden path leading to the light grey double storey house.

"Well, without it, the surprize would be ruined, and that would ruin my fun." Nathan smiled.

"I don't like surprizes, Connor." Emilie muttered, but Nathan just laughed.

"I know." Nathan lifted her up onto the steps and opened the door. He led her through the foyer, down the corridor and into the dining room. "Okay. Are you ready?"

"I think so." Emilie frowned and clasped her hands together.

"Okay, so here goes. One, two, three!" Nathan grinned.

He took the mask off and Emilie blinked.

"Happy birthday!"

Emilie laughed, as streamers flew through the air and she clasped her hands together. "Ah, you guys!"

In front of her was a long table, covered in a white table cloth with a white sparkly cake, with twenty two candles on it. White balloons were floating against the ceiling and there were candles everywhere. Emilie smiled as she saw Spencer and Shannon, holding Socrates. Socrates had a bright pink bow around her neck and was chewing on Spencer's finger. Zoe and Kelly was there, taking photographs of everything. She even saw Samantha, Maria, Brandon and Nathan's twin cousins, Scott and Jason from California.

"I can't believe you're all here!" Emilie exclaimed and giggled.

She walked to Shannon and Spencer and held her arms out to them.

"Happy birthday, Emmy!" Spencer smiled and hugged her.

"Happy, happy birthday, my beautiful friend!" Shannon hugged her as well.

"Thank you, Shan." Emilie smiled at them. "Hey Socrates." Emilie rubbed the bulldog's nose and Socrates playfully shoved her hand away.

"Stop hogging the birthday girl!" Kelly exclaimed and pushed passed Spencer and Shannon. "Happy birthday, girl." Kelly hugged her and she laughed.

"You and Nate should come surf with us next month, the swells are sick this time of year." Jason smiled as he hugged her.

"I don't know, I'm not much of a swimmer." Emilie grinned and winked at Scott.

"Well, girl, you can't possibly be worse at surfing than Nate." Scott laughed at he pulled her in for a hug.

"Hey!" Nathan exclaimed and Emilie and Scott laughed.

"We can't be good at everything, can we, Nate?" Jason nodded.

"Exactly." Nathan grinned and high-fived his cousin.

Emilie and Scott exchanged glances and frowned. "Sound like something a loser would say." Emilie grinned at them and Scott cheered her on.

Nathan and Jason playfully narrowed their eyes at them and Emilie laughed. Zoe walked over to Emilie and put her arms around her and hugged her as well.

"Happy birthday, honey." Zoe smiled at her.

"Thank you so much, for everything." Emilie tilted her head and looked at Zoe.

"You're welcome, Honey." Zoe nodded with a smile.

Emilie turned and looked at everyone in the room. Nathan was standing next to the table, his hands n his pockets, looking at her with a crooked smile. Emilie smiled at him and sighed happily.

"Wait a minute..." Her smile was quickly replaced by a frown as she looked around her.

"Connor?" Emilie narrowed her eyes at Nathan.

"Yes, my love." Nathan grinned, looking very satisfied with himself.

"Where are we?" Emilie asked him.

Nathan simply smiled and took a deep breath, still looking at her.

"Nathan didn't tell you?" Zoe asked and Emilie looked at her.

"Tell me what?" Emilie looked back at Nathan. "No, it can't be..." Emilie looked around her and frowned.

Nathan looked at Shannon and Kelly and gave them a small nod.

"Is this the Garfield street house..." Emilie watched as they walked to the far end of the room and opened the double glass doors. "Oh my god..." Emilie said breathlessly and slowly walked to the open doors. The patio came into view as Emilie came to a stop and covered her mouth with her hands. She felt a tear run down her cheek and she spun around. "This is the house...." She whispered.

"Correction, my love. This is our house." Nathan walked to her with a smile and gently touched her cheek.

"Are you serious? We got it?" Emilie asked, surprizingly calm and Nathan nodded.

Emilie let out a loud, high-pitched scream and threw her arms around his shoulders. "Oh my god! I can't believe this!"

"Happy birthday, pretty girl." Nathan laughed.

"I don't know what to say. I can't believe you bought us the house." Emilie looked at him. "Thank you so much."

"Come on, I want to show you something." Nathan smiled and pulled her outside.

Emilie's eyes widened as they stepped outside onto the patio. She looked at the pool and smiled. "It's so beautiful."

Nathan smiled and they walked around the back of the house. Emilie gasped and stared out in front of her.

"I thought it would be a good idea." Nathan smiled and Emilie took a few steps forward. In front of her, was their very own tennis court. She turned and smiled at Nathan. "It's perfect!" She ran up to him and he put his arms around her.

"Thank you so much! I love it!" She whispered to

him.

"You're welcome, my love." He smiled and kissed her head.

"Nate!" Kelly called from the patio and he looked over his shoulder.

"We're coming!" Nathan waved to Kelly.

"You go on ahead." Emilie smiled and watched as Nathan nodded and walked up the steps and into the house.

Emilie sighed happily and looked around her at the beautifully landscaped garden. She gently touched the different leaves and smiled.

"Happy birthday, baby sister...." Jeremy's voice rang in her ears. His voice was soft, barely a whisper.

Emilie looked around her but she could not see him. "Jer?" A tear ran down her cheek and she dug her hands into the pockets of her white linen pants.

"Em?" She heard Nathan behind her and she looked at him, over her shoulder. "Are you okay?"

"Yeah." Emilie shrugged and looked at him.

"Are you sure? You look like you saw a ghost." Nathan smiled, but his smile quickly faded.

"No, not this time." Emilie gave him a small smile and he nodded. "Everything is good."

"I got you something." Nathan gave her a crooked smile.

"Really?" Emilie turned to him and narrowed her eyes at him.

"Hear me out. I have four good reasons. I promise." Nathan defended.

"Okay, let's hear them." Emilie laughed and crossed her arms.

"One, because you are my girl." Nathan said and showed Emilie the black rectangular box. "Two, because it's your birthday, obviously." He opened it and inside was a white gold sapphire bracelet.

"Oh my god! It's so pretty!" Emilie gasped and brought her hands up to her face.

"Three, it matches your eyes." Nathan smiled at her.

"It's really beautiful." Emilie looked at him.

"And four, because it reminds you of the lights." Nathan smiled and put it on her wrist.

"I don't understand.." Emilie frowned at him.

"I know that the lights will always remind you of Jeremy, so I wanted you to have something that reminded you of him, so you can keep him close." Nathan said.

Emilie looked at it, fingering the sapphires gently, tears forming in her eyes. "Nate, I don't know what to say. Thank you." She felt a tear run down her cheek.

"You're welcome." He pulled her close and ran his fingers through her hair. "Happy birthday, pretty girl."

Emilie looked up at him and he smiled at her. I love you so much." She whispered.

"I love you too, Emilie." Nathan smiled and pulled her close. He kissed the top of her head and pulled away slightly. "Now, come on. I believe there's a party inside."

"Have you heard from Tom?" Nathan asked Spencer.

"I spoke to him the other day. He's in Marseille, sorting out some family stuff. Sounds like he won't be back for a while." Spencer leaned against the wall and looked over at Kelly, Shannon and Emilie on the other side of the room. "How's Emilie holding up?"

"Better than I expected, actually. Sometimes she

gets that famous faraway look of hers when a certain song plays on the radio." Nathan said.

"I know that song." Spencer nodded and smiled as Shannon, Kelly and Emilie walked over to them.

"Hey, girls." Spencer grinned.

"What are you boys talking about?" Shannon grinned.

"Oh, you know. Guys stuff." Nathan laughed and put his arm around Emilie's waist.

"Right, guys stuff." Emilie nodded.

A loud knock came from the front door and Emilie frowned at Nathan.

"I wonder who could that be?" Nathan frowned.

"No more surprizes, Connor. I mean it." Emilie smirked at him as she walked over to the door and opened it.

"Evening, I am sorry to bother you." A tall, lean man with sandy brown hair and light eyes stood on the porch.

"That's no problem. I hope we're not making too much noise." Emilie said apologetically. "My friends threw me a birthday party...."

"Is it your birthday today?" The man asked.

"Yes." Emilie frowned.

"I'm sorry to be rude. My name is Marcus Gordon. Are you Emilie?" The man asked.

"Yes, I am. Do I know you?" Emilie looked at the man. Something about him seemed very familiar, but Emilie could not figure out what.

"No, you don't know me, I knew your mother, Paige." Marcus said, studying her expression.

"My mother." Emilie frowned, feeling her heart pounding in her chest.

"Who is it, Em?" Nathan called from inside.

Emilie turned around and looked at Nathan. "I don't know. He knew my mother."

"Really?" Nathan frowned and walked closer to her.

"Yes, I did, many years ago. She used to teach with me. Look, I know this is not the best time, but there's something that you need to know, Emilie." Marcus said.

Emilie turned her attention back to Marcus and looked at him. "Okay."

"This may sound completely insane, but I think that I might be your father." Marcus said.